That Kiss

Kate Squires

ISBN-13: 9781499134292
ISBN-10: 1499134290

In loving memory of William and Christel.

I love you and miss you every day.

Acknowledgments

There are so many people to thank, and I'm sure I will miss a bunch. Some of them didn't even know they helped me. First and foremost, I would like to thank God for giving me the talent, the desire, and the means to share my stories with the world. Second, thanks to Frank K. and Bryan M. for letting me pick your brains regarding technical stuff that I couldn't Google. I appreciate every word. Next I'd like to thank Jennifer P. for giving me encouragement and advice when I needed it. Because of you, I don't feel quite as alone in the world of writing and publishing. A big thanks goes to my surrogate "Gram," Thelma J. You listened to me jabber on for hours on end as I read every last word to you. Your input was very much appreciated and extremely helpful. I love you. Smooches! Thank you to my kids, who gave me ideas for names of people and places. Some were good, some not so good. As always, I love you, now get to bed! Lastly, thanks to my husband, Len. Without you wrangling the kids on nights and weekends, it would've taken me years to get this project done, if ever. I love you!

one

Here I am, stuck in the slowest line in the grocery store. It didn't seem like the slowest until I got in it, and then all movement ceased and the dreaded blinking light came on. Ugh! Just one time I would like not to be the curse that makes all checkout lines stop. I run my hand through my shoulder-length hair in exasperation as I glance down at the miscellaneous items for sale in the small aisle leading to the cashier.

There are all sorts of candies, gum, and chips, but my eyes land on the latest issue of a tabloid magazine. As I readjust the shopping basket in my hand, I pick up the magazine and gaze at the cover. Ah yes, another star who has fallen into rehab and a picture of another star on a beach in her bathing suit that does anything but flatter her post-baby body.

As I shuffle along, waiting my turn, I remember that Jenna asked me to pick up some red wine on the way home.

Jenna is my roommate, best friend, and the only one I can vent to when my day has not gone according to plan. I've known her for nine years now, but she is more like a sister to me. She is outgoing and beautiful, and her sense of fashion is spot on; she is everything that I am not. Oh, the things I could do if I only had an ounce of her self-confidence.

The line moves again, and the baby in the shopping cart behind me begins to scream. Why would you bring your infant out to a store at ten o'clock at night? Shouldn't she be asleep well before now? We move again, and it's finally my turn. On the conveyer belt I place all of my items and then add a copy of *Rolling Stone*. The very bored girl behind the counter rings me up, and I'm out the door.

After stopping at a small liquor store, I walk through our apartment door and I'm greeted by Chiffon, Jenna's cat.

"Hi, girl," I say, stroking her soft white back as she purrs like an engine. As I make my way to the kitchen, Chiffon weaves in and out of my legs. I almost trip twice. She has a habit of doing this, and one of these days I'm going to fall flat on my face.

Jenna comes out from her bedroom in a shimmery hot pink top and skinny jeans that hug her perfect little figure. She must be going out tonight.

"Chloe, you're back!" Jenna says. "Did you get the wine?"

"Yes, I got it. Is this okay?" I ask her, holding the bottle out for her to inspect.

"Yes, that'll do. Trent and I are going to celebrate our one-month anniversary tonight!" she says as she winks.

"That's great, Jenna. I hope everything goes well. Don't do anything I wouldn't do," I chuckle, knowing full well she's already done way more than I would do.

"Oh, Chloe, you really need to get out more. Trent has a friend. I could set you up," she says with a devious grin.

"Jenna, stop. You know I'm not into blind dates. Besides, I'm just not interested in dating right now," I say. I try to look as convincing as I can.

"Chloe, is it old what's-his-name again? You need to get over him. He had his chance years ago, and he blew it. I know if you just put yourself out there, some hot, young guy would snap you right up," she says matter-of-factly.

"Yeah, maybe. I don't know," I reply as I put the groceries away. Jenna is always trying to set me up with her latest boyfriend's friends. I always make excuses as to why I can't go out. I know she is onto me, but she never says so and neither do I.

"So where are you going tonight?" I ask her out of politeness.

"Trent's picking me up. We're going out to the pub and then probably back to his place."

I know exactly what that means, and I give her a have-fun kind of smile as she saunters back to her room.

By ten thirty, Jenna and Trent are out the door, and I'm left alone again. Just me and the cat. Is this how it's always going to be? Me, sitting at home with the cat, crocheting an afghan while listening to sad music on the radio? Is this really my future? The crazy cat lady—great. Why is it that men just seem to fall into Jenna's lap? What makes her different than me? Sure, she's very beautiful with her long auburn tresses and her figure puts Barbie to shame while I'm thin and kind of pale. And my face...well, it isn't awful, but still nobody seems to notice me. There is that guy at Starbucks, but I'm pretty sure he's gay. The fact is that there's nobody who I'm attracted to either. I haven't dated much because most men are the same. No one has ever made me feel as though I wanted a second date...except for one.

Matt was my best friend from a very early age. We used to play outside all summer long. The two of us were inseparable, splashing in the pool and making mud pies during the day and catching lightning bugs after dark.

There were other kids in the neighborhood to play with, but something always drew us together. Early in high school, even though we both had new friends, we still hung out once in a while. Matt eventually got into sports, and a very popular, very pretty cheerleader turned his head. After that, we didn't see much of each other. They broke up after a few months, I think, but we never had the same friendship. Then one night, we both ended up at the same graduation party. I'm not sure how that happened because we just didn't run in the same circles anymore.

As I sit on the couch, next to Chiffon, who is purring quite loudly now, I close my eyes and remember that fateful night as if it were only yesterday. Even though I try not to let myself go there again, I just can't help it this time. My thoughts begin to drift.

"Hey, Chlo! What are you doing here?" Matt asks with the definite scent of having had too many beers.

"Hi, Matt. Jenna dragged me here. Apparently I need to get out more. So are you still planning to go to OSU in the fall?"

"Nah, I've decided the only thing I want out of school is me. I'm gonna go into the family business. Besides, electricians make decent money," he says casually.

"I see. I thought you wanted to do something in music." I try not to seem too excited that he will not be moving away.

"Yeah, well, plans change," he replies. "How about you? Where are you headed?"

"Baldwin Wallace. They have a pretty good dance program there. I don't want to stray too far from home, you know?"

"Well, it looks like we both are staying local. Maybe I'll see you around," he says as he walks away, and I can't help but feel as though the whole conversation was just bland small talk.

Jenna finds me and hands me some kind of concoction that smells of cheap liquor. Hmm, I've never been much of a drinker, but after that unfulfilling chat between Matt and me, I take the proffered drink and gulp it down.

"Whoa, Chloe! Slow down, or you'll be sick!" Jenna says. "You don't drink that often, and these things will catch up to you quick."

"I'll have another then. It's a celebration, right? Let's get drunk," I say with a halfhearted smile on my face. I chug down the tainted beverage.

We drink several more until I can no longer walk straight. My eyes don't focus as they do normally. I know that I am hammered. Jenna is not in any better shape than I am, and some guy, who I think is one of the jocks, is hovering around her trying to keep her upright.

I need air; maybe that will sober me up a bit. I glance around the room and spot a door, but there are too many people crowded around it. I don't want to take the chance of falling into them like bowling balling into a set of pins. After a few minutes I decide to try the back door. Bingo! There are only two people by it, so I make my way through the kitchen trying not to disturb the make-out session going on. I'm almost there when I suddenly trip over my own two feet. I'm bracing myself for the fall when out of nowhere two arms grab me and prevent me from crashing to the floor.

"Chlo, be careful!"

It's Matt. He must have followed me in here knowing I might need help.

"Where are you going? You can't get out that way. It just leads out to the deck," he says, still holding me in his arms. I gaze up at him and he at me, and I am lost in his intense stare.

"Um, yeah. I know that. I was trying to get some air, that's all."

I am mesmerized by his beautiful green eyes. With his arms around me I feel so safe, so cared for so...what? Loved? No way! This is Matt after all. I've known him most of my life. If he had feelings for me, surely he would have revealed them by now, right? But I can't help this overwhelming need to kiss him. I want him to kiss me, kiss me in a way that lovers do. Full-on passionate, no holds barred, tongues entwined kind of kiss.

"Are you okay, Chlo? You have a strange look on your face," Matt says softly after a beat.

I say nothing, still entranced, caught like prey in his web. "Come on. Let's get you that fresh air." He stands me up and walks me outside to the deck. I hold on to the deck rail as if it were a lifeline for what seems like forever. My head is still fuzzy even though we've been outside for a while. It's getting chilly, but somehow I am very warm. The spell that I was under is gone now, but I find that I am still speechless.

"Tongue not working?" he says with a snicker.

What? How did he know what I had in mind for my tongue? I sweep my head up and look at him in a panic. Oh wait, he's referring to my lack of communication. Say something, anything!

"Um, thank you...for helping me with my, um, clumsiness," I say and try not to look flustered. I am shaking now, and I'm not sure if it's because of the chill in the air or the close proximity to my best friend, who for some reason is making me feel jittery.

"You cold, Chlo?" I give him a small nod. "Here take this." He takes off his black sweatshirt and wraps it around my shoulders, keeping his arm around me.

"Thanks," I say shyly. It's warm and soft and smells like him. It's very comforting. "You don't have to babysit me, you know." I say it, but I'm not sure I mean it.

"I know, but you're like my sister, so someone has to protect you from your clumsy nature," he says with a half grin.

The word *sister* burns into me like a branding iron. Sister? Really? He thinks of me as a sister? Could I feel any worse? Ugh! I jerk away, and he flinches.

"Well, I think I'm warm enough," I say more forcefully than I mean. "You can have your sweatshirt back."

"What's wrong? What did I say?" He scans my face, but I keep my expression as neutral as possible. I hand him his shirt and turn to walk away.

"Chlo, stop!" he shouts. He seems confused and bewildered, so I stop and turn my head to the side to show him I'm listening. "Please come back. Did I say or do something to upset you?"

"No. I'm fine. I just want to find Jenna and get out of here," I say in a calmer voice.

"Well, if you're sure you're okay," he mutters.

"I'm fine, I told you. I need to hunt down Jenna. See you later."

I stalk off in the direction of the last place I saw her. She's on the dance floor with the jock. It's a fast song, but there they are, locked in an embrace, slow dancing in the middle of the rest of the drunken crowd. I tap her on the shoulder.

"Jenna, it's time to get going. Let's go home."

"What? The party is just getting good. Let's stay just a little while longer, please?" She has the most contrite look on her face, and I roll my eyes and cave in.

"Fine. Just half an hour more, and then I'm putting your butt in a cab." She smiles at me and nods.

"Sure, Chloe, anything you want." Jenna is very drunk. I'm not much better, but I make a promise to myself to keep an eye on her, knowing I might have to save her from herself.

I look around for a place to sit so I can watch her. A very wasted guy approaches me.

"Hey, sweetheart, how 'bout a dance?" he slurs. Ugh, I really don't like sloppy drunks. I'm about to say no thanks when Matt walks into the room. He's looking around. Is he searching for me? Our eyes meet, and he makes a beeline straight for me.

"Sure, I'd love a dance," I say to the sloppy drunk guy. I take his hand and lead him onto the dance floor before Matt can reach me. He stops in his tracks and watches us carefully. I seize this opportunity with both hands. This should be fun. A song with a pounding beat comes on, and I get to work. I am dancing my ass off all over Sloppy Drunk Guy. In fact, if you didn't know better, you might think I was about to start stripping off clothes. Sloppy Drunk Guy, whose name I think is Dave, is very willing to accept my advances and gladly reciprocates. I glance over at Matt, and he looks seething mad. Ah yes, exactly the reaction I was hoping for. He comes barreling toward us and grabs Dave by the back of the shirt, effortlessly tossing him across the room.

"Go sober up outside, asshole!" he says with a fury I've not seen before. Then he turns his anger at me. What? Why the hell is he mad at me? "Let's go, Chlo! I'm getting you out of here—now!" He takes me by the arm and leads me into a hallway. We stop halfway down, and he stares at me. If looks could kill, I'd be at the morgue. "What the hell were you thinking? That wasn't you out there, Chlo," he shouts. "Do you really think acting that way is gonna get you anything but trouble? Dave is a sleezeball. He's fucked every girl in school who would let him, and he tosses them aside afterward. What were you trying to prove? You're not like those other girls." His tone softens.

"I don't know. I was waiting for Jenna, and, well, I figured I'd try and entertain myself," I say guiltily.

"Entertain yourself?" He's livid and yelling again.

"I'm sorry. I wasn't thinking," I reply and hang my head in shame.

"Clearly," he says. I can tell he's trying to reign in his temper. "Let's go. I'm taking you home."

"I can't go yet. I have to make sure Jenna gets home."

"Ugh! Fine, but I'm gonna make sure you stay out of trouble." He grabs my hand again and leads me into a bedroom where several coats are laid on the bed. "Find your jacket. I'll find Jenna."

"You're awfully bossy today," I add bravely.

"And you're a handful. Just find your coat so we can go."

He leaves the room on his mission, and I sift through the plethora of jackets strewn all over the bed. I need to sit, as I am still dizzy from all the alcohol. Drinking this much is never a good idea. Matt rushes back in the door as if he were on fire.

"Get up!" he shouts at me. "We gotta go—now!"

"Why, is the house on fire?" I say sarcastically.

"Worse! It's the cops!"

The police are here, and we're all underage and drinking. I grab my jacket and stand up quickly. The room spins. Oh jeez, this can't be good. Matt sees me sway and puts his arm around my waist.

"I got you," he murmurs as he looks down at me. For a moment our eyes lock again. That feeling is back, but it's fleeting. We have to get out of here.

Matt tears his gaze away—reluctantly?—leads me to the door, and peeks out.

"We can't get out this way," he says. "We'll have to go out the window." Matt smiles at me, and it's a childlike expression. It's almost as though he's enjoying this. Well, in a way, it is very exciting. He opens the window and gestures for me to go first.

"Good thing we're not far off the ground, eh, Chlo?"

I nod, give a small smile, and sit on the windowsill. After swinging my legs out, I turn onto my belly as I dangle out the window, gripping it tightly. Matt grabs both of my hands to lower me gently down. His touch makes my hands tingle. I drop awkwardly onto my feet and then land on my behind. He quickly follows, but his dismount is much more graceful.

"Come on, Chlo. I know where to go."

He takes my hand again and we run...well, he runs. I stumble along behind him trying to keep up. We continue to make our escape until we come to a graveyard. It's a very old cemetery. We duck through a hole in the fence.

"This is creepy," I say as we weave through the headstones.

"Yeah, I guess it is a little bit. Let's rest over by that mausoleum." He points in the direction of a small stone building. We make our way over to it and sit, leaning our backs against its side.

"That was exciting," I breathe, trying to slow my panting.

"Yes, it was." He frowns down at me. "Since when are you into that kind of excitement?"

I frown back at him, a puzzled look on my face. "I don't know. Since now, I guess." And then I remember my drunken best friend. "Jenna!" I exclaim. "I forgot about her. I hope she made it out before the cops got to her."

The thought of her being arrested makes my stomach roll. How could I leave without her? Well, I wasn't exactly in a position to help myself, let alone someone else. In fact, if Matt wasn't there to help me escape, I would've been calling my parents from jail right now. That would've been a moment of pride for them.

"Relax," he says. "I'm sure she's fine. I'll take you home in a bit. You can call her in the morning. Well, maybe in the afternoon would be better," he chuckles.

We sit in silence for a while, neither one of us feeling the need to say anything.

"This is nice, you know?" I say softly.

"What, being at an underage drunkfest, drinking way too much and almost falling on your face, jumping out of a window, and running through a graveyard? Yeah, *nice* isn't exactly the word I would use to describe this evening," he says.

"That's not what I meant. I mean we haven't hung out in a long time. This is nice. It's just us, like it used to be."

I close my eyes, lean my head back, and smile wistfully, thinking about some of our past adventures as kids. "I miss it, you know? I miss... us."

"Me too. And you are right. This is kind of nice. But now we've graduated, and everything's going to change." There's a sad tone to his voice. I look at him, and he's staring at me with a heavyhearted expression that changes to...what? Then I feel that pull again. We are two magnets being drawn together. There's no controlling it. He leans forward. His face is getting closer to mine. I glance down at his lips. They are slightly parted, and then, slowly, they are on mine. He's kissing me very gently. I gasp for precious air, and he eases his tongue in my mouth. Oh my God, this is so...good. I wrap my hands around the back of his head and entwine my fingers into his hair. He snakes his arms around me and pulls me further into him. We are both putting everything we have into this wonderfully passionate kiss. I'm floating. Despite the chill, my body is on fire. We are nothing but hands and tongues. He moans into my mouth, and it's the sexiest sound I've ever heard. Just as I think my heart will burst from my chest, he pulls back and regards me with shock on his face.

I blink up at him, stunned. He pulls back further and shakes his head as if to clear it.

"Chlo, I'm...sorry. I don't know what came over me. We need to go. I have to get you home," he says after a beat. I'm struck dumb, speechless once again. He stands and holds out his hand to help me up. I take it and shakily get to my feet. I know the buzz from the alcohol hasn't yet left me, but my legs feel like Jell-O, and I don't think I can blame the alcohol. He starts to walk, still holding my hand.

"Wait just a minute. Let me steady myself."

He looks back at me and halts his progress.

"Okay, I'm good," I mutter quietly, and we're off, headed back to my house, I think. What happened back there? Whatever it was, it was fantastic. We don't speak the whole way home, which gives me nothing but time to think about our kiss.

We never spoke of that kiss again and even now, five years later, I touch my lips reflexively and think to myself, *That was the best day of my life.*

two

It's early on Saturday morning when I wake. My arm dangles off the bed, and Chiffon rubs her body against it, purring loudly.

"Good morning, girl. You must be hungry," I say as I stroke her a few times. She runs to my bedroom door and looks back as if to say, *Are you coming?* I slide out of bed into my slippers and yawn and stretch before making my way to the kitchen. After getting the coffee pot going, I grab the newspaper from in front of the door.

"There is nothing like the smell of fresh coffee in the morning, Chiffon," I say as I put a scoop of cat food in her bowl. She runs over, and even as she hungrily gobbles up her food, she's still purring. I smile. A simple bowl of food makes her so happy.

Jenna must have come home late last night—or early this morning, more likely—because her shoes and jacket are sprawled out on the floor. Hmm, I hope she was careful.

I pour myself a cup of coffee, grab the newspaper, and sit down at the kitchen table. Leafing through it, I find the comics first. This should brighten my day. Ah yes, Marmaduke. He's been my favorite since I was a child; maybe it's because we had a dog similar to him.

I continue reading the funnies and then skip to the employment section. I need to find my next show. Living in New York City and being a dancer means you're a dime a dozen, so I audition for every part that I think I have any chance of getting. I don't usually go after the lead dancer role because I just don't think I'm that good. I've seen what other dancers bring to the auditions, and they are exceptional. I know

I can move better than the average person, but I've always been sort of an introvert and would much rather just blend in with the ensemble.

I hear someone stirring in the hallway leading to the bedrooms. Jenna comes walking out with her bed head look. Her mascara has migrated slightly south, and her pajama top is buttoned up wrong.

"Good morning, Jenna. What time did you get in last night?"

"Good morning, Chloe. It was more like what time this morning," she chuckles. "And I'm not really sure. What did you do while we were out?"

"Oh, Chiffon and I had a lovely evening just hanging out together. We watched a little TV, and we had long, meaningful conversations about life. You know, the usual," I say with a grin. "What did you do?"

"We went dancing, drank way too much, and ended up here. You know, the usual," she says, and a glint of mischief is in her eyes. She heads over to the kitchen and pours a cup of coffee. "I ran into someone we know at the bar last night."

"Oh? Who?"

"Well, someone you know better than I do," she replies, and now I'm really curious because she has a really big smile on her face as if she has a whopping big secret. Who the hell could she be talking about? I can't think of anyone who...

I don't know for sure, but now I have a guess.

"Matt Masen!" she shouts and seems pretty damn happy with herself.

I feel the blood leaving my face. Matt Masen is in my city. I could actually bump into him somewhere. Why is he here? Does he know I live here now? What if I see him? What the hell would I say to him? A combination of absolute elation and paralyzing fear rush through my body.

"Chloe, are you okay? Say something." Jenna's concerned words bring me back from my thoughts.

"Does he know I'm here?"

Please say no; please say no.

"Yes, I told him."

Crap.

"What else did you tell him?"

"Um, not much." And by the look on her face, I think she realizes that I'm not happy.

"Oh, Chloe, should I not have said anything to him? I'm sorry if I said too much. I just assumed you'd be happy I ran into him. Are you angry?"

Am I angry? No, not really angry as much as...nervous. Nervous? Is that what this is? Why should I be nervous about seeing Matt? I mean, he's been a close friend for most of my life. We've seen and done so much together and...

Then I know what my problem is. It's that kiss all those years ago. We've never discussed it, and the meaning behind it still haunts me. Why is that damned kiss keeping me from the happiness I should feel at the thought of seeing my very good friend? This is ridiculous.

"No, I'm not mad. Just surprised, that's all. *Shocked* might be a better word. What's he doing in New York anyway?"

"I'm not sure exactly," Jenna says with relief written all over her face. "He said something about coming here for work. I don't know, maybe there's an electrician's convention going on," she states with an eye roll and a giggle. "Besides, New York is a big city. What are the chances that you'll actually run into him?"

"Yes, that's true," I reply hesitantly.

"But," she says.

But? Oh no, this can't be good.

"Just in case you do run into him, I think you need a little makeover."

I frown. "What's wrong with the way I look?" I say with a pouty lip.

"Chloe, you're beautiful just the way you are. But I know we can enhance what God has given you. Come on. I know just the place to go."

We pull up in the cab in front of a salon. The sign reads, The International Salon of New York.

Jenna hands the driver some cash, and we step out into the sunshine. She takes my hand, and we glide inside. Everything is white. The walls are white, and the floors are white. The only things that aren't white are the chairs. Pictures of all types of monuments from around the world cover the walls: the Eiffel Tower, the Great Wall of China, the pyramids, and more. Jenna speaks with the receptionist and then sits down with me.

"They know me here. It'll be just a few minutes," she says as she smiles.

I nod my head in compliance. "This place is nice. It looks exclusive," I say while glancing around the large, open room.

"Exclusive? Yes, I guess you could say it's exclusive. I've been coming here for a couple years now, and they always do a great job," she says.

As I sit and wait for my turn, I leaf through hairstyle magazines and look for a style I might like.

"Chloe?" a very perky young woman says. She is tall and attractive with long, bottle-blond hair. I smile and stand. "This way, please," she says as she leads the way to the sinks.

We are passing chair after chair of people getting haircuts and highlights and a couple of silver-haired women getting perms. Miss Perky gestures for me to sit at one of the chairs in front of a sink. I sit. Putting a towel around my neck, she starts the usual small talk you get in a salon.

"My name is Kendall. So how long have you lived in the Big Apple? I moved here a few months ago," she says as she wets my hair.

"Um, I've lived here about three years. I transferred to NYU in my junior year."

She keeps talking, but it's hard to hear her over the noise of the water. Her voice seems to echo around the sink bowl, so I just smile and nod as she works my hair into a lather. Soon she's done, and I'm in the styling chair.

"So, what are we doing with your hair today, Chloe?"

"Well, I want a haircut, something stylish and cute. You know, maybe a little edgy." This is out of character for me. I hand her the magazine I've been looking at. "Here, this is what I want." I am pointing to a picture of Ashley Greene, the character named Alice from the movie *Twilight*. Her hair is almost pixie-like. It's short and has jagged points strategically sticking out everywhere. "It's dark brown though, and I like my natural blond color. But this is basically what I want."

She grins.

"This is a great look for you."

And then she gets to work, lifting my hair and cutting it this way and that, all the while making small talk.

"And then I said, 'Oh yes, you look lovely with green hair! '" She laughs and snorts at the same time.

"You must come across some strange people here. New York can be an interesting place to be."

"Yes, I do," she replies with a you-have-no-idea kind of smile on her face.

"So are you getting this new style to impress someone? A new guy maybe?"

More like an old friend—and how does she know?

"How can you tell?" I say, astonished.

"I don't know. I guess I just know how to read people. So what's he like?" she asks.

What is Matt like? Hmm, I really don't know, do I? It's been five years or so. I'm not sure how much he's changed. What can I say? "Well, he's an electrician, I think, and he's very kind and sweet, and he was my best friend forever."

"Sounds mysterious. You're not sure what he does for a living? Why is that?"

I explain I lost touch with him after high school and the last thing I knew was that he was working with his dad in Ohio. I left out the part about the kiss because the truth is that after all these years and never having a discussion about it, I'm beginning to think I imagined the whole thing.

"Wow, well, I'm sure it'll all work out. So, what do you do for a living, Chloe?"

"Well, I'm a dancer mostly," I say with a small smile. "But I have a day job too. I'm a waitress at"—"

"A dancer?" Kendall interrupts. "I'm a dancer too! Have you been in anything I might know?"

"Um, probably not," I say shyly and shake my head. "I mostly stick to smaller productions."

"Oh. Are you in a show currently?"

Why is she so interested?

"No. I'm actually looking for my next gig. My last show ended a couple of weeks ago."

Her eyebrows shoot up in surprise.

"I have the perfect audition for you! The cast of *Chicago* is hiring new dancers to fill some spots. The auditions are on Friday. Why don't you come try out? It'll be fun! Maybe we could work together." She says it with such enthusiasm that it's almost impossible to say no.

"Friday?" Well, I don't really have anything else going on. "Okay, that sounds good. You'll write down all the information for me?"

"Yes, I will!" And again, she's just way too happy.

She finishes up and hands me a mirror so I can look at the back.

"It's perfect," I tell her.

"Yes, and it really suits you," she adds.

I walk with her to the front desk and give the receptionist my credit card. Then I turn to Kendall and hand her a tip. "Thank you so much, Kendall. You did a great job. I really do love it."

"You're welcome," she says and hands me a small piece of paper. "And don't forget Friday."

"Yes, Friday. I'll be there." I walk back toward Jenna.

three

"Oh, Chloe!" Jenna gasps. "I love it. That haircut looks wonderful on you." She claps her hands rapidly.

I blush what is probably a lovely shade of scarlet.

"You really think so?" I ask meekly.

"Absolutely. It frames your face so well. Now let's go home, and I'll do your makeup."

We take another cab back to our apartment. Within an hour or so, I am treated to a mud mask, mini manicure, and a lecture on the correct way to apply makeup.

"Remember, less is more," Jenna says. "You don't want to look like you tried too hard."

After a few more finishing touches, she steps back to look at her masterpiece.

"Perfect! Now all we need is an outfit," she says, grinning.

"Why do I need to change clothes?"

"Because," she replies, "I am taking you out tonight. You spend far too much time by yourself."

I open my mouth to argue, but she quickly silences me by holding her finger up in a "don't mess with me, I'm on a mission" kind of look.

I sigh and accept my fate. I'm going out with Jenna tonight, and apparently, I'm going to have a good time whether I want to or not.

⟵⟶

The club is loud. I can feel the beat of the music in my chest. Bright lights flash and swirl all around us. As I look around, all I can see is wall-to-wall people. Ugh, this is so not my thing, but I have agreed to humor Jenna and come with. It appears that the melting pot of New Yorkers have all converged in this place, everyone deciding that tonight is the night to party. Some of the people have multicolored hair and strange piercings. Some look as though they should be walking the streets professionally, and some, I'm pretty sure, really do. Others look relatively normal, and I wonder why they are here. Oh wait, maybe they have an overly concerned, interfering best friend who played dress up with them too.

We find two seats at the bar. They're at the far end of it, and I'm glad because that means we are not going to be in a high-traffic area. Jenna flags down a bartender.

"What do you want to drink?" Jenna shouts over the music.

"Seven-Up?" It's more of a question than a statement.

Jenna grins wickedly.

"Fine." She turns to the barkeep. "One beer and one sloe gin Seven-Up."

"Jenna! That's not what I"—" I don't even get my full protest out before she scowls at me. "Okay, fine." I bow my head slightly in defeat. When she sets her mind to something, she really is a force not to be reckoned with.

The bartender hands us our drinks, and Jenna raises her glass. "To an unforgettable night," she says, and we clink glasses. I take a sip.

"Oh, this is good. I can't even really taste the alcohol in it." I take another swig. It's sweet, red, and a little bubbly from the Seven-up.

"Be careful, Chloe. Sloe gin can and will catch up to you quickly. Hmm," she says, "I think I've told you that before." Then she snickers. "Yes, the night of the graduation party!"

"Oh, Jenna, don't remind me. I was so sick the next day." My stomach recalls the unpleasant aftermath of my binge drinking that night.

"Your hangover might have been ugly, but at least you got to kiss Matt!" she teases.

"Jenna!" I shout, then nudge her arm and smile.

She's right. That was such a wonderfully confusing night. I can't count how many times I've replayed it in my head over the last five years.

We continue to drink. She's had three beers, and I'm on my second sloe gin when I look through the crowd and see...Matt? My heart stops beating. I stare for a few minutes, willing my eyes to focus. Relief washes over me. Nope, not him. I haven't seen my childhood friend in five years, but that's definitely not him. I am really starting to feel giddy. The alcohol is taking effect, and I probably should stay seated as much as possible. I turn around and catch another glimpse of someone who looks just like Matt. Same sandy brown hair, but he turns out to be much older. I can't believe how many men at the bar resemble him. It's like he's everywhere. Jenna has me all worked up; that must be why I keep seeing him and why my heart goes crazy until I realize it's just another imposter. And now I have a problem.

"Where's the bathroom in this place?" I ask Jenna, who is holding her beer and swaying side to side in a subtle dance.

"It's over there." She points to the far corner of the large room. "Do you want me to come with you?"

"No, I'll be fine. I'm a dancer. I will just bourrée right through this crowd."

Jenna smiles and then shrugs. "I'll stay here and hold our seats. Besides, I'm not ready to break the seal yet."

I nod and start my trek toward the facilities. It's hot in here, and it's hard to penetrate the crowd. As I look at the intoxicated faces of the bar goers, I see another faux Matt. And just as I come to the hallway leading to the restroom, I see another. Jeez, I must really be anxious about the possibility of bumping into him. Finally, I get to the door of the bathroom. After standing in a small line, it's my turn.

I exit the graffiti-clad stall and wash my hands while looking in the mirror.

Get a grip, Chloe. Jenna's right, this is a huge city. The likelihood of seeing Matt is so remote that winning the state lottery would have better odds. Still, it's always a good idea to freshen up a bit. I run my fingers through my hair a few times and then give up.

When I pull open the bathroom door, two very drunk girls almost fall on me. "Sorry," they slur and giggle as they continue to stumble toward the end of the line.

I really do hate the bar scene. I start to make the long journey back to Jenna when I see she has company. Not one, but two men are standing in front of her with their backs to me. I'm not surprised. She is very beautiful, and I can tell by the look on her face that she likes at least one of them. They are laughing, talking, and having a good time. Then the thought occurs to me, is Jenna trying to set me up with one of Trent's friends? Ugh, I hope that's not her plan. I hate blind dates, and I'm in no condition to entertain anyone. I've had way too much to drink and would probably be unable to fight off any advances he might make. I look behind me. Maybe this place has a back door I could escape out of. But then again, New York at night is no place for a single woman to walk around unaccompanied. I roll my eyes, surrender, and continue to rejoin my traitorous friend. As I approach the trio, Jenna leans into one of the men and talks into his ear while smiling and looking at me.

Crap. This is a setup. Damn it, Jenna!

The man abruptly turns to look my way. I stop in my tracks. My heart forgets to beat and then pounds thunderously in my chest. Holy shit, it's him. It's Matt, for real this time. He's got a huge grin on his face, and he's gorgeous. I mean, like male model hot! I stare, dumbfounded at the beautiful creature who stands just ten feet away from me. I'm pretty sure my mouth is open, but I can't seem to figure out how to close it. I cover it with my hands in disbelief.

"Hey, Chlo!" Matt grins from ear to ear.

The power of speech has failed me. I am unable to move. He walks toward me with his arms open, and my feet finally figure out their purpose. I run at him, slamming into him hard while wrapping my arms around his neck. His strong arms envelope me and hold on tight. Oh, this feels good. I close my eyes and breathe in his intoxicating scent. He smells freshly showered. In fact, his darker brown hair is still slightly damp as I grab a fistful. As I savor his embrace, I note that he feels the same, yet different. He's muscular, very muscular. And his hair is longer and somewhat tousled. It's beautiful. Matt lets out a long-held sigh, and I can feel his body relax.

Still holding me and twisting ever so slightly from side to side, he whispers in my ear, "I've missed you."

four

We are standing in the middle of hundreds of people, but it feels as though we're alone in the room. He feels so comfortable, like an old blanket. I feel complete in his arms somehow. I don't quite understand it, but I'm just so glad he's here. Finally, after what seems like an eternity but also only a fleeting minute, he breaks our hold but keeps my hands in his. Staring at me, his huge face-splitting grin mirrors mine. He takes a step back, though he doesn't let go.

"Look at you, Chlo! You turned out to be a real hottie!" Matt says as he looks me up and down.

I must be blushing furiously, because I feel my cheeks heat.

"Oh jeez, I'm a mess...but thank you. And you look more than great."

"Thanks. So what have you been doing since high school, Chlo? Have you won a Nobel Peace Prize yet?"

I laugh.

"Not quite. Who's your friend?"

"Oh, Jake, this is Chloe and Jenna. Ladies, this is Jake, my best friend and business partner."

"It's nice to meet you, Jake," I say as I shake his hand.

"It's great to meet you both, especially you, Chloe. He's been going on and on about you forever." Jake rolls his eyes in an exaggerated manner. Matt shoots him an exasperated look and nudges him with his elbow.

"Enough small talk," Jenna shouts. "You can catch up later. We need another round of drinks." She catches the eye of the bartender and gives her our order. Jenna and I sit on our stools while the guys stand in front of us.

While waiting for our drinks I lean into Jenna. "We will have a little chat about this when we get home," I say in a menacing tone. She smiles guiltily.

Our drinks arrive, and Matt raises his glass.

"To finding old friends and making new connections!"

We all take a sip and begin catching up.

"So, what have you been up to, Chlo?" Matt asks. He seems as though he's genuinely interested.

"Um, where do I start?" I tell him how I started out at BW as a dance major but moved to New York in the beginning of my junior year. "I've been in several musicals, though I'm sure you've not heard of most of them."

"Wow, you've come a long way in five years."

"Now it's your turn. Spill it," I say, curiosity eating away at me.

"Well, there's not much to tell actually. I started out working under my dad as an electrician, and then I decided it wasn't enough for me. I enrolled at OSU, got a degree in theatrical lighting, and did that locally for a while. I met Jake on the job, and we started our own company. It takes us all over the country sometimes."

"Wow, that's amazing! But I thought you'd decided not to go to college," I reply.

"Yeah, that was my plan, but my dad talked me out of it. He said I would always have his trade to fall back on, but he knew I would never be completely happy doing that for the rest of my life. Turns out he was right. I'm doing what I love now. Not many people can say that." He wears a contented smile.

"And you're here in New York. How long have you been here?"

"About two or three months now. Jake's parents have a place here. We pay next to nothing for rent. It's an interesting city, isn't it?" he chuckles.

"It's worlds away from Brunswick, Ohio." I take a sip of my drink.

For the next two hours or so, we talk about everything and anything. I know Jenna and Jake are conversing with us too, but it feels as though Matt and I are the only ones in the room. I am fascinated when Matt talks about his job and the places it has taken them. He knows so much about the theater, and it's amazing to see how animated he becomes. I can see his passion for it.

"I see there is no ring on your finger, Chlo. No one has swept you off your feet yet?"

What? I know that I am fifty shades of red right now. "Um...no. No one has measured up, I guess. Why do you ask?" I say rather boldly, I think.

"Well, a beautiful girl like you living in New York City and being a dancer, I just assumed you'd be with some guy you'd danced with on stage or met at work."

He thinks I'm beautiful? Well, he has had a lot to drink.

"To tell the truth, most men I've partnered with are gay, and the ones who aren't are too arrogant for me. How about you? Some woman hasn't snapped you up and dragged you to the altar?" Okay, now I'm talking too much. Do I really want to know this? Let's get real: I'm hoping that he hasn't had anyone in his life since that day because nobody compares to yours truly. Wake up, Chloe. That's never going to happen.

"No."

I wait for him to continue, but he doesn't.

"No?"

"No," he repeats. And that's all he has to say about it. Hmm, how frustrating and how perplexing. Now I want to know more. Why doesn't he elaborate? Jake breaks into our conversation to announce to Matt that they should go. Apparently they have work to do tomorrow. My heart sinks. I don't want Matt to go. It's been so long since we've seen each other, and I've missed him, really missed him.

"Jake's right. We need to get going. Can I give you my number and maybe get yours?"

Without hesitation I grab a pen from the bar and scribble my number on a napkin. He rips it in half, writes his on it, and hands it back to me.

"It's been so good to see you, Chlo. You have no idea how glad I am to have...um...run into you like this." He smirks.

"Yes, what a coincidence," I say with a wry smile.

"Please, don't be a stranger. I really am happy we got to hang out tonight."

"Me too, Matt." I hug him tightly, not wanting to let him go.

The cab ride home is quiet as I am giving Jenna the silent treatment. As soon as we walk into our apartment, I let her have it.

"How could you take me out to the club all the while knowing that Matt would be there?" She opens her mouth to speak, but I interrupt her. "Why didn't you warn me?" I growl.

"You know why. If I had told you who was going to be there, you would have freaked out and been a disaster all day."

She has a point.

"Yeah, but it would've been nice to know so I could girl it up a bit more."

"Chloe, you looked fantastic. Everyone at the bar was staring at you. Matt couldn't take his eyes off of you, for Pete's sake."

Really? "Jenna, you're exaggerating."

"No, I'm not. He was watching your every move. I'm not even sure he was aware that Jake and I were in the room."

"Please don't say things like that. I am so afraid to have feelings for him. I could easily fall for him, and I have no idea how he feels about me. He's always been vague. I mean, talk about mixed signals. Just when I thought he was looking at me in a romantic way, he would say or do something that screamed friends only."

"And men say we're impossible to understand," she giggles. "I'm sorry, Chloe, but actions speak louder than words, and I think he likes you. I mean, I think he *likes you,* likes you. How will you ever know unless you talk to him?"

She's right, of course. I know that deep down, but it's so scary. What if I screw up our friendship? I would never forgive myself. Then again, if I do nothing, then I'll never know what could have been.

"Ugh! I know. You're right. But what the hell do I say? 'Hi, Matt. How was your day? Would you like to discuss the two of us having a long, meaningful relationship?' Somehow, I think that would backfire on me."

"You'll find the right words and the right time to talk to him about it. I don't think it'll be as hard as you think. After seeing his reaction to you tonight, I have no doubt he's into you."

"Maybe. I'm going to take a shower and go to bed. See you in the morning." I give her a small "thank you for being there for me" hug and head off to my bedroom.

After grabbing my pj's, I walk into the bathroom, set my stuff on the sink, and turn on the shower. Looking at myself in the foggy mirror, I try to imagine what life could be like in five years. I imagine Matt standing behind me in the mirror, his arms wrapped around my waist and smiling as he kisses my neck. He's wearing only a towel. I can almost hear it hit the floor as he climbs in the steamy shower and beckons me to follow him. And then reality hits me. If things go terribly wrong between us, I can picture myself alone in my bathrobe, curlers in my hair and a lonely feeling in my heart.

I physically sink, my shoulders slouching forward in defeat.

"Please don't screw this up," I say to the pathetic girl who stares back at me. I step into the shower and begin to wash the images out of my head.

five

It's Sunday morning. My head is foggy. I'm still in bed and reluctantly open my eyes. The light that filters in through the window is too bright, and I squint in protest. Why does my head hurt? Oh yeah, the alcohol last night. I roll over and grab my iPhone to look at the time. Holy shit! I'm late for work! I scramble out of bed in double time, pulling a brush through my hair and then trying to pull my pants on quickly. Why, oh why did I do this to myself? I run to the bathroom while buttoning my shirt. There's that creature in the mirror again. Wow, she looks like hell. Some mascara and lip gloss and I'm off to the kitchen. Jenna sits at the breakfast bar looking equally disheveled.

"Good morning, Chloe. Sleep well?"

"Morning," I mumble as I stuff a piece of bread in my dry mouth.

"Late for work? That's not like you. Were your dreams about Matt too hot to wake up from?" she says with a smirk.

I almost choke as I inhale sharply, and crumbs come flying out while I cough and hack, trying to take in a breath. I swallow.

"I do not have time to discuss my dreams from last night with you. I'm late, and you know how much I hate tardiness." I grab my bag and head out the door, one arm up in a wave as I go.

The Sunday breakfast rush is nothing to mess with when you work for the most popular mom-and-pop restaurant in New York City. Mangolina's is owned and operated by Sal and Ana Mangolina. They serve authentic Italian and American food that is to die for. They have a very good reputation in the city, and even people who have moved away find themselves walking back through their doors for the famous cuisine. Sal is an expert businessman, and Ana gives the place a homey feel. Together they have run the restaurant for over forty years with much success. Ana decorated it herself with items from her birthplace, Sicily. When I see the two of them, they remind me of cute little salt and pepper shakers. Each of them short and round, jolly-looking in an old-world way. They are good people and great employers and have been nothing but generous and kind to me. I don't know if I could ever quit working for them.

"Good morning, Chloe! I hope you had a good time on your days off. I see you got a new haircut. It looks very nice," Ana says in her thick Italian accent.

"Good morning, Mrs. Mangolina. Yes, I had a wonderful couple of days, thank you. And I'm sorry I'm a little late today."

"Nonsense, child, it's only five minutes after. You've heard of the five-second rule? Well, here we have a five-minute rule." She smiles and hands me an apron.

"Thank you, Mrs. Mangolina. It won't happen again."

The mornings here are very busy, but even more so on Sunday. The after-church crowd means double the work but double the tips too.

I'm most of the way through my shift. I'm exhausted from the late night and the amount of alcohol I ingested. My hair, which I'm not used to dealing with, is pinned back in a very small ponytail. It has started to loosen, and small pieces are hanging down the sides of my face. Between brushing it aside with my hands and blowing it out of my way, I'm sure I look just stunning—or not. I look up to see my next set of customers being seated at table nine, three men. Two of them look as though they're probably in their mid-twenties, and the other one looks much older. I watch them sit and take my cue. "Good morning...er...afternoon. Can I get you gentlemen something to drink? Coffee maybe?" I say as I am looking down at my notepad. When I realize there is a hesitation, I peer up to see one of the younger men blatantly staring at me. I freeze, instantly caught in his gaze, then flush crimson and tear my focus away. He is attractive, very attractive, and I have to bite my bottom lip to keep from smiling. His hair is jet black, and his eyes are a stunning blue, the same color you'd see in the ocean while vacationing somewhere tropical. He has a slender build, but I can tell he works out regularly. His button-down shirt is barely containing the pectoral muscles threatening to burst out from beneath. The older man finally speaks up.

"I think we'll all have coffee, don't you boys think?" They both agree, and their heads bow to search the menu.

"Okay then, coffee all around it is. I'll be back to take your order in a few minutes."

I walk off in the direction of the coffee pots and can't help but feel as though I'm being watched.

"Wow! You got the best-looking table of the day," Olivia says. Olivia is another waitress who I work with often. She's in her fifties, I think, and sort of a mother figure. I always get advice about life from her, whether I want it or not. "I do believe he has himself a little crush on you, honey," she says with her Southern accent.

When I look back toward the table, I see the younger man with jet-black hair watching me, but he abruptly looks away and down at his menu.

"Oh, Olivia, you always think everybody has a crush on me. He's probably just wondering what's taking me so long to get them their coffee."

"I know I've been known to say that before, but this guy keeps staring at you like your something to eat, darlin'. I think he's sweet on you."

I give her an exasperated look, grab the coffee pot, and head back toward the now awkward feeling table.

In silence I pour three cups of coffee, all the while noting that the tension in the air is growing thicker.

"Are you ready to order?"

"Only if you're on the menu," says the other younger man with lighter hair, as he snickers.

The dark and handsome one throws an elbow into to his friend's side, making him wince and chuckle. They're obviously brothers.

"Shut up, Adam. Have a little respect," says Dark and Handsome, and then he gets elbowed back.

"Boys! What are you doin', huh? This beautiful young lady is just tryin' to do her job, and you two are carrying on like this. I'm sorry..."

He looks at my name tag. "Chloe. Please forgive my sons. We only let Adam out of his cage once a week, and he's obviously forgotten how to behave in public." The older man gives his son a knock-it-off look.

"It's fine," I reply. "I had a little brother. I know how much of a pain in the butt they can be."

The older man chuckles, and I giggle.

Dark and Handsome glances up at me. "You have a lovely laugh and a beautiful smile."

I feel my cheeks heat.

"Oh jeez, bro, really?" Adam snorts.

"Adam, that's enough," says their father.

Adam slouches in his chair at the scolding.

"Oh...um, thank you." I feel my face flush again. "Have you decided what you want?"

They recite their choices, and I scurry off to the kitchen to put the order in.

I am flustered the rest of the time the men are in the restaurant. Even when I'm waiting on another one of my tables, I feel as though they're watching me. Well, I feel like he's watching me.

Their order is up, and I walk toward them, feeling shy as Dark and Handsome stares at me. I start placing the dishes in front of them.

"I'm sorry. I think we got off on the wrong foot. My name is James. You're Chloe, right?" says Dark and Handsome.

"Yes, and it's nice to meet you, James," I say.

"This is my dad, Jerry Hale, and of course my little brother, Adam."

I smile at both of them. Jerry seems like a genuinely nice kind of man, gentle but stern when necessary. His graying hair tells me he's probably in his fifties, and his typical New York inflection says he has been living here for quite some time. Adam has the same tone to his voice. I'm sure they are lifers here. James, on the other hand, sounds as though he's been outside of this burg, at least temporarily. He sounds as if he's tried hard not to sound indicative of the area. Maybe he went to college out of state. Whatever the case, his voice sounds smooth like melted caramel, and I am entranced by it.

"Hello, Jerry, Adam." I nod to each of them. "If you need anything else, please let me know. My shift is just about over. After that, Tammy can get whatever you'd like. It was a pleasure to meet all of you." And as I say it, I look at each of them but linger a little longer on James's handsome face.

I begin to walk away.

"Wait!" James interjects, a little louder than he probably meant to. "Um...do you come here often? I mean...how often do you work here? I'm just curious because the service you've provided was excellent... and...I was hoping that the next time I come in to eat here, you'd be... um...here." His voice is shaky, nervous, and charming. My smile broadens, and I blush for the hundredth time.

"I'm here about four to five days a week during the daytime," I say. "I'm sure we'll run into each other again." And with that, I turn away and walk into the back.

When I get home the first thing I do after petting Chiffon is kick off my shoes, sit on our plush couch, and rub my aching feet. It's funny how I can practice for hours on end in painful pointe shoes but eight hours waiting tables makes my poor battered feet throb terribly. I am too exhausted to move, so I lean back, close my eyes, and...drift.

I wake to the sound of Jenna cursing as she almost trips over Chiffon who is, as usual, weaving affectionately between her legs. It is her way of welcoming Jenna home but annoying if you are in a rush to get in the door.

"Chloe, did you just get home from work?" she asks, surprised.

"No. I've been home for...what time is it?"

"It's seven o'clock in the evening."

"Wow, really? I must have been extremely tired to have slept that long."

"I guess. So did you call Matt back?" she asks.

"Back? I didn't realize he called."

"Well, he's called and texted me several times today, so I can only assume he's done the same to you. Have you checked your messages?"

"No. I mean, I was late for work this morning, and it was a typically busy Sunday at the restaurant. I came home and fell asleep." What would I find when I looked at my phone? I turn it on. Five text messages and three missed calls!

It was good to see you last night.

Call me when you can.

I hope you made it home safe.

Are you okay?

??

The three calls were spread throughout the day. The messages go from the first one sounding casual to the last one dripping with concern.

"Oh my God, what was possessing him?"

"Um, Chloe? I think maybe *you* are possessing him."

What? No way. He was just really glad to see me after all these years.

"Jenna, I don't think so." But all the way in the back of my mind a little voice says that maybe she's right.

"Are you going to reply?"

"You think I should? I mean, what would I say?"

"How about, 'Hey, Matt. Do you want to meet up for coffee?' That might be a good start." She rolls her eyes in exasperation. "You know, you should give yourself more credit. You're gorgeous, Chloe. I'm betting that Matt noticed that too."

Ugh.

"Okay, fine, I'll do it."

I pick up my cell phone and dial his number, but I hesitate to press send.

"What are you waiting for? Call him already," she says impatiently.

I press call, wince, and squeal as the phone reads, "'Calling Matt Masen'."

six

It rings once. My heart beats wildly. It rings twice. I imagine him walking toward his phone. It rings a third time. Is he ever going to answer? And then...

"Chlo?"

His voice is deep and breathy, kind of like it would be if he had just woken up. Oh my, his voice. It sounds just like I remember from when we were kids. It's familiar, and it's like every other sound in the world has been muted for a little while. Like my ears can only register the soothing, sexy sound of Matt's vocal cords.

Say something, stupid!

"Err...yeah, it's me," is all I can muster.

"Oh, thank God." His relieved exhale strikes me as odd. "Is everything okay? I left a lot of messages...and, well...I'm glad you called."

Why does he sound so worried?

"No, I mean, yeah. Everything is fine. Why wouldn't it be?" I manage to find my voice again.

"Well, last night, we surprised you and...after I didn't hear from you...I thought maybe...you might have been upset about seeing me," he says.

'Is he nervous?

"Oh, no," I say while forcefully exhaling. "I was happy you guys showed up. I gave Jenna a little hell for keeping the secret from me, but overall, I was pleased to see you."

"Okay, good. That's a relief. I'm glad I came out. You really looked great, you know, so grown up. And that haircut. You don't look like a kid anymore, Chlo." He pauses. "The whole package was wonderful."

My cheeks flush at the compliment.

Jenna eyes me closely, and I feel the need to move this conversation to my room. When I get up and start walking in that direction, she scoffs, but I don't care. I'll fill her in after I'm done. I just know that if I talk in front of her, I will be unable to concentrate, and I really need to concentrate. I give her a sorry-I'll-be-back-in-a-minute kind of look, and I shut my door. Flopping onto my stomach across my bed, legs bent up and crossed at the ankles, I continue my conversation.

"Thank you. That's nice of you to say. Sorry I didn't call or text you back. I was busy at work all day and never checked my phone for messages."

"It's okay. I was hoping it was something like that. So when can we get together again? It's kind of late now, but how about tomorrow? Coffee maybe? I found this great little café down the street. Do you drink coffee?"

I giggle inwardly. He's babbling.

"Tomorrow. What time?"

"I should be free after five. What time do you get off work?"

"I'll be off by then. Just give me time to get home, shower, and change. Seven, maybe? I'll meet you there if you tell me where it is."

"Perfect!" he says, and his voice seems to relax.

Matt explains where the cafe is, and it turns out it's within walking distance of my apartment. We hang up with a promise of meeting up tomorrow.

I emerge from my room, and Jenna pounces. "Sooo, how'd it go?"

"It was good."

"Good?"

"Yes, good. We're having coffee tomorrow evening."

Jenna claps her hands once with a huge grin on her face.

"We need to figure out what you're going to wear."

She grabs me by the wrist and drags me back into my room.

After we try on practically my whole closet, we settle on a pair of skinny jeans and a black shirt that crisscrosses in the front so you can adjust the amount of cleavage you want to show. I plan to pair it with a sweater with a three-quarter-length sleeve just in case it gets a little cool.

My phone rings, and I'm happy to see that it's Drew Morgan. Drew is a good friend and just happens to be a dancer too. I met him years ago at an off-Broadway audition. They were calling for partners, and neither of us had one, so we auditioned together. We both got parts in the show, although they didn't pair us together. Since then, whenever there's an audition coming up that sounds interesting, one of us calls the other one to tell the where and when.

"Hey, Drew," I say, excited to hear from him.

"Hey, sweetie! How's it going?"

"Oh, you know, same stuff, different day. How have you been?"

"I am just peachy, honey. Andrew and I have just adopted the cutest little Yorkie pup. His name is Simba. We picked that name because of his ferocious growl." He laughs.

"Aww, that's great, Drew. I can't wait to see him. Send me a picture."

"I will definitely do that as soon as we hang up. I have an adorable one of the three of us."

"Sounds good. So what's up?"

"Well, sweetie, there's an audition coming up this week on Friday. I know it's kind of short notice, but it's a good one—*Chicago!*"

Oh jeez. I'd forgotten all about that audition. Kendall told me about it, but I guess I was so busy thinking about Mr. Wonderful that my brain filed it into my short-term memory. I should've been the one calling Drew to tell him about it since I've known for two days.

"Oh, Drew, I'm so sorry. I heard about that two days ago, and it totally slipped my mind. I should've called you about it. I'm sorry."

"No sweat, sweetie. I have that day off anyway. I'm glad I reminded you though. It would be a shame to have missed the opportunity."

"Yes, that's for sure. I'll have to see if Olivia will swap shifts with me, but I'll be there...with bells on," I chuckle.

"Skip the bells, sweetie. They're so last year." He laughs, and it's infectious.

"Okay then, I'll see you Friday, Drew. Give Andrew and Simba kisses from me."

"Will do. See you then." He hangs up.

I love talking with him. He is always so upbeat and happy. And he's a great partner to dance with. We were paired up for only one show. It was the most fun I've ever had on stage. His life partner is pretty great too. Andrew is less flamboyant than Drew, but equally fun to hang out with.

A text message comes across my screen. It's a picture message of Drew, Andrew, and Simba. I stare at it almost enviously. I wish I had a relationship like theirs. They look so happy together. And I'm happy for them. They each found their own Mr. Right. Maybe someday I'll have that too.

Then, as if on cue, another text from Matt:

Can't wait 2 see you 2mro.

I smile and hug my phone to my chest. I can't wait either. I reply:

Me 2. We have catching up 2 do. See you then! :)

A little later, despite the fact that I had a nap, I am exhausted and ready for bed. As I snuggle in under the covers, I begin to drift. Thoughts of Matt fill my mind.

I'm at the restaurant. I look around and see Matt and some woman sitting in my section. That's curious. Why is he here, and who is he with? I saunter over to them to take their order.

"Hi, Matt. Can I get you anything to drink?" I say as I look at him and then turn to her.

"Oh, Hi, Chlo. Yeah, I'll have coffee, and Miranda will have..."

"Water. Just iced water, please," she interrupts in an annoyingly squeaky, high-pitched tone.

I watch in disgust and almost slow motion as Matt seemingly hangs on her every word. Eww. What is this about?

"Hey, Chlo, I'd like you to meet my date. Chlo, this is Miranda. Miranda, meet my *sister*, Chlo." His voice echoes around the room. The word *sister* seems to be emphasized.

What? No! Did he just say...? I'm not his sister! I look at the tables around us. They're laughing. They're all looking at me and laughing. I want to run far away. Oh, why don't they stop laughing at me?

I wake with a jolt, bolting upright. I am covered in sweat, and my heart is racing. I look at the clock. It's five thirty in the morning. I'm in my bed, that image still lingering in my brain. Thank God it was just a dream. I throw back my covers and head for the bathroom.

Watching the pale girl in the mirror, I splash water on my face in hopes of washing away any mental picture that might be clinging to me. I am more nervous about my coffee date than I originally thought. Wait, date? Not a date. A meeting? That sounds too formal. Ugh. I'm putting way too much thought into this. It's just two old friends getting together to talk about old times. That's all. If I think of it in any other way I'll drive myself crazy. I have to assume that's all he wants from me, idle small talk. Yes, let's just go with that. Well, I'm awake now so I might as well stay up and start my day. Moving toward the kitchen I feel Chiffon at my feet. I reach down to stroke her, and she purrs loudly.

"You need some food, you fat little kitty cat?"

I straighten up and walk toward her food dish. Suddenly she's weaving between my legs, and I sidestep to avoid stepping on her. She reads my mind and moves in the same direction. In an instant I am losing my balance, careening toward the corner of the wall.

A couple hours later Jenna comes out to the smell of freshly brewed coffee. She takes one look at me and gasps.

"What the hell happened to you?" she shrieks.

"Chiffon and her gymnastics. I fell into the wall."

"Your arm looks awful, and you have a bump on your forehead. Are you all right? Do I need to take you to the ER?"

I roll my eyes.

"No, I'm fine. It looks much worse than it actually is."

"When did you do this?"

"This morning, about two hours ago."

"It's already bruising. You're going to have a huge black and blue mark." She inspects my arm and head.

"It's okay. It doesn't even hurt that much, and I'll just pull my bangs all the way down to cover the one on my head," I state matter-of-factly.

"I really need to retrain that cat," she says, and we laugh.

"So what's on the agenda for today?"

"Just working and then having an incredibly nerve-wracking, heart attack–inducing, nail-bitingly excitable coffee with Matt later."

"Is that all?" She bursts out laughing, taking me with her to her giddy place that we go to sometimes. It feels good.

Work is the same as it always is—busy.

"Honey, what on earth happened to you? You look like you got in a fight with a wild animal," Olivia says with concern written on her face.

"Oh, Olivia, you certainly have a way with words."

I explain what happened, and she just shakes her head. I then ask her if she would change shifts with me so that I can make it to Friday's audition. She agrees as she usually does. She's one of my biggest cheerleaders. Every time I go on an audition, she prays for me to get a good part.

When I walk in the door at home, Chiffon is her usual self, winding and twisting between my legs.

"Chiffon, I really think you're trying to kill me," I say as I pet her. I reach into my pocket and check to see if I have any messages. There's one from Matt.

C U @ 7!

I reply:

I'll B there :)

Pretty soon Jenna comes home, and my dress-up session begins.

"We need to cover that nasty bruise on your head."

And with that, she douses me with cover-up and loose powder.

"There." She steps back to admire her work. "All finished. Take a look and tell me what you think."

I turn toward the mirror and inspect her work.

"Not bad, Jenna. It's not completely covered, but I'll just make sure my bangs come down over it and then it'll be harder to spot."

She smiles and hugs me.

"What's that for?"

"I'm just so excited for you, Chloe. I know you've been dreaming about having Matt walk back into your life for years, and now it's final happened."

"Yes, I have. I just hope I don't do or say something to screw it up."

"Think positively. Everything happens for a reason and in its own time. Maybe there's a reason you two didn't get together five years ago. Maybe both of you had to go through some things and learn from life to be ready for each other."

"Jenna, it's not an actual date. It's just two old friends getting together to have coffee and reminisce. He's not going to ask me to marry him or anything." I chuckle but realize that in the far reaches of my mind, I'm hoping for more.

By the time six thirty rolls around I'm ready to go. As I step outside of my apartment building, the late summer evening sun caresses my face and instantly gives me a calm feeling. I walk down the steps and stand, looking up at the sky while closing my eyes. I take in a deep breath of fresh air. As I exhale, I repeat a mantra in my head: stay calm, don't sound stupid, and don't ramble on about nothing.

I begin the ten-minute walk to the coffee shop, thinking of things to say. A few people sit on the steps of their apartments enjoying the beautiful weather. They don't say anything to me as I pass by. They look at me and nod slightly as I keep walking. I give them a small smile in return.

The closer I get to the cafe, the more urban the buildings appear. The street is lined with small shops: a butcher, a small grocery store, a barber shop. I smile inwardly when I see the red and white striped barber pole in the window. This city I have adopted is so vintage but so modern at the same time.

Before I can see the quaint little café, I can smell it. Arabica aroma fills my nostrils and infiltrates my brain, giving me a caffeine rush, or so it seems. I look up at the sign. It has a picture of a cup with steam rising from it. I take one more deep breath, and I head inside. The interior has a soothing feel to it with dark woodwork and a muted wall color. There are tables with chairs and big fluffy couches to sit on. Soft music is playing in the background, though I don't recognize the artist. As I scan the room looking for Matt, I feel a pair of strong arms wrap around my waist from behind. I gasp and instinctively try to pry them off.

"Hey, Chlo. It's just me. Relax."

I turn around to see Matt's face up close, as he still has me trapped in his embrace. I throw my arms around his neck and squeeze, grateful that it's him and not some deviant.

After too short of a hug, he releases me.

"Matt, you nearly gave me a heart attack." I laugh.

"Sorry, Chlo. I forgot things here in the Big Apple are different than in Brunswick."

"Yes, they are. You can't go around molesting people randomly around here, you know," say in jest.

"Don't worry, I wouldn't dream of molesting anyone but you like that. Err...you know what I mean."

The air surrounding us suddenly feels thick. Our awkward silence feels as though it goes on for hours. In actuality, it's probably more like seconds.

Matt breaks the strange tension.

"Shall we sit?" He gestures toward the seating area. "Would you like a couch or a table?"

"Um, how about a table. That way there's a better chance I won't wear my drink," I state with a chuckle.

His empathetic grin reminds me that he knows me well. God, that smile does things to me.

We take a seat at a small table with two chairs by the wall.

"What would you like to drink?" he inquires.

"Caramel latte, please."

He stands and makes his way over to the barista and places our order. It takes a few minutes, but soon enough he's back with two paper cups with our names written on them. He hands me one as he sits back down. It smells so good, and I take a tentative sip. It's very hot, which means I'll have to nurse it for a while and we'll have more time together. I wonder if subconsciously I chose a hot drink in the summer for exactly that reason.

"I've missed you, Chlo," he says as he looks directly into my eyes, green to blue.

Holy crap! That came from nowhere.

"I know the feeling. I've thought about you a lot over the years. I never imagined I'd run into an old friend here in New York though."

He sips his coffee and stares unapologetically into my bewildered face. What is he thinking about?

"I don't think you understand. I've really missed you. I went to your parents' house looking for you a few years ago. They said you'd moved away, and I was crushed."

What?

"I asked them where you went, and when they said NYU, I knew I had to come here...to find you." He pushes his hand forcefully through the mop of hair on his head in frustration and sits back in his seat. I am speechless once again.

"Chlo, we need to talk...about what happened after high school."

Oh shit. Is this really happening? I open my mouth to speak, but nothing comes out. Shit! I wish I had anticipated having this conversation. I could've gotten my thoughts together so I wouldn't sound like an idiot.

"Do you know what I'm talking about?"

Still nothing comes from my lips.

A long pause and then...

"Yes."

And that's all I've got.

"I'm sorry. I know the timing of this conversation is five years too late, but I need to know." He pauses as if he's not sure what to say next but then continues. "Do you hate me because of what happened? Did that kiss ruin things between us? Do I need to worry about our friendship?"

We are really going to talk about this. It really did happen.

"No!" I shout, a little too loud. "I mean, I'm okay with it. More than okay with it. I was surprised when you didn't talk to me about it afterward, but I'm not mad. I've never been upset about it." Quite the opposite, actually. "I thought you were upset."

"I was...confused," he says, and then I notice he hasn't looked me in the eye since he brought it up.

"Hey," I beckon. "Look at me."

I place my hands on top of his and gently squeeze. His head swings up, and his eyes slowly meet mine. "We're good, okay? No worries. Please don't feel guilty about something that happened so long ago."

He nods his head and exhales with relief.

"Thank you, Chlo. The truth is, I don't know what I'd do if I had hurt you. You're still my best friend in the world, and I need you in my life. When I ran into Jenna, I thought I'd died and gone to heaven. That didn't sound right." He laughs. "Because I accidentally found her, I knew you couldn't be far away, and I was right. I begged her for your number and wouldn't let her leave until I got it. I can't lose you again. I mean it, I can't."

I am floored. I had no idea I was that important to him even years after we used to hang out. Nervously, I brush my hair out of my eyes and inadvertently expose the rather large blue lump on my forehead. He audibly gasps.

"Chlo, what happened to you?" he asks a little too loudly. "Your head!" Then he looks at my arm. My sleeve had fallen up my arm when I raised my hand to my head. Abruptly he grabs for my arm and pushes my sweater up to inspect it further. "And your arm! What the hell, Chlo? Who did this to you?" His concerned eyes stare at mine, willing me to talk.

I turn beet red.

"Um...me."

I explain about the cat and the wall and tell him I'm okay.

"Jeez. You really did a bang-up job."

I giggle. "Really?"

He chuckles.

"Pardon the pun. Are you okay? Do they hurt?"

"Not much." I shake my head.

Then he gingerly lifts my arm to his lips and plants a soft kiss on the bruise. He repeats the process with my head, but when he's hit his mark, our faces are so close to each other, I feel as though I'm being drawn into him. I stare, unable to move, entranced. One of the baristas drops a metal coffee pot, and the spell is broken. We both sit back in our chairs. I am too stunned to do anything but contemplate what just happened.

seven

When I get home, Jenna, who has been anxiously awaiting my arrival, leaps off the couch, ready for me to give her the details of my, um... encounter.

"Details! Give me every last detail! I mean it, Chloe. We'll sit here all night if we have to." She practically vibrates with excitement.

"Okay, okay, jeez, Jenna. Can I take off my sweater first?" I snicker.

"You can talk while taking it off. Now spill it."

I sit on the couch as I remove my outer layer and begin to tell her all about it. We chat excitedly for more than half an hour and analyze every word that came from Matt's lips.

"Oh, Chloe, he likes you."

"You really think so?"

"Are you blind and deaf? Wake up and smell the love, girl. He wants you. He's just unsure of how you feel about him and probably doesn't want screw it up again like he did after high school. Trust me, Chloe, I've been here before."

She squeezes my hands, and we squeal with delight.

That night I can barely get to sleep. My mind is racing through everything that was said and wondering with hope if my gut instinct could be right. Could Matt really have feelings for me? I mean beyond just friendship? I'm afraid to believe it. Soon I drift off into a world where anything can happen.

I wake to my phone alerting me that I have an e-mail message.

Good morning beautiful! Hope you slept well. I had fun last night. Please be careful as you move about your apartment so no more walls come out and hit you lol. Have a wonderful day!
- Matt Masen, Theatrical Technologies Inc.

I smile and feel a warmth come over me as I press the phone to my chest. I need to reply.

Good morning to you too! I slept fine, although I was a little reluctant to nod off. These walls are plotting against me, you know. And please have an equally pleasant day.
-Chloe G. Shepherd's iPhone

Do I need to come over there and put padding on all the walls? I will if it keeps you safe and free of hideous blue spots.
-Matt Masen, Theatrical Technologies Inc.

I would love for you to come over and would use any excuse to make that happen. Are you game?
-Chloe G. Shepherd's iPhone

Unfortunately, I'll have to take a rain check. I have a meeting tonight. I'll call you later.
-Matt Masen, Theatrical Technologies Inc.

My heart is beating out of my chest, and I can't get this Cheshire cat smile off my face. I feel as if I'm floating while I go about my morning routine.

At work, I am all smiles, and Olivia can't believe my mood.
"You must have really gotten a good night's sleep or else you've got a man in your life," she's says with a wink.
"Well, I barely closed my eyes, sooo..." I reply.
Her knowing smile makes me chuckle.

Back at home, I'm sitting on the couch eating my Ramen noodle soup when my phone rings.

"Hello, Gram!"

"How's my baby?"

"I'm so happy to hear your voice. I'm good...great actually. How's your new place?"

"Oh, you know, it's not like my own house but the aids and nurses are nice to me. There's one aid here who sits and visits with me and even says she wants to adopt me as her gram. At least I avoided a nursing home when I chose this assisted living facility."

Thelma Shepherd is my grandmother. She's my dad's mother and one of my best friends. She's wonderfully wacky and fun and not the usual elderly woman type. Her wardrobe looks more like my mom's because she says she's an old lady but that doesn't mean she has to dress like one. I love her.

"That's great, Gram. So what's going on?"

"Nothing much. I had a dream about you and figured I'd give you a call. Is there someone you need to tell me about?"

Oh my. How does she do that? She has always had a gift of seeing things before they happen, especially when it comes to me. We have this weird connection that's hard to describe.

I tell her about my evening with Matt, and she's excited for me because I used to talk to her about him all the time. She always said he'd come around. Looks like she might be right again.

"Well, baby, I have to go. They're trying to get me to come down for dinner, but the food here is awful, especially their chicken. It just tastes terrible. I'll probably end up eating something in my room, drinking some coffee, and watching one of my favorite movies. Love you, honey!"

"I love you too, Gram. I'll come by and see you next time I come home."

"You better!" she adds, and then we hang up.

I smile as I snuggle into my bed. Matt doesn't call, but he texts me an apology that explains that his meeting has taken longer than expected.

I'm a little disappointed not to hear from him, but I'm hopeful that I'll hear from him tomorrow.

The stage is black except for the dim ghost light. Suddenly the music starts, and the lights pop on. I know that I should know the dance, but I am clueless as to any of the steps. Panic sets in as I realize not only do I not know the dance routine, I'm in the wrong costume. Dozens of other performers enter the stage, and all are doing the same choreography except for me. Then I see him. Matt stands in the middle of the audience watching me make a fool of myself. He is shaking his head with a disappointed look on his face. Tears trickle down my face as I realize that everyone is laughing at me and pointing. Crying hysterically, I bolt, full throttle, off into the wings. The laughing begins to echo as I keep running backstage and through the double doors, out into the street.

I wake with a scream as Jenna shakes me violently.

"Jeez, Chloe, wake up! You're having a nightmare!"

I sit up suddenly and see her sitting beside me. I'm drenched in sweat and panting. Tears still roll down my cheeks, and I wipe them with the back of my hand.

"Chloe, it's okay," Jenna says calmly. I look around the room. The stage is gone, the laughing has stopped, and panic subsides. "Another dance dream?"

I just nod my head.

The smell of coffee fills the apartment. The shower feels like just what I needed as I let the deliciously warm water pour down my body. I had managed to fall back asleep for a few hours after my disturbing slumber. I'm still haunted by my dream, but it is nothing new. Most times before an audition, I have dance-related nightmares. It's pretty much the same dream every time. I don't know the dance, wrong costume, people laughing. It's all horrifying, except this time Matt was involved. That was new.

"Feeling better?" Jenna asks.

"Yeah, I guess so. I must be more nervous about that audition on Friday than I thought."

"Aww, Chloe, don't be afraid. You'll be great. You always are. You just need to see what everyone else sees."

Hmm, I'm not convinced.

"It's not that I think I'm not good at it. It's just that I know what everyone else brings to the audition. The competition is fierce, and I'm not cocky like most of the others. They intimidate me sometimes."

"Well just pretend it's an acting audition, and act like you're arrogant. It just might work. What do you have to lose?"

She's right; it's annoying. I'm going to try it because it's worth a shot.

Before I leave for work I shoot Matt a quick e-mail.

Hi there, handsome! I just wanted to say I hope you have a wonderful day today, whatever you are doing. I wish I could've talked to you last night but I understand. You're probably busy. Please call, text, or e-mail me when you have time today. I look forward to hearing from you. ;)
-Chloe G. Shepherd's iPhone

While at work, I periodically check my phone. No reply yet. I am growing impatient by the hour. What is he doing that's so important that he can't take a few minutes and answer my e-mail from this morning? The longer the day gets, the more my frustration turns to anger. He has a smart phone, so I know he got the e-mail a few seconds after I sent it, so what the hell? Maybe I should send a concerned text.

Is everything okay? Haven't heard from U all day. Please call me ASAP.

By the time my shift is over and I arrive back at home, there is still no word from Matt. I am a mixture of worried for his safety and really angry at him. I fluctuate between the two. I want to text him again, but I don't want to seem too desperate either. My gram always said if you chase after a man, he'll lose interest. If you let him pursue you, he'll eventually catch you. So with that advice, I holster my iPhone and endeavor to take a long, hot bath.

While I'm soaking in the tub, my phone rings. It's Drew.

"Hi, Drew. What's up?"

"Hi, sweetie! I'm just calling to remind you about the audition Friday at ten o'clock."

"Oh, don't worry, my sub conscience has already done that."

"Dance nightmare?"

"You know it!"

"Yeah, I had one too. I choose to think of them as good-luck dreams. You know, only the most talented dancers get them."

We both laugh.

"Drew? Do you remember me telling about a guy named Matt?"

"Of course I do. He's the best friend you kissed after high school but never resolved what it meant. You haven't seen him in about five years and secretly you're waiting for him to ride in on a white horse, sweep you off your feet, and ride into your happily ever after." He's breathless. "Did I get it right?"

"Um, yeah, that pretty much sums it up." I am astonished at how good his memory is.

"Well, what about him, sweetie?"

"He's here...living in New York."

"What?"

I catch him up on the soap opera I've been living lately.

"Oh goodness. Let's do lunch after the audition. We can talk more about it and drown our sorrows a little too."

I snicker and agree, and we end our conversation.

eight

I walk into the Palace Theater in a daze. It's breathtaking with all of its majestic archways and finely carved pillars and moldings. The walls are uniquely teeming with life, and my eyes are reluctant to focus solely in one spot for fear of missing a single detail. The arches just under the ceiling dip down and rest on top of the stately skyscraping columns. Where the arches and columns meet, single lights hang down like tired tulips. The fabric on the thousand or more seats is crimson red to match the massive curtain that has closed in front of too many Broadway stars to count. The balcony section is equally ornate as it sprawls from wall to wall, seemingly floating above. I am in awe of the possibility that I might grace this sacred place where countless plays and musicals have come and gone for decade after decade. Productions like *West Side Story, The Phantom of the Opera, Grease, Wicked, Hair,* and many, many more. I am humbled, feeling unworthy to stride into a place full of so much history.

Dancers fill the massive building, all hoping to get a part in the show. With duffel bags hanging from shoulders, they sign in at a table and take a seat to wait their turn. Some have unpacked and are stretching on the floor, wherever there's room. When signing in, I notice Drew's name, and I look around to find him.

"Hey, sweetie," Drew exclaims as he comes from behind me. "Cute haircut! Are you as nervous as I am?"

I turn, smile, and give him a friendly hug.

"Yes, I am. This place is gorgeous. Have you been before?"

"Not for a job. I once saw *South Pacific* here," he replies. "The acoustics are out of this world."

As we wait our turn, I see a familiar face in the crowd.

"Hey, it's Kendall," I tell Drew with a smile and an overhead wave. She waves back and heads in our direction.

"Who's Kendall?" Drew inquires.

"She's the woman who cut my hair and told me about this cattle call."

"Hey, Chloe, you made it."

"Hi, Kendall. Yes, I did. I'd like you meet my good friend Drew. Drew, this is Kendall."

They shake hands and exchange pleasantries.

"Well, I can't talk long but maybe I'll see you afterward? My boyfriend is auditioning too. If you want, we could go get a bite to eat. We can all discuss the horrible stress we're experiencing while waiting to hear some news. It'll be like a double date."

I look at Drew. "Um, okay. We'll talk about it."

And with that she disappears into the crowd.

After waiting nervously for what seems like an eternity, it's finally my turn. I enter the stage and take my beginning position. The lights flicker from dim to bright and then back to dim, although they are not as dim as before and it's a soft light that I'm hoping enhances my appearance. The music starts. As I move through each step, I dance as if no one is watching, as if I'm the only one in the entire theater. My moves are fluid yet properly placed and strong. At precise moments I close my eyes and surrender myself to the rhythm. At the end I sink into my last pose, and I'm still.

As I get to my feet, I lift my gaze into the seats and find Matt standing alone looking almost lost. Reminding me of my dream, I inhale sharply and stumble a bit. We stare at each other, and it seems as though we are the only two people left in the world. His eyes are big and round like saucers; his expression is one of astonishment. Neither of us tear our gaze away from the other. Then I glare at him, and he frowns. Finally I look away and turn to walk off the stage. Out of the corner of my eye I see him throw something down and run full throttle across the row of seats and down toward the exit. Backstage is crowded, but I make my way through and head down the hallway. I have no idea what the judges said because I was mesmerized by the site of Matt. Every step I take makes me angrier and angrier. I don't hear from him for two days, and he has the nerve to show up here? Ugh!

"Chloe Shepherd!"

I stop in my tracks and look down the long hallway to see Matt barreling toward me pushing through people like a salmon attempting to swim upstream.

"Chlo! Wait!"

I let him catch up to me. I want an explanation. He reaches me.

"Chlo," he pants "Don't go. We need to talk."

"This should be good," I snap.

He stands in front of me with his hands on my shoulders.

"Listen, please. I know I left you hanging the other day. I should've called you or texted."

"It was over two days ago to be exact," I snap again.

"Yes, you're right, and I'm sorry. I've been busy with...things. But I promise I wasn't ignoring you. Please believe me, Chlo."

I begin walking again, and he is keeping up beside me.

"I don't know what to believe anymore. First you tell me you can't live without me, next you tell me you'll call but I don't hear from you for two days, and then you show up here." I stop walking and turn to face him. He turns too. "Why are you here, Matt? What do you want from me? This game doesn't work for me. I feel like a yo-yo. I have felt like this for five years!" I say forcefully.

A look of hurt crosses his face, and I feel a little sorry that I caused it.

"I know. I'm sorry. But I can explain if you let me. I...it's a long story, but I want you to know. I need you to know." He rakes a hand through his hair in frustration. "God, you looked beautiful up on that stage. You were perfect. You *are* perfect. I couldn't believe what I was seeing." He takes a step toward me, and I step back. I am now against the wall as he moves in closer. He puts his hands on the wall on either side of my head. "I need you. I need you like I need the air I breathe, like the sun needs the sky, like"—"

"Matt, baby! There you are!"

A familiar female voice comes from a side door. We both turn our heads and see Kendall walking through the door.

What the hell is this?

Matt takes his hands off the wall and turns to face her.

"Chloe, I see you've met my boyfriend, Matt."

What?

I turn my head back to Matt with a look of confusion. His expression is one of horror.

"It's not what you think, Chlo. Please. Let me explain," he pleads.

I have no words. He touches my arm, and I jerk away.

"I have to go," I say in a hushed voice. I feel numb as I walk away.

"No! Chlo, wait! Don't leave! Please!" I hear her say something to him. "Damn it, Kendall, shut up!" They're arguing, but I don't care. I hear him calling me, and my pace gets quicker until I'm running down the hallway and out of the building. When I hit the fresh air and I know I've escaped, my tears start to flow full force down my cheeks. My knees feel weak, as if they may stop supporting me. Drew, who had been following me, runs up behind me with my dance bag in hand.

"Hey, sweetie, let's get out of here right now." He hails a cab, and we jump in. As it pulls away, I can hear the strained muffled voice of Matt as he tries to get to us. I don't look back. Drew puts his arm around me, and I weep uncontrollably into his neck.

nine

Drew mumbles something to the cab driver and then sits back again.

"I don't want to go home. I'm afraid he'll go there. I just can't see him right now."

"I know. That's why I'm taking you to my apartment."

I look up at him. "Thanks, Drew."

"Anything you need. We've all been there over a man."

Drew's building is in an expensive area and comes complete with a doorman. My phone rings; it's Matt. I let it go to voicemail and then shut it off. I don't want to talk to him right now. We step out of the cab and into an elaborate lobby. The elevator is just as impressive as the rest of the place.

"Nice place, huh?" Drew says with a wry smile. "Andrew is a lawyer and pays most of the rent. I'm just lucky enough to be with him."

"No, Drew, he's the lucky one."

He puts his arm around my shoulder and squeezes. "Thanks."

Their apartment is amazing. It's decorated in rich dark woods with splashes of bright colors as accents. Everything is very modern and almost over the top—almost.

"Your place is beautiful, Drew. You have great taste in furnishings," I say as I take it all in.

"Thank you. We like it too. Would you like something to drink?"

"Yes, please, just water."

He heads off to the kitchen and comes back with two glasses of ice water. He gestures toward the couch and we sit. With one leg folded underneath him, he twists to face me.

"Are you okay?"

I nod as I look down at my hands in my lap. "I will be. I just don't understand why he was even there. I mean, he's not a dancer, and I didn't tell him I was going to the audition. So what on earth was he doing there?"

I turn to face him.

"I think I can shed some light on that. When I saw him, he was wearing a headset. I thought he was a hottie so I moved closer to get a better look. That's when I overheard him talking to some guy named Jake. He was calling out lighting cues for each audition. I think he might have been on his own audition of sorts. Is he a theatrical lighting tech?"

A light bulb pops on.

"Oh. Yes, he is. So that's why he was there. I saw him throw something down when he came looking for me. I bet that was his headset. He may have blown his job opportunity...because of me."

I put my face in my hands.

Drew puts his hands on my leg.

"Hey, it's okay. It's not your fault he picked the wrong time to want to talk. He should've done it two days ago."

"More like five years ago," I say bitterly. I tell him about our latest encounter.

"He's just so damn confusing, you know? And now I find out he has a girlfriend? To top it off, she's the one who gave me this haircut. I lost a great hairdresser and my best friend all in one day."

"Oh Sweetie, talk to him. He really doesn't seem like the type to juggle women. I bet there's a rational explanation if you give him a chance."

"I've given him so many chances though. Tell me, when do I just throw my hands in the air and give up?"

"Don't give up until your heart says it's time."

"But my brain is on overload. It keeps telling me to run in the other direction."

"I said your heart, not your mind. What does your heart tell you?"

I think for a minute and sag into the couch. "My heart says to fight for him. But I'm still too mad right now."

"Then let him stew for a few days. Maybe he'll understand how you feel."

Drew orders a pizza, and we sit on the floor of his living room debating the pros and cons of Cecchetti ballet positions.

"I should probably check my phone in case Jenna called me."

I switch on my iPhone, and there are four text messages, six missed calls, four voicemails, and an e-mail. Holy shit!

I check my missed calls. Four of them are from Matt. One is from Jenna. And the other is from a number I don't recognize. Then I check my voicemail. The first one is from Matt.

"Chlo, please don't hate me. I need you. I need to talk to you, tonight. Call me."

Another from Matt:

"Please, please call me. I'm so sorry."

One from Jenna:

"Chloe, I don't know what's going on with you or where you are, but Matt has been blowing up my phone, and he showed up here looking for you. He looks terrible, and he's desperate to find you. Call me, or I'm gonna really start to worry."

I skip the unknown number.

The text messages are all from Matt.

Please call me.

Chlo, please don't be mad. Let me Xplain.

Where R U??

I M worried. Please call me!

And finally the e-mail:

Chlo, I know you're really upset with me and for good reason. But it's not what you think, and I need to talk to you about it. I can't find you, and I'm very, very worried. Call or text me that you're okay. New York is a big place, and if something has happened to you because of me I'll never forgive myself. If you won't text me then at least call or text Jenna. She's worried too. Please just let us know you're all right. Matt

I call Jenna right away.

"Chloe? Thank God, where are you?"

"I'm fine. I'm at Drew's apartment."

"What the hell happened between you and Matt? I mean, he burst in here in a full-on panic and searched every square inch of our apartment looking for you. What's going on?"

"I'll explain it to you when I get home. Right now I just wanted you to know that I am safe and I'll be home sometime tonight. If Matt calls or comes back, just let him know I'm okay. I just don't want to see him or talk to him right now."

"I'll tell him to give you some space. That should keep him from coming back tonight."

"Thanks, Jenna."

"Whatever you need, you know that."

We hang up.

Drew sees to it to put me in a cab. "Go get him, girl," he says with a wave, and I'm on my way home. I am nervous. I'm afraid Matt is going to show up, and I'm not ready to face him. What am I supposed to say to the man I'm in love with who has a girlfriend? I wince just thinking about it.

Poor Kendall, she must have been shocked to see us standing there like that.

The cab pulls up, and I hand the driver some money as I get out. Standing on the curb, looking at the front door, I take a deep breath and go inside.

Jenna greets me with a hug. "Are you all right, Chloe?"

"I'll be okay. I just need a hot shower and my iPod...not at the same time, however."

"Probably a wise decision." She snorts. "Can we talk about what's going on after you're done? I'm dying to know how he screwed up this time."

"Sure."

The shower feels good, cleansing, in more ways than one. As I stand under the warm water, I contemplate the events of the day.

I'm towel-drying my hair as I come out into the living room. Jenna is waiting for me on the couch with two cups of peppermint tea.

"So what happened?"

I explain it to her in detail.

"What? A girlfriend? How could he? That man has no class."

"In his defense"—"

"Defense? What defense could he possibly have? He practically tells you he's in love with you during coffee and you nearly kiss, and then he ignores you for days only to show up and pour his heart out again. Oh, and we can't forget his girlfriend walking up on the two of you. He was probably going to try to kiss you if she hadn't caught him!"

She's out of breath, thankfully.

"Jenna, believe me, I'm not happy about any of this. In fact, I'm pretty pissed off. But...I don't know. There has to be some explanation for his behavior. He keeps saying there is. It better be a damn good one."

"Yes, it better be good. So what are going to do? Are you going to listen to his excuse?"

"Well, if I talk to him right now...I...I just can't handle seeing him. I need to gather my thoughts."

I'm exhausted, and we agree to talk about this some more after a good night's sleep. I walk down the hall to my room and get ready for bed, but as I pull the blankets up to my chest, I know that a good rest will not be easy to achieve. I slip into a very troubled sleep.

Today is Saturday. Most of my morning is spent avoiding Matt's repeated attempts to contact me. I call in sick. I should've called in lovesick, but I don't think Mr. and Mrs. Mangolina would appreciate it. I was sure that Matt would try to show up at the restaurant, and I knew I couldn't deal with him there.

My suspicion is confirmed when Olivia calls me on her break to tell me some guy named Matt came in looking for me. He doesn't call or text through the afternoon and evening though, which is both a relief and a heartbreak at the same time. I'm not sure if any feelings he has for me are beginning to dissipate or if he is truly trying to give me space to think.

Jenna invites me to go out with her and Trent, but I'm just not in the mood. Besides, being a fifth wheel will only make me feel worse. I wish Matt were here with a perfectly logical explanation for his behavior, but I'm not sure I'm strong enough to hear it. What if he has turned out to be some sort of womanizer? He could have countless girlfriends. The more I think about it, the more I feel used. Maybe I've been reading him wrong all this time. Maybe when he said he needed me, he just meant that he wanted me to show him around the city or he needed a buddy. After all, he did say I'm like a sister to him. The thought depresses me. I don't want to be his sister. I think I'm in love with him, and he obviously doesn't feel the same—or does he?

Ugh, this is so confusing. I need to get my mind off of things. Maybe I should take a few days and go back to Ohio to see Gram and my parents. Maybe a little time away will help me think. The one bright spot in my day is when someone calls to offer me a position in the ensemble for *Chicago*. I immediately call Drew, who has also been offered a part. We laugh and cry and promise to have lunch soon. I then called the restaurant to tell Mr. and Mrs. Mangolina that I'll need about two weeks off for rehearsals. They're used to my calling in with this news and gladly congratulate me and grant me the time off. Jenna comes home and then goes out with Trent. I sit lifeless on the couch until I start to get tired. Day one ends with me sobbing into my pillow until I fall asleep.

ten

Day two. There is no option to stay home. It is Sunday again, and we are always busy. It would be wrong to be selfish on the one day that I am needed the most. I just pray that Matt will be kind and stay away today.

I wait on my tables with a forced smile. Once in a while, one of my regulars notices I am not my chipper self and asks me what is wrong. I laugh and say the rainy weather always affects me. Olivia is even more helpful than usual. I think she can tell something is going on but she never asks. Then my next customer comes in.

"Chloe, right?"

I look up to see the dark-haired man I had waited on just one week ago.

"Yes and you're...James?"

I flush because I remember how awkward our first meeting was.

"Yes, you remembered," he says with a boyish grin. "How have you been?"

My response is automatic. "Fine, thanks, and you?"

"I'm good. Hey, um...I wanted to apologize for last week. My brother is an ass and—"

"Oh, no worries." I snort. "I know the type. So can I get you some coffee?"

"Yeah, sure, that'd be great, thanks."

When I bring the pot back he continues to make small talk, asking about my life and jobs, and for some strange reason, I tell him. I know better than to divulge too much information, but for a reason I can't pinpoint, he feels safe.

"So what does your boyfriend have to say about you getting a part in the musical?"

"Um...I don't have one...but I'm sure he'd be proud if I did." I chuckle.

"Really? How is it that the most beautiful and talented waitress in New York City is still unattached?"

I blush furiously. "Oh, you know, just one of those things." I wave my hand dismissively in the air.

"Well, that's a shame, but it's good for me because I would like to take you out sometime."

My heart stops. Holy shit, I didn't see that coming.

"Well, my life is a little complicated right now. I'm not sure I'd be very good company."

"I bet you'd be perfect company. We could just start off with coffee."

"No coffee," I say a little too quickly. "I mean, I'm trying to cut back on caffeine."

"Okay, how about dinner later this week? You could relax and let someone else serve for a change."

He's trying hard. I have to give him credit for that.

"James, I'm just coming off of this weird...thing with a guy. I'm not really ready to start something new. I appreciate the offer, but I'm afraid it's not possible right now."

"Okay, what if we just go somewhere as friends? Would that be okay? I promise I won't try to coerce you into marrying me."

I laugh unintentionally and recover quickly. "You're funny."

"I try. So what do you say?"

I think about it for a moment. I am not attached to Matt at all. He has a girlfriend, for God's sake. Why shouldn't I go out and have some fun?

Who knows what Matt even wants from me? And this guy is handsome and seems sincere.

"Okay."

"Okay? Really?"

"Yes. I'll go out with you...as friends. Here's my number. I'll have to let you know exactly when because I need to get my rehearsal schedule." I scribble my cell number on the back of a napkin.

"Great! I can't wait," he replies with an all-American-boy smile.

When I get home later, I jump immediately into the shower, dress in my pajamas, and hit the couch for a little evening television. I note with a heavy heart that Matt hasn't called or texted all day. In fact, the last time I heard his name was when Olivia called to tell me he was at my job. That was yesterday morning. I fall further into my depression. I'm Matt's yo-yo again but this time it's my own fault. I told him to stay away so I could think, and now that he's actually taken my advice, I'm upset about it. I hate this. I hate all of this. Why does this have to be so complicated? Why can't Matt and I fall in love and be together? Why can't he love me as I love him? Is there something wrong with me? Am I not pretty enough? All of my negative thoughts start welling up inside me, and a floodgate bursts. I begin sobbing uncontrollably on the couch.

As my crying releases some of my tension, I sit and wonder if he thinks about me in the same way I think about him. I mean, he couldn't, because if he did we'd be together. Matt and I would be together as a couple. I know he has his company to run and it takes up a lot of his time, but still. Maybe I'm overthinking this whole thing. Maybe he does think about me, but he's too afraid to try. Our friendship means a lot to both of us. The fact is I don't know if things would work out between us, and then what? Would our friendship suffer because we tried to make it more than it was meant to be? All of this thinking gives me a headache. I wish Jenna could give me some insight, but I just don't think she would be able to help me in this area. She's busy swooning over Trent. Ugh, relationships come so easily to her. And if one doesn't work out, there's always another guy ready and willing to step in and take his place. I have never had that problem. Jenna is a guy magnet, I am not.

At ten o'clock in the evening, there's a knock at the door. Jenna comes out of her room to answer it, looks at me, and shakes her head with a sorrowful look on her face. She no sooner unlocks it when Matt comes bursting through, startling both of us.

"Matt! What the hell?"

"Where is she, Jenna? I need to see her now, and I'm not leaving until I do!" he says with desperation in his voice.

His view of me is blocked by Jenna, so she steps aside to reveal me looking frightful on the couch. The look of regret and concern is written all over his face as he rushes over to me. Matt sinks to his knees in front of me, grabbing my hand with both of his and burying his face into my leg.

"I'll leave you two alone. Chloe, if you need me, just let me know." She walks into her bedroom and closes the door.

Matt's strained voice is muffled, but I can still hear him.

"Chlo...please...I need you." He lifts his head to look at me. "Let's talk, okay?"

I nod, and he visibly relaxes.

He gets up and sits on the couch, facing me but keeping a hold of my hand.

"I know you're upset. Please let me tell you what I started to say at the Palace." He looks at my hand and begins to stroke my fingers. "Chlo, all those years ago, I mean what happened after high school...well, it was a confusing time for me. I never had feelings, other than friendship, for you until you fell into my arms. I'm not sure why that incident changed my perspective, but it did."

"Then why did you say I was like a sister to you afterward?"

"I know I did. I'm not sure why. Maybe I was fighting this new view of you because if you didn't feel the same way then I would be crushed. Anyway, when you were dancing with that drunk guy— Dave, I think it was—I was suddenly stricken with concern and... jealousy."

What?

"The thought of him touching you in any way that mattered made me absolutely furious. Then when the police showed up, my protective instincts kicked in again and nothing else was more important than getting you out if there."

Oh.

"Are you okay hearing this so far?" he asks sweetly.

"Yes, please continue."

"Okay, well when we got to talking in the graveyard about the good old days, it was a huge reminder that we would soon be going our separate ways. I felt panicked. I was afraid I'd never see you again. You were my best friend, Chlo. I didn't know how to fix it. And then I saw this look in your eyes, and I knew what I wanted to do. I really wanted to kiss you. And you know what? It was the best kiss I've ever had, even to this day."

Oh my.

"So after I finished college, I knew I had to find you. I prayed that you weren't with someone. I accidentally bumped into Jenna here. What pure luck that was! She gave me all the information I needed... that you were still single. When I saw you for the first time again, when we hugged, I felt sparks just like before and knew what I had to do."

He puts his fingers gently on my chin, lifts my head slightly, and softly places a gentle kiss on my lips. My head is swimming with jumbled thoughts, and I feel dizzy. He pulls back slightly and looks into my eyes looking for...my reaction?

Then seeing that the idea didn't anger me, he leans forward again and with his mouth open a fraction, kissed me again. I close my eyes and absorb the feeling of him wanting me, wanting me enough to be so worried about losing me. His lips are soft yet firm and my head is spinning.

"Was that okay?" he whispers.

Our faces are still inches apart as I nod slowly. My heart is pounding out of my chest so hard that I fear he can hear it. I am in love with this man. How could I not be?

"Chloe Shepherd, I think I've been in love with you for five years, maybe more. Please tell me I didn't just ruin things between us."

I blink at him through a haze of thoughts. Am I dreaming? I must be dreaming. Did he really just...? And then reality hits me. I pull back and he frowns.

"You have a girlfriend. What about Kendall? Where does she fit into all this?" I stand up and walk toward the kitchen. He follows.

"Kendall and I were dating when I first got to New York, yes...but—"

"But what, Matt? Were you in love with her or was she just something to do because you were bored?" Where is this anger coming from? "I can't let myself be with you if every time I turn around you're either hot or cold. I don't know which way is up with you sometimes, and it hurts me."

"I know, and I'm sorry. The truth is that I broke it off with Kendall the day after we had coffee. I called her up after I got back from the café and told her we needed to talk. She probably guessed what I was doing and put me off until the next day. When I finally told her we were done, she didn't take it well at all. She refused to accept it. That's why she said I was her boyfriend, not because I really was. I suspect that when she saw us together after your audition, she figured she would stop something from starting between us. She couldn't have known that she was five years too late."

I'm in shock. It makes sense, though I'm not totally convinced.

"When you ran out of the building, I chased you so that I could explain, but you left. Then I tried and tried to contact you. I felt as though I were dying inside. I was so desperate to see you, to tell you how I felt. It was all I could think about. I showed up here and at your job. Chlo, it drove me to near insanity to know that you were so close but I couldn't get to you. I was absolutely panicked. Please believe me."

He reaches for my arm. I take two steps back, but Chiffon is behind me and I trip over her. Before I know it, Matt tugs me by the wrist and pulls me to him, preventing another clumsy event. I'm in his arms again, and a warmth spreads. Our eyes are locked and then so are our lips. I pour all the anxiety from the last few days into our kiss, and I think he does too. It's a desperate wanton release of pent-up sexual tension, and it's fantastically passionate. Our tongues are entwined, as are our hands, twisting and fisting in each other's hair. He pulls away fractionally. With his forehead leaning against mine, his eyes closed, and panting breathlessly, his breathy words flow into my parted lips.

"Please say you'll be mine. I can't live without you anymore."

eleven

Can I be Matt's? How will it work? I mean, I've always thought of him as a best friend, not a lover. Lover? Is that what we would be? Oh my God, I'm not sure we're ready for that title. Yet, I don't think I could live with myself if I didn't give it every effort it deserves. I can't believe I'm about to say this.

"Yes," I say as my heart attempts to slow its rhythm.

"Yes?" He pulls back and looks at me, unsure of what he just heard.

"Yes, let's see where this goes."

Matt inhales sharply. He wraps his arms around my waist, buries his face in my neck, and swings me around in a circle. I grab on to his shoulders for balance, and I giggle. He sets me on my feet again and gently puts both hands on either side of my face.

"Oh, Chlo, you won't regret it. I promise. I will do everything I can to make you happy. God knows you've made me the happiest man alive."

He kisses me again and then pulls back enough to rub noses. He smiles the biggest smile I've seen and I mirror him. I had never thought this would be a reality.

"Let's go out and celebrate."

"Matt, I have to work in the morning. I can't."

"Okay, then we'll order in. Chinese?"

I smile shyly. This is so normal, what normal couples do.

"It's almost eleven o'clock in the evening."

"Hmm, okay then. We'll just sit and watch the news together. Chlo, I don't care what we're doing as long as we're doing it together."

"I agree, but what are we, forty? Let's watch a movie."

We sit on the couch watching a movie we had lying around the house when Jenna comes out. Matt's arm is around me, and I am snuggled in beside him.

"You two look cozy. What gives?"

"We've decided to see what would happen if we started dating," I say, and her face lights up.

"What? That's fantastic! I'm so excited for you. Now you two can double date with Trent and me," she squeals.

All too soon, the movie ends. It's very late. We kiss good-bye but with the promise that we'll see each other tomorrow.

As I lie in bed and begin to drift, thoughts of the day dance around my head. So much has happened that it's hard to take it all in. And then there's Kendall. I feel awful for her, but what can I do? Matt chose me, and I'm glad he did. I hope she finds someone who makes her feel as good as Matt makes me feel. Then a thought crosses my mind. What will happen if Kendall gets a part in the show too? Will I be able to work next to her knowing she thinks I'm the reason Matt broke up with her? It's definitely going to be awkward.

The morning comes, and even though it's a Monday, I am in a great mood. The first thing I do us check my phone. There's a text from Matt.

Good morning, baby! I trust you slept well. I had the best dream.

I reply:

Good morning, yourself! In fact I did sleep well, like a baby actually. What was your dream about?

Matt's response:

I dreamed you were my girl, 4 me to kiss and hold anytime I wanted 2.

My response:

You didn't dream that, silly. That really happened!

He replies:

Yes. You're my dream come true!

I reply:

Melt...

I hug my phone. What a difference a day makes. Yesterday I was boiling mad at him. Today all I can think about is when I can see him next.

My day goes on as usual, work and then home. Jenna and I invite Matt over for dinner. I am cooking a teriyaki stir-fry. When he arrives I am in the middle of making the rice. He sneaks into the kitchen and wraps his arms around my waist.

"Still into molesting random people, I see."

"Not random, only you," he says, and he kisses the side of my neck. "I brought you something."

I turn around to watch him pick up a single red rose from the counter.

"Aww, Matt, it's beautiful. Thank you."

"It doesn't have any thorns because it's perfect that way. Just like you."

I blush.

"Matt, I'm far from perfect. I bite my nails when I'm nervous, I slept with a blankie longer than I'm willing to admit, and I sometimes talk in my sleep."

"Do you now? I'm fascinated as to what you say. Do you talk about me?" He's grinning like a loon.

"Maybe. I don't know because I'm asleep when I do it." I tease him and stick out my tongue.

"Did you just poke your tongue out at me, Chloe Grace Shepherd?"

"I believe I did, Matthew Aaron Masen." I grin back at him.

"Do you remember what I do to rude little girls like you who stick their tongues out?"

"You wouldn't."

"Better start running, Chlo."

At those words I take off, out of the kitchen into the living room. Matt follows in hot pursuit. I round the coffee table and stop. He stops directly opposite of me. We both lunge side to side as the other one moves.

"Just give up now, Chlo. You know I always catch you."

"Not this time, slowpoke."

"Slowpoke? I'll give you a slowpoke." He reaches across the table for me, and I narrowly escape, hopping up onto the couch and to the chair. I make a mad dash for the kitchen again. I'm almost there when his incredibly long arms snag me at the waist. I squeal with surprise as he pulls me onto the floor. I'm on my back, and he's on his knees, his legs on either side of my body. He begins tickling me, mercilessly.

"Matt!" I scream as I try to drag in precious breathes in between fits of laughter.

"I told you I'd catch you. And now I'm going to tickle you until you wet your pants."

"Matt! Uncle! Uncle!"

"Now, you know those aren't the words I want to hear. Say it."

"No!"

"Say it, Chlo. I can do this all night."

"Aaaagghh! Okay, okay! You're the king of the world!" I blurt out.

He stops, but I can't let him win, so I try to grab his sides for a little revenge. He grasps my wrists and holds them on either side above my head. Still sitting on me, he leans down, inches from my face.

"Are you done yet?"

I try to struggle out of his hold, but it's useless. He's too strong, and I surrender.

"Yes," I reply, panting.

"Good." And he leans in the rest of the way and kisses me. Slowly he releases my arms and leans on his elbows above me. I rake my fingers across his back as I pull him deeper into our embrace. As we kiss, I can feel his erection growing, so I stop.

"Let me get back to cooking. It's probably burnt by now."

"Okay." He agrees, and lets me go, but smacks my behind in warning.

"Ow!"

"That's so you remember who the boss is," he says in jest.

"Only because I let you." And I almost stick out my tongue again, but I see him raise an eyebrow so I keep my tongue inside my mouth.

We finish dinner, and Jenna cleans up.

"So what's your rehearsal schedule look like for the show?" Jenna asks.

"Well, it's every day this week at ten in the morning, and they can keep me there until six in the evening. Then I'll have to go to Saturday's show to see how it all comes together." Matt frowns. "What?"

"Nothing. I just thought I'd get to see you more than that this week."

"Aww, it's okay. We'll be able to hang out after I get home at seven-ish."

"What about Saturday though? I thought we could do something together."

"Well, we could go see *Chicago*." I snicker.

Jenna laughs. "Can you get me in too, Chloe?"

"I'm not sure."

"I was kidding. I've seen it before. At least you have the evenings free to do what you want." She winks, and when I give her the shut-up look, she mouths, "'What?'"

"Yeah, that's true. We can plan to hang either here or at my place," he says optimistically.

"Well, I'm off to bed. Good night, lovebirds." Jenna half-yawns.

"Good night, Jenna," Matt and I say in unison. We turn to each other with a smile on our faces.

"Oh, brother." She rolls her eyes and disappears into her bedroom.

"So what do we do now?" Matt asks and raises his eyebrows suggestively.

"Well, we could play Monopoly or maybe a little Parcheesi, Chinese checkers perhaps?" I say with a small giggle.

"Or we could do this." He lifts his hand to caress my cheek. I close my eyes and lean into his touch to absorb the sensation. He gently presses his lips to mine. A warm feeling runs down my body and rests between my thighs. I am both too warm and chilled at the same time. He pulls me closer to deepen the kiss, and I resist slightly. He pulls back to look at me.

"What's wrong, Chlo? Are you okay? We can stop if this is weird for you."

"No, it's fine. I'm fine. It's not weird at all. It's just that I don't have much...experience with...things, and I'm a little nervous."

"And considering that yesterday we were just friends, I'd say this could be an interesting transition. We can take things as slow as we want. It's taken me this long to get you. I am willing to wait as long as you need. Besides, what do you think I am, easy?" He acts as though he's indignant, but I know better.

"Thanks, Matt. This is all so new for me...I mean us. I'm glad we're on the same page."

He kisses me again and again. I am comforted by the knowledge that he will take his time with me. So I let go, and I am lost in the sensuality that is Matt Masen.

twelve

"So did you?"

"No, Jenna, jeez. We just made out...a lot." I smile.

"Are you seeing him tonight?"

"Yes, after rehearsal."

"His place or ours?"

"His, I think. Why?"

"Well, Trent and I"—"

"No need to finish that sentence," I state, waving my hands at her.

When I get to the theater, I see Drew. He is stretching and doesn't see me come in. I seize the opportunity to have a little fun. Sneaking up behind him, I jab two fingers into his sides. He screeches like a twelve-year-old girl, and I cover my mouth and giggle.

"Was that necessary, Shepherd? I think I just peed a little," he snaps, but he doesn't sound angry.

"No, you didn't, but sorry, Drew, it just couldn't be avoided."

"Well, try harder to resist next time," he says with a wry smile. "So what's got you in such a good mood this morning?"

My huge grin gives me away.

"You and Romeo talked, didn't you! So how'd it go? From the look on your face I'd say very well."

"Yes, it went very well. In fact, we have decided to see where this goes."

He fans himself with his hand.

"Sweetie, that's wonderful! I'm so happy for you. Did he kiss you? Tell me everything, and don't skimp on the details."

I give him the full story, and he claps rapidly. "Good for you, honey. You deserve it."

As we sit and stretch, a couple more dancers come in, one of which is Kendall. Ugh. This is not what I need today, but I figure I'll go with being polite.

"Hi, Kendall," I say sheepishly.

She looks down at me with a small, sad smile and nods. I wonder if she knows. "Are you okay?"

She thinks for a moment.

"Not really. You know that guy you were talking to after the audition?" I nod and then swallow. "Well, that's my boyfriend...was my boyfriend. We broke up not too long ago. I want him back," she says with a look of desperation.

"Oh. I'm sorry to hear that."

"Thanks. I think he may have moved on already, but I'm not sure. I would love to know who he's with now. It's good to know your competition, you know?"

"Competition?" I swallow again.

"Well, naturally I'm going to get him back, but I need to know her weaknesses so I can have the advantage." She chuckles, and I get a sudden chill.

"Maybe the one he's moved on with is the one he's supposed to be with and you should just move along," Drew interjects as he waves his hand, dismissing her. I shoot him a take-it-easy look.

"Oh, I'm pretty sure I'm the one for him. I just need to remind him of that," she retorts. The look she gives Drew is scary. "Besides, he's not into boys anyway, honey."

"Ugh! As if!" Drew spits back. And with that, she walks away.

"Drew, don't wind her up. We have to work with her for who knows how long, and I'd like to keep Matt and me a secret from her if possible."

"You don't think she'll figure it out when she sees him pick you up or drop you off here and your faces are stuck together?" he asks with one eyebrow raised. I elbow him, and he pretends it hurt.

"Over actor," I state.

"Home wrecker," he replies.
I gasp and elbow him again.

When I get home it's nearly seven. I check my phone.

RU home yet?

I reply:

Yes, I'll B ready by 7:30.

Matt's response:

Ok. Can't wait! I'll B there soon.

I quickly jump in the shower, and within minutes I'm washed, shaved, and done. Jenna walks in as I am blow drying my hair. I stop.
"Whoa! You look nice, Jenna. Trent is going to devour you."
She curtsies.
"Thank you. That's what I hoping for. How late are you going to be tonight?"
"Um, I'm really not sure. I have rehearsal again in the morning, so I don't imagine I'll be out past eleven."
"Okay, good. That should give me plenty of time to work my magic," she says with a wink.
"In that outfit, you won't need magic."

The doorbell rings, and I run to get it. It's Matt, and he looks so handsome in his blue jeans and tight black T-shirt. I'm practically drooling. I am wearing a green fitted halter top which dips down in the front to show just the right amount of cleavage. My tight navy capris hug my backside without flattening it.
"Wow! You look gorgeous, Chlo." He smiles and motions for me to spin, and I do.

"You clean up well yourself," I say as I take a step forward and smooth the fabric on his chest. Oh my, he works out.

"Ready to go?"

"Yep just let me get my purse."

I duck into my room and grab my clutch. Jenna walks by. Leaning into to me she whispers, "I put a few condoms in your bag, just in case."

I turn red.

"Thanks, but we're not there yet."

"You can never be too prepared," she says with a smirk.

We leave my apartment. It's raining so we have to run into a waiting cab. Matt gives the driver an address and sits back.

"That doesn't sound like an apartment address."

"It's not. I'm taking you out to dinner in celebration of your first day of rehearsal."

"Really?" I squeak.

"Yes, really. I'm very proud of you, and I have some good news myself."

"What is it?"

"I'll tell you over dinner. I want to see your reaction, and it's just too dark to see in this cab."

Hmm, my mind races with possibilities.

Lombardi's Pizza is a quaint little restaurant. It has a typical New York–style front except for the giant Mona Lisa holding a pizza in the front window, which I guess could be considered typical too. We get out of the cab and quickly run underneath the red awning.

"After you," Matt says as he holds open the door for me.

"So chivalrous Matt, thank you." I smile and walk in.

The place is really cute inside and the smell is amazing. We take our seats, and I notice the brick pizza oven.

"Now that is authentic Italian cooking, no doubt," I point out.

"Yes, I've heard this place has been around since eighteen ninety-seven or so."

"Then it must be good."

Our waitress comes to take our drink order. She's very attentive to Matt. She walks away, and I roll my eyes.

"What?" he asks.

"Oh, please. Like you didn't notice the waitress's googily eyes flirting with you."

"Actually, the only eyes I'm interested in looking at are your baby blues."

I smile shyly.

"Matt I had no idea you were such a romantic. Flowers, compliments, holding open the door. Where was this when we were kids and swimming at Brunswick Lake? We raced to the lake, and you never let me win. You were always in the water before I could even hit the shore."

"Ahh, that's because I had heard there were snapping turtles in there, and I figured if I jumped in first, they would either bite me or swim away before you got in."

What?

"You're making that up."

"No, Chlo, I'm not."

Huh.

Our waitress comes back with our drinks, and we order our food.

"One pizza with your homemade meatballs, please."

"Coming right up." She winks at him, but he ignores her.

Ha!

"So tell me about your news."

"Impatient as always, Chlo."

"You know how I am, now spill it."

"Okay, okay. You know how I was at the audition at the same time you were?"

"Yeees."

"Well, I was on my own audition of sorts. Jake and I were there to interview for a position with the lighting crew."

"Oh?"

"Yep. And I wanted to be the one to tell you that I got the job."

"Oh, Matt, congratulations! That's terrific! I'm so happy for you."

"Thanks, and you know what that means? We'll get to work together, kind of."

Oh no. My face falls. We'll be working together. That means he'll also see Kendall. And worse than that, she'll see us together.

"Chlo, what's wrong? You look pale," he says.

"Oh, Matt, I'm happy we'll get to work together. It's just...well...it's Kendall."

"What about her?"

"She also got hired at the Palace, and she's going to try to get you back. She told me so. But she has no idea that you and I are together and...I'd like to keep it that way as long as possible."

He frowns. "Why? Are you ashamed"—"

I take his hands in mine and interrupt him. "It's only because I don't want animosity and tension between Kendall and me. I am proud to be your girlfriend. Please don't ever think otherwise."

He lifts my hand to his lips and plants an understanding kiss on the back of it.

"Don't worry about Kendall. I'll take care of it."

That's what I'm afraid of.

We get done eating our pizza and ask for a box to take the rest home.

"Wow, that was so good."

"Yes, it was," he agrees. "So what do you want to do tomorrow night?"

"Um..." My phone alerts me to a text message. "Excuse me a minute." I pull it out and start to read.

Hi, it's James. How about our dinner date this week? Is tomorrow night okay?

Sent from James Hale's iPhone.

Oh shit. I forgot all about him. Ugh. I agreed to have a friendly dinner with James before Matt and I were together. How the hell do I handle this? Honesty, for both men. I quickly put my phone back and focus my attention back to Matt.

"I sort of...have plans."

"Okay." By the look on his face I know Matt would like more information.

"With...a friend of mine."

"Jenna or Drew?"

"Neither, actually. His name is James."

His face turns serious suddenly. Oh boy.

"I don't remember hearing about anyone named James. Who is he?"

Oh no. Here we go.

"Well, I was working at the restaurant when this customer came in. To make a long story short, he asked me out as friends, and I said yes because I didn't have a boyfriend at the time." I look down at my hands, which I'm wringing at the moment.

"But you have one now," Matt says slowly.

"Yes."

"So thank him for the offer, and tell him to take a hike."

"Matt."

"What, Chlo? What else do you want me to say? I mean, I don't want my girlfriend going out with some loser just because you feel obligated to."

"I understand what you're saying, but I already made it clear that he and I are just friends."

He snorts.

"The only female friends men have are the kind they haven't slept with yet."

"Oh, come on. That's just not true."

"It's very true, and the fact that you don't know that makes you naive and vulnerable. No, Chlo, I don't like it."

"Excuse me? Last time I checked I was my own person with my own thoughts and feelings. I can do what I want, and if that means holding true to a commitment to my friend, then so be it."

This is getting louder than I'd like.

"Fine. Do whatever the hell you want, but if you get in trouble, don't—"

"Don't what? Don't call you? Well, that's just great, Matt. Thanks a lot."

I make to stand up and leave, but he grabs my wrist and holds on to it.

"I'm sorry. You can always call me, whether you're in trouble or not. I didn't mean that. Please sit."

After a beat, I do as he asks, but I still don't look at him.

"Go out to dinner with him. I trust you. I know you are your own person, and I didn't mean it to sound as if I can make any decision for you. Forgive me?"

I take a deep breath and exhale.

"Yes, I do." I touch his hand and look into his eyes. "It's late. I'm exhausted. Take me home."

We get into our cab, and even though we don't speak, our body language lets each other know that we'll be okay.

thirteen

I kiss Matt good-bye in the cab and promise to call him tomorrow. When I get upstairs, Jenna is walking Trent to the door. They pause at the exit and stand nose to nose, embracing. By the lustful looks they give each other, I don't want to be near them for the next five minutes.

I lay my bag on the dresser and plop down on my bed. I hate fighting with Matt. It just feels like my life is off somehow. I need to text James back, but I'm hesitant. I have to tell him something though. I heave a sigh and begin my message.

Hi, James. Dinner tomorrow night will be fine. What time?

I get an immediate reply.

There you R! How about 8? I'll pick U up.

Pick me up? I don't think that's a good idea. I'd much rather meet him somewhere. Besides, he doesn't need to know where I live. I just met the man after all. I text him my reply.

Let me know where, and I'll meet U there.

There's no response. Five minutes later a text finally comes in.

Okay, but can I at least drive U home?

Hmm, persistent, isn't he?

I text:

I'll think about it.

His reply is clipped but confident.

Good enough. Park Avenue Restaurant. 100 E. 63rd C U @ 8.

Park Avenue? That's expensive. I hope I'm not making a mistake. James seems nice, but Matt is obviously against this. I'm not sure why I don't just tell James I've changed my mind. I get ready for bed and fall into a troubled sleep.

My second day of rehearsal is brutal. There is so much choreography to learn and in such a short amount of time. It's a little overwhelming. It's Matt and Jake's first day, but I don't see them much. Kendall, however, notices Matt immediately.

"If she bounces around here, flipping her hair and batting her eyelashes any more today, I'm going to bitch-slap her, I swear," Drew announces.

I chuckle. "I know, right? Kind of makes you wonder what Matt sees in that kind of girl."

"My guess would be all the T and A," he says as he flutters his eyelids.

Ugh. The thought of it makes me ill.

We break for lunch, and I am sort of expecting Matt to come over and talk to me, but he doesn't. The twinge of disappointment I feel is surprising. Instead, he and Jake go off with the other guys from the crew. I sink into a nearby chair, heartache written on my face.

"Aw, sweetie, he's only doing what you asked him to do." Drew takes a seat beside me.

"What's that?"

"You told him you wanted to keep your relationship a secret from Kendall. He's doing exactly that."

In my heart I know that.

"I know, but after the fight we had last night, I just don't have a good feeling. Maybe I was wrong to ask that of him. Maybe Kendall would just get over it."

"Sweetie, with all of this going on"—he pretends to flip his hair and mockingly puckers his lips—"I'd say she won't just get over it easily."

He continues to make kissy faces and mocks her flirtation. I laugh.

"Stop it. You look ridiculous. "

"So does she. You have nothing to worry about, so just relax."

Lunch break is almost over. I'm feeling a little sad, so I shoot Matt a quick text.

I miss u. Wish we could b together right now.

His reply is instantaneous.

Me 2. Meet me in the control booth in 5?

I inhale sharply and reply.

Yes, I'll b there!!

I close out my texting app and go in search of the booth. When I get there, Matt is waiting outside the door.

"Hi," I say quietly.

"Hi," he replies. "So you miss me, eh? Thinking this charade might not be such a great plan now, are you?"

"No. Yes. I don't know. I just needed to see you. After last night I"—"

"Hey." He lifts my chin. "It's okay. We're okay. Go out tonight. I'll be fine. Just be careful. Where are you going and what time?"

"Park Avenue Restaurant at eight."

He whistles. "Sheesh. That's expensive. Now I'm a little nervous."

"Don't be. I'll be thinking of you the whole time" I smile and I give him a short peck on the lips.

I can't believe the reaction my body has to his touch.

"Make sure he knows that you're taken," he says authoritatively.

"Don't worry. That'll be the first thing out of my mouth. I wouldn't want him thinking this is anything more than it is."

With that, he smiles shyly and wraps his arms around me, pulling me tightly to his chest as I hug him back.

"Please be careful, and call me the minute you get home."

"I will."

"Promise?"

"Yes, I promise."

He takes a deep breath and releases me, but before I leave his arms completely, he dips me backward and plants a very ostentatious kiss on my lips.

Holy shit, I suddenly feel very warm.

He releases me. "Now go, be gorgeous on that stage, and I'll talk to you later."

I blow him a kiss and make my way back to rehearsal.

"Feel better now that you got a nooner?" Drew says with a mischievous smile.

"Drew! I did not get a nooner!" I try to keep a straight face, but I'm in such a good mood now that I just crack up.

It's sometime after seven, and I'm about ready to go to dinner with James. I have chosen a light blue wrap dress and two-inch pumps to match. It's an expensive restaurant, so wearing jeans is not an option. Jenna has deemed my look acceptable for a friendly get together and takes my picture just in case Matt's jealous side doubts my intentions. I make sure that there is no unnecessary cleavage showing—not that I have much to show anyway—and I'm off.

When I arrive, I see James standing near the door to the immaculately impressive facade. He is wearing a black suit jacket that was obviously tailored to fit him and a thin black tie. His pants are also black with patent leather shoes that I'm hoping don't reflect up. He's stunning. He smiles broadly when he sees me and, walks closer. Taking my hand, he kisses the back of it and I smile.

"Good evening, Miss Shepherd. You look absolutely beautiful tonight."

I blush.

"Thank you, James. You look very handsome as well."

He nods his appreciation and ushers me inside.

The maître d' checks our reservations and leads us to our table. The dining room is rectangular with recessed lighting inside the tray ceiling. The room is filled with small square tables that sit upon a modern checkerboard-type floor. To finish the look, sprays of long branches seemingly shoot out of contemporary vases. It's all very chic, and I am intimidated. As our dining experience begins with drinks and hors d'oeuvres, I can't help but feel like our small talk is forced. I cut to the chase.

"Before this evening goes any further I need to tell you…I've started seeing someone. I wasn't when you asked me out, but I am now. I just wanted to be clear. You did agree to just be friends," I say and hope it doesn't end the evening.

He winces very subtly but recovers quickly.

"Yes. I agreed we'd go out as friends, and that still holds true. I'm glad you were up front and honest with me about it, though I won't say I'm happy to hear it. My intention is to get to know you and eventually, if the opportunity arises, to ask you out again…as more than friends. I'll be honest, Chloe, if your guy screws up, I promise you I'll be the first in line to pick up the pieces. If you can live with that, then so can I."

Oh my.

"What if the opportunity doesn't arise?"

His breath shoots out in a short burst. "We'll cross that bridge when we get there."

I smile and feel as though a little of the tension has left.

"So, how were your first couple days of rehearsal, Chloe?"

"It's been stressful but fun. Luckily I have a friend who also got a part in the ensemble. That makes it easier."

I look around for some kind of inspiration to start another conversation.

"So what exactly do you do for a living, James?"

"I'm in broadcasting and voiceovers."

My eyebrows shoot up.

"I can tell by the tone of your voice that you're very good at it."

"I'm not bad, I guess. I don't do it to make a fortune. I do it because it's my passion. My wealth came from my mother's second husband. She and my father divorced when my brother and I were young. She found a very wealthy man who died only three years after they were married. He had no heirs, so a trust fund was set up, which I received after the age of twenty-one. That's how I am able to bring you here," he says with a smile.

I'm a little, no, very embarrassed to be told about his history in such detail. Surely it's none of my business.

"I'm sorry. I didn't mean to pry. It's just that you didn't look like... What I mean to say is I had no idea you"—"

"You had no idea I was rich?"

I nod slightly.

"I like it that way. It keeps people honest. If they knew right away how wealthy I am they'd treat me differently than they would if they assumed I wasn't. Because you had no idea where I was planning to take you to dinner when I asked, it told me that you wouldn't care if it were here or at the corner pizza shop."

"Well, that's true."

We eat our meal and make small talk. I have the slow-cooked Chatham cod with dill, lemon, and baby carrots, while he orders the honey miso-glazed pork with Easter egg radishes.

He asks me about my family and work, and I tell him because he's easy to talk to. I find out his dad lives here in New York while his mom lives in California. The waiter asks us if we're interested in dessert, and we both decline.

"It's getting late, and I have rehearsal again in the morning. I should probably go."

"May I offer you a ride home?"

I think for a minute. He's been a perfect gentleman, and I'm not getting any danger vibes.

"Okay, thank you. I would love a ride home," I acquiesce.

"Wonderful, let's go then." He stands and takes my hand, leading me out to the street. His limo arrives just as we get to the curb. Wow, a limo and curbside service. If this is what he drives, I can't imagine where he lives.

We get in the back and take off toward my apartment.

"Thank you so much, James, for a lovely evening. I really had a good time."

"You are very welcome, Miss Shepherd. I would love to do it again sometime."

I smile and flush.

"Me too."

fourteen

I walk in the door of my apartment and immediately check my phone for any messages. There is one from Matt.

Just want u 2 know I'm thinking about u and that I miss u. Don't forget to call when ur home.

I smile reflexively and start typing.

I'm home safe and sound. I've missed u more than you'll know. C U tomorrow. XOXO

Just after I press send, my phone rings. It's Matt.
"Hey," I answer.
"Hey, baby," he replies softly.
I melt at the endearment.
"How was dinner?"
"It was good."
"He didn't try anything, did he?" He sounds protective.
"No, of course not. And I told him right away not to bother because I have a boyfriend who I am very happy with."
"Good girl." I hear the smile in his voice. He pauses. "I'm glad you're back home. I was worried." He sounds exhausted.
"I knew you would be. In fact, I'd be upset if you weren't."
There's another break in the conversation.
"Matt?"
"Yeah?" he whispers.

"Thank you."

"For what?"

"For understanding and being so gracious about tonight. I know you didn't want me to go, and I thank you for not demanding that I stay home."

He sighs. "I was close."

"I know, but you didn't. It's late. I should go."

"Okay then, hang up."

"No, you hang up."

He laughs softly. "Oh, Chlo, don't ever change."

"Back at you, Matt."

And with that, we both hang up.

For the next week or so it's the same routine: get up, go to rehearsal, come home, spend a few hours with Matt, and go to sleep. I get a text message from James the day after our friend date, thanking me for a wonderful evening. He's asked me for another chance to take me out as friends, but I think it might push Matt a little too far. I tell him I will keep in contact, but for now I am very busy with the show and all. Matt and I continue to get closer. We've even started to finish each other's sentences, but then we've always had that weird connection.

Tonight is my first performance with an audience of over seventeen hundred people. I am nervous but mostly because Matt and Jenna will be in the seats. Everyone backstage is getting ready for the show. At any given moment, dozens of half-naked dancers walk around as if it's no big deal. Stage makeup is painted on so thick that if they were to walk outside anyone would think they were in the circus, but because they'll be on stage it looks perfectly natural. Every so often someone will walk around yelling how many minutes it is until show time. The closer it gets, the more my bladder falsely informs me that it's in need of being emptied. I understand my body well enough to know that ignoring it doesn't work, and I make yet another trip to the facilities.

Show time is in five minutes, and everyone is in place. One of the stagehands finds me.

"Chloe Shepherd?"

"Um...yes?"

"Here, I was told to give this to you."

He hands me a piece of paper and then gets lost in the crowd.

I blush as everyone seemingly stares at me, but I open it anyway.

You are the most graceful and beautiful dancer on the stage. I'll be cheering only for you. Break a leg, baby!

Love, Matt XOXO

"Oh my God. How sweet is he?" Drew leans over my shoulder to be nosey.

"He's the best." I hold the note close to my heart.

We go on to perform *Chicago,* and end with a standing ovation. As I take my final bow during the curtain call, I swear I hear Matt's voice screaming and whistling for me. It makes me smile even bigger. The curtain closes for the last time, and we're done. Drew and I hug and congratulate each other on a job well done. When I leave the dressing room area, I see Matt standing against the wall talking to someone. Shit, it's Kendall. What the hell does she want? As if I don't know. I watch from a distance at the two of them. She is all smiles, but Matt looks irritated. It looks as though he's trying to politely tell her to buzz off. Finally she leaves, and that's my cue to move in closer.

"Hi." I greet him with a peck on the lips.

"Hey, there's my dancing girl! You looked wonderful up there, baby. You were definitely the best dancer on the stage," he says with pride and hugs me with one arm.

I blush scarlet and thank him for being too kind. Then he pulls his other arm out from behind his back to reveal a small bouquet of roses.

"I believe this is customary. Well, it's my custom anyway."

"Thank you so much!" I inhale their sweet scent. "I love them." I hug him again; this time he uses both arms, and it lasts longer. But reality sets in, and I'm all too aware that Kendall could come back at any time and find us together. I release him.

"Come on, baby. Let's go home," he says.

Instead of going back to my apartment, he asks the driver to take us to his place. It's dark outside, but it looks a little more like a downtown area with tall buildings. He hands the cabby the fair, and we get out. As he holds my hand, he takes a deep breath. He looks...nervous. Why? We step inside the main door and enter the lobby. As he presses the small round button to call the elevator, it occurs to me that he hasn't said much since we left the theater.

"Is everything okay?" I ask.

"Fine, why?"

"You seem nervous."

"Not nervous, anxious to get upstairs where we'll have the place to ourselves."

Oh? Hmm.

We step across the threshold into the apartment that he normally shares with Jake. It's impressive with its stark white walls and hand scraped, teak hardwood floors. The ceilings are high and the large windows reach down from them to the floor. There is one accent wall made of red brick with recessed lighting shining onto it. In contrast to the pale white walls, the kitchen cabinets are a dark coffee color with sleek brushed-silver handles. The pendant lights that hang over the breakfast bar are one of the only splashes of color besides a few throw pillows. Looking around I can see a bedroom through a sliding, frosted glass door. It looks equally modern with its platform bed and contemporary headboard.

"Wow."

"Wow?" He thinks a minute. "Yeah, wow could describe it I guess. I'm so used to it now that I don't notice how beautiful it is. Hmm, there's a metaphor in there somewhere." He smiles down at me, and I feel my cheeks heat.

"Would you like a drink?"

"Yes, please, just water."

He goes into the kitchen and brings back two bottles of Aquafina.

"So, is that where you sleep?" I point into the bedroom.

"No, that's Jake's room. Mine is down the hall. Luckily we were able to convert some unused space into a second bedroom. Are you hungry?"

"No, not really. Can we sit though? I'm exhausted from the show. I do need the powder room, if you don't mind first."

"Can it wait a few more minutes?" he asks.

What a strange question.

"Um, yeah, I guess. I just wanted to freshen up a bit. I'm sure I stink like sweat." I chuckle.

He puts his arms around me and buries his face in my neck and inhales.

"You smell like hard work and determination, and it's intoxicating."

I raise one eyebrow.

"And sweat," I add with a wry smile.

He smiles, rolls his eyes, and shakes his head.

"I'll be back in a few minutes. Don't go anywhere." He turns and walks toward the hallway.

After what seems like an eternity, he appears at the edge of the hall. With one finger he points at me and then flips his hand over and bends and straightens that same finger to summon me to him. His smile is mischievous and sexy as hell. Perplexed, I stand and walk over to where he waits. He takes my hand and leads me to the bathroom. Matt steps inside just before I do, and I notice a strange glow. When he sidesteps, I see where the strange light is coming from. The entire four-piece bathroom is lit up by candlelight. Tea lights and votives line the double sink vanity and the windowsill surrounding the jetted soaking tub. It smells like a meadow full of the most fragrant flowers, and red rose petals float on top of the foamy bathwater.

"Matt, what is this?" I ask after I lower my hand from my gaping mouth.

"It's for you, Chlo. It's all for you. I knew you'd be tired from all of your hard work, so I wanted to give you something special for your debut."

"I'm speechless."

"Well, I think that's a first," he teases.

I smack his arm in mock disapproval.

I turn and hug him. "Thank you for everything you do for me," I say into his neck.

"Anything to make you happy, Chlo. Now, you'd better get in before the water cools off."

I look at him awkwardly.

"Don't worry, this bath is private. I have no intention of crashing your time in here. But I do hope that once you've soaked as much as you want, you'll come out and join me for the rest of our evening."

I reach up on my tiptoes and kiss him on the cheek. "You are the best, you know that?"

"I know that. I just hope you always remember. Now go on, in you go. I'll be out in the living room when you're done. Have fun!"

I nod excitedly, and he closes the door behind him.

The bathroom is warm and dimly lit. I quickly disrobe and test the water with my toes. Mmm, it's the perfect temperature. As I climb in, I slowly sink beneath the foam. I notice there are several hair care products waiting for me to use. I unleash my hair from its small ponytail and tilt my head back to get it wet. After squeezing a small amount of shampoo from the bottle I begin to massage it through. It smells like an orchard full of lilacs in full bloom. I note that he might have picked this bouquet on purpose; it is my favorite floral scent. After washing and conditioning my hair, I work on the rest of my body. Then I just soak.

I contemplate the time I've spent with Matt since we've reconnected. It feels like a dream or a fairy tale. I'm in love with him; I know that I am. I want so much to tell him, but if he rejects me, then what? I can't be the first to say it—I won't. I know it's the coward's way, but I love him so much and I can't risk losing him over three little words.

What have I done to deserve this? I had no idea he was so thought-ful and romantic. I wonder what else, if anything, he has planned for tonight. I bolt upright as I speculate and slosh water on the floor. What if he's expecting…sex? Oh God, are we ready for that? I'm not sure I'm ready for that. A panic sets in through my body, and now I can do any-thing but relax. He's been very sweet about everything, but he's a man and even Matt has his limits. If I don't put out, is he going to say forget it and then leave me? Oh God, what would I do then? A bead of sweat forms on my brow, and I know I have to get a hold of myself. Okay, Chloe, calm down. You don't know if that's what he's expecting. The best thing you can do is bring up the subject before he does. I sink back into the warm water and try to bring my riotous thoughts and my rapid heart rate under control.

fifteen

As I emerge from the bathroom I see Matt in the kitchen. His back is to me, so I take the opportunity to observe his muscular physique. He has changed into sweatpants but has no shirt on. My eyes can easily access his muscles as they flex while he moves. He really takes care of himself, and it suddenly feels very warm in here. I walk toward him slowly and quietly so he doesn't hear me. Reaching out, I lightly touch his back and feel his muscles reflexively ripple beneath my fingers.

Oh. My.

He turns suddenly, and then a slow, creeping grin develops across his finely chiseled face.

"I see you found the clothes I laid out for you."

"Yes, I did. Thank you. Although, putting two and two together, I note that the pants, which are yours, are too big and the fact that I am currently going commando might not be a coincidence."

He laughs.

"Yes, I see what you mean. But I can assure you that was never my intent. I have to say though that my clothes have never looked that sexy on me."

I flush.

"I beg to differ," I retort. "What are you doing?"

"This is called cooking. You take raw food and heat it in a pan, put herbs and spices on it, and then eat it," he says sarcastically.

"Really?" I say with one eyebrow raised and a sardonic tone. "I meant, what are you cooking?"

He smiles. "I know it's late and you probably don't want to eat a bunch of carbs right now, so I just whipped up some rosemary chicken with green beans on the side."

"It smells wonderful." I close my eyes and inhale. "I had no idea you could cook."

"I can't. Well, I can, but not much. I've learned a few things here and there. When you're a bachelor, you really get tired of fast food and Ramen noodles."

I nod in agreement. It's not unlike being a single woman. He dishes out the servings onto plates and carries them over to the dining table. We sit.

"Would you like some Chardonnay?"

"Yes, please." I am shocked at his sophistication.

I slice into the chicken and take a bite. It's really good, but then again, I'm starving.

"Matt, this is delicious."

"Thank you. It's my mom's recipe. She gave me a few of her easiest dishes to make, figuring if she didn't, I would probably either starve to death or look like a Whopper."

I laugh but then turn serious.

"So, I saw Kendall talking to you this evening after the show. What did she want?" I say wrinkling my nose.

"Ugh. What do you think? She wants me to give her another chance. I told her that I have moved on, but I don't think she cares."

My stomach roils.

"Do you think she will continue to pester you?" I hope not.

"I don't know. Without physically showing her I have someone else, I'm not sure she'll believe me and be able to move on."

I must make some sort of facial expression that I don't know about because he puts his hand on mine.

"Chlo, you have nothing to worry about, okay? If I wanted her, she'd be here instead of you. She's part of my past. A past I couldn't change if I wanted to, so stop worrying about her. I'm with you and only you."

He rubs his thumb back and forth softly across the back of my hand, and I suddenly feel better.

We eat our meal and make small talk, but in the back of my mind I am thinking about what comes next. How can I bring up the subject of intimacy without being embarrassed? What if I'm the only one contemplating it. If I talk to him about it before he does, will it make me seem too eager? I don't know.

When we are finished, we take our plates to the sink and then snuggle up together on the couch in front of the fireplace.

"Chlo?" he says softly.

"Yes?"

"I need to talk to you about something."

"Okay. What is it?" My heartbeat picks up speed.

We turn to face each other.

"Um...I want you to know how much fun I've had these last few weeks. It's been...the best. And I think you've enjoyed my company as much as I've enjoyed yours."

I nod in agreement.

"Chlo, I've never felt this way about anyone else in my life. I don't know what it is about you, but I just can't get enough. I...think we should take this to the next level."

Oh no.

"Chlo, I think I...I mean I'm pretty sure that..." He sighs and takes my hands in his. "Chlo, I love you. I think I've always loved you. You are the first thing on my mind in the morning and the last thing I think about at night. When I'm not with you, I wish I were, and when I am with you, I want to be so close to you that I'm practically wearing you. I hope this doesn't sound creepy. I'm not expressing myself very well." He rakes his hand through his hair.

"You're doing fine," I reassure him. "I feel the same."

"And I don't know what I'd do if I lost you. I mean it. I can't lose you. What did you say?" He looks bewildered.

I giggle. "I said that I feel the same. I love you too."

He inhales sharply and then, a few seconds later, pulls me into an embrace, squeezing firmly.

"I was so worried that you'd leave if I told you that too early. I was gonna wait until you said it, but I just couldn't hold it in any longer." He pulls back and kisses me with a passion that takes my breath away. I reciprocate full force, pouring all the love I feel into our kiss. Soon I am falling on my back onto the couch cushions, Matt's body descending onto mine. We are all hands and mouths and completely tangled around each other. The space between my legs is warm and wet, and I have an urge to be touched there as I've never had before. I groan as the urgency grows. Matt's erection is rubbing against me, and reflexively I push my hips up to meet him and to relieve the yearning I'm feeling. When I do, he moans into my neck, which he has been licking and kissing, and that makes my need grow even further. I want him. I want him to touch me more than I've wanted anything else. I writhe beneath him as I try to get some welcomed friction. He begins to grind his pelvis into me. I moan again. I'm throbbing now and can feel the blood rushing to the area, making me swell. He starts working his way down, kissing and sucking as he goes. He gets to the top of my breast and pulls my shirt down slightly. He hasn't quite reached my nipple when something inside me yells stop.

"Wait!"

He stills.

"Matt, wait. This is too fast. Please stop."

He immediately halts his progress and looks down at me.

"Chlo, what's wrong? Are you okay?"

He sits up and pulls me up too.

We readjust ourselves and sit facing each other. I notice his rather large erection through his sweatpants.

I'm staring timidly at my hands in my lap when his hand covers mine.

"Talk to me, Chlo. What's wrong?" he says quietly as his other hand gently lifts my chin. I keep my eyes cast down even though he's willing me to look at him.

"Chlo? Baby, I can't read your mind. You're gonna have to talk eventually."

I sigh and try to find the right words.

"I want you. I really do, but I need to move slowly with this. I've never felt this way before and it's...foreign. I know you've been through this, but I haven't and"—"

"No, Chlo, I've never been in love before, until now. These feelings are foreign to me too. There's a learning curve, but I think we've managed so far, and I have no reason to think we can't continue on our journey, wherever that takes us." He smiles sweetly and runs his thumb down my cheek.

"Matt, you misunderstood. I wasn't just talking about being in love. I was referring to sex. I've never done it."

His eyebrows shoot up.

"Oh," he says, and now the look he has on his face is...what? Shame? Oh no, is he disgusted that he's dealing with someone with no experience with sex? Is he rethinking this whole relationship? What is he thinking?

"Matt? Now I can't read your mind. Talk to me. Please tell me I didn't just screw this up."

His eyes shoot straight to mine.

"Screw this up? You? I'm the one who should be saying that, not you. Chlo your virginity doesn't have the power to screw anything up. In fact, it makes it better."

What?

"I'm so sorry, Chlo. I had no idea you had never...and then I...ugh!" He buries his face in his hands. "I'm sorry."

"Hey." I pull his hands from his face, forcing him to look at me. "I liked what you were doing. It felt good. I wanted more but...I'm afraid. I've heard it can be painful the first time, and besides, I had always thought that I would wait for marriage. Now I'm not so sure."

"I don't want you to fear sex with me, Chlo. I never want you to compromise your morals or put yourself in a position where you're not comfortable. Please don't ever do that, even for my sake. I love you, and the last thing I would ever want to do is hurt you."

"I wouldn't. I won't. Please believe me, when the time comes, I'll be ready and you'll know."

He kisses me once on the lips and again on the forehead. We sink into the couch, snuggling once again.

I wake to the feel of Matt's arms around me, lifting me from the couch. "Shh, baby, I've got you," he whispers as he carries me to his bedroom. I protest a little but the truth is that I'm too tired to argue about it. I lay my head on his shoulder as he walks over and deposits me on his bed.

"Sleep now, baby," he says as he covers me up. "I'll see you in the morning."

"No," I mumble sleepily. "Stay with me."

"I'll just be on the couch if you need me."

"No, please sleep here." And I flip the bed covers out of the way.

"Chlo, I...I don't know. I don't think I should."

"It's fine. Please, get in." I pat the mattress beside me. He acquiesces with a sigh and climbs in.

"Roll over," he requests, and I comply. He snuggles up behind me, and like two spoons in a drawer, we drift off.

I hear a noise. It's loud, and I just want it to stop. Without opening my eyes, I extend my arm and smack my phone several times until all sound stops.

"What time is it?" I mumble into my pillow.

"Time to get up, sleepyhead," I hear Matt's soothing voice say.

"Noooo," I protest.

"Come on, Sleeping Beauty. It's time to greet the world," he says as he throws the covers off of me.

"Hey!" I exclaim and try to wrestle the covers away from him. "I'm still tired, and now I'm cold. Give me back the blanket."

"Whoa, you're really not a morning person, are you?" He laughs.

"No, I'm not." I pout. I grab the covers and pull them over my head. The room is silent for a few minutes, so I peek out to see what Matt's up to. All of a sudden he pounces on me and starts to tickle my feet. I am lying on my stomach, yelling and thrashing around, but he's sitting on me backward with my feet in the air.

"Matt, stop!" I half-scream, half-laugh. "You are so gonna get it!" I laugh some more.

I manage to spin beneath him so I'm on my back. I grab onto his sides and start to tickle him. He jumps up suddenly, grabbing my hands, and turns around. Still sitting on me, he holds my hands above my head and waits until I'm calm. When I stop struggling he leans down and softly kisses me.

"Good morning, baby."

I growl.

"Hmm, looks like I have a wildcat here. I guess I'll have to tame her," he chuckles. "Are you awake now?"

"Yes," I reply, defeated.

"Are you done trying to get me back?"

"For now," I confess, but a small smile plays on my face.

"Okay then, I'll let you go." He lets go, and I lace my hands behind my head with my elbows out to the sides. "Are you hungry? I could cook." He has a sincere look.

"A little. You cooked dinner; how about if I cook breakfast?"

"That sounds great. What are you going to make?"

"I thought maybe French toast. Do you have eggs and bread?"

"Yes, and if I didn't, I'd go get it for you." He smiles sweetly and kisses my head.

We are in the kitchen starting breakfast together like a well-oiled machine. I'm breaking eggs in a bowl and scrambling them while he starts a pot of coffee. As we move about, it occurs to me that this feels right—ordinary and mundane and yet so comfortable. I am flipping the bread when a text message comes in.

I just wanted 2 say good morning and I love u.
That is all. ;)

My eyes shoot straight to Matt. He's smiling at me with a boy-next-door grin on his face.

"You're silly, and I love you too."

I step closer to close the gap between us, wrap my arms around his neck, and plant a long, soft kiss on his waiting lips.

"There's nothing silly about the way I feel about you, Chlo. I want to show you every day how much you mean to me."

I hug and kiss him again.

"Are you ready to go?" Matt inquires.

"Almost," I reply as I dig through my closet for a heavier jacket.

When I appear back in the living room, I am dressed for a typical day of New York weather, which could include sun, rain, snow, or all three in the same day. Matt grins widely and laughs when he sees my attire.

"Chlo, are you expecting a sudden blizzard?" He's poking fun at me, jerk.

"Well, frankly, yes," I say indignantly.

"I always knew you were a freeze-baby, but it's not that cold out today. Don't you think you're a little...um...overdressed?"

I knit my eyebrows together as I look down at my outfit. It doesn't seem too over the top to me. I have on blue jeans with leggings underneath, a tank top under a red sweater with an OSU hoodie over that and my winter coat. I have gloves and earmuffs in my pockets, but he can't see that. It's fall in New York City, for heaven's sake. The weather could change at any given moment.

"No, I don't. In fact, when you are freezing your ass off outside in Central Park today, you'll be begging me for one of my layers."

His look is skeptical as he chuckles.

"Not likely," he mutters and walks toward me. Matt snakes his arms around my many layers and squeezes. "I love you and all of your quirks."

"Humph!" I pout and try to look offended but the truth is that I can't stay mad at this man. I give in and hug him back.

"Okay then, let's get going," he says, and we head out the door.

The cab ride there feels too short as I enjoy my quiet alone time with Matt. We sit together in the backseat holding hands and leaning against each other slightly. I lay my head on his shoulder and feel him squeeze my hand now and then. I look up at him a few times and smile. When he questions as to why I am so happy, I just shake my head and smile again. How is it that we ended up together? I still feel like I'm in some kind of surreal dream that I will surely wake up from at any time.

The driver pulls over and lets us out. As I step out of the car, I am stunned into silence at the beauty of this place. The air is crisp, and the summer leaves have already begun to change colors. There are millions of varying shades of red, orange, and yellow mixed in, with green being the definite minority. Each tree seems to have its own color scheme, and collectively, they look a little like cotton candy, though not the traditional colors. Even the smell is intoxicating. The deeper we walk into the Garden of Eden, the less I can hear the noises of the city. Horns that honk almost constantly in rush hour traffic fade into the background and disappear, and revving engines and exhaust fumes are nonexistent. I smile as I imagine I'm in a Disney movie and expect Snow White to step in front of us with a bird in her hand. I had forgotten how much I've missed this environment. It reminds me of home and makes me think about all the years I spent doing fun things in one of my favorite seasons.

Matt speaks up. "So what do you think? Nice, huh?"

I nod my head. "Heavenly," is all I can say as I take in every inch of this oasis.

"Yeah, I don't come here often enough. Have you been before?" he asks, bringing me back to the now.

"Yes, a handful of times, but each time I see the beauty of it, it leaves me speechless."

He blows out a short breath. "Is this all I have to do to get you to stop talking?" he teases.

My head swivels in his direction briskly to shoot him a dirty look, but I know he's just kidding. He's trying to get a rise out of me and make me laugh. He succeeds, and I smack his arm in faux irritation.

As we walk along the path looking for a place to picnic, we pass by dozens and dozens of people on their lunch breaks. Some are sitting on benches, people watching no doubt, some are using their breaks to get some exercise, and a few are sitting on the ground or just lying there looking up at the sky. I note, self-consciously, that Matt may have been right about my outfit, but I refuse to give him the satisfaction of saying "I told you so," so I just keep that thought to myself. We walk until we come to a lake. Matt unfurls the blanket he brought with us and smoothes out the wrinkles. It's a little windy, so I place the picnic basket on one of the corners, and he finds a small rock to put on another corner. Sitting, I begin to unpack the lunch that Matt made for us, and I giggle as I peek inside at the contents.

"Peanut butter and jelly sandwiches? How old are we, six?" I tease.

"Hey, I figured it was a sure bet. I remembered that you like them but only with strawberry jelly. Has that changed?"

He remembered; how sweet.

"No, it hasn't changed. I am just a little shocked that of all the things from our childhood to remember, this stuck in your brain."

"Chlo, I remember lots of things about you."

"Oh? Like what?" I'm intrigued.

"Well, I remember that you don't mind spiders but hate ants. In fact, you refuse to kill spiders because they took care of an ant problem your folks had years ago."

That's still true, the vile little creatures.

"True, go on."

"And I know that your favorite animal is the Bengal tiger. You used to have posters up in your room, dozens of them, plastered all over your walls. I'm not even sure I could see what color your walls actually were."

I smile as I recall my childhood bedroom.

"And I also know that you invented an imaginary friend who you affectionately named Spike so you didn't feel so alone when you moved your bedroom upstairs into your parents' attic. You claimed he protected you from vampires, werewolves, and other monsters that hid in your closet."

"Hey! He was not imaginary! Spike and I had long meaningful talks of which you will never know the contents!" I say petulantly.

"Okay, okay, I'm sorry. I was just trying to prove my point." He scoots closer, reaches out, and runs his thumb down my cheek. "I know you better than anyone else, Chlo, and now that I have the opportunity, I'm going to get to know you even better."

A slow smile creeps onto my face until I am grinning like a loon. I cannot contain my joy any longer. I launch myself at him, knocking him onto his back as I follow, landing on top of him.

"You are a giant mushball, you know that? Since when did you go soft?"

I squeal as he shifts, and suddenly I am the one on the bottom and he's got me pinned underneath him.

"Soft? You think I've gone soft?"

I giggle.

"I'll show you soft!" he says and starts his usual tickle torture.

We carry on like this for several minutes until I surrender, then he tenderly kisses me and I melt in his embrace.

sixteen

It is Saturday night, and the New York clubs are teeming with life, as usual. Matt and I want to go out, but we don't really want to be pushed and knocked around while trying to have a good time, so we opt for an evening in. We have invited Drew and Andrew to come over, and Jenna has asked Trent to join us. Matt arrives early to help me prepare for our impromptu party.

"I brought the items you requested," Matt informs me as he enters my apartment. He places the grocery bags onto the kitchen counter and turns to greet me.

"Hey, baby!" Matt says as he snakes his arms around my waist and kisses my cheek.

"Hey, yourself!" I say, grinning from ear to ear. "Thank you for going shopping for me. I wasn't actually intending on having a full-blown party, but here we are."

"Anything for you, baby. You know, I think you are the only person I know who can accidentally have a party." He laughs.

"I see what you mean." I giggle, and he swats my behind.

I protest, but don't really mind his form of endearment.

"Has anyone else arrived yet?"

"No, just you. Drew said he and Andrew would be along in about thirty minutes, and Jenna said Trent will be here in forty-five."

"Good, we're alone." Matt raises and lowers his eyebrows suggestively.

"Never mind that," I reprimand him gently. "We have things to do before everyone gets here." I say it, but I'm not sure I mean it.

"I know. I just wanted to take a few minutes to enjoy each other before we become hosts."

He takes my hand and leads me to the couch. We both sit. Matt pulls me into his side, and I snuggle in close. He feels warm, and I melt into him. This is my favorite place to be, snuggled up to the man I love.

"Matt?"

"Yes?"

"Always do this."

"Do what?"

"Insist that we slow down and enjoy moments like these."

"I will, count on it."

Our guests arrive, and our spur-of-the-moment party is in full swing. Drew and Andrew bring a delicious black raspberry Merlot, and Jenna and Trent bring beer. I lay out several types of chips with dip and also make a layered taco salad. Since Andrew is very health conscious, I also prepare a large tray filled with veggies and cheeses with crackers on the side. We are all having a wonderful time, and I'm astonished at how many different conversations are going on.

"And then he stormed out of the room in a huff!" Drew says, chuckling.

We all laugh loudly at his story, and Andrew rolls his eyes.

"If I haven't heard that story a million times, I haven't heard it once," Andrew declares, but he can't help but laugh a little.

"Oh, Andrew, you know that being with me requires that you listen to my jokes over and over again."

Andrew looks at me and mouths the words "Help me" and then winks. Drew nudges him affectionately.

"So, Matt, how's your job? Is it hard working at the same place as the old ball and chain?" Trent speaks up.

Matt's eyebrows shoot up in surprise.

"It's great actually. I get to see my best friend at work and at play. Why would you think it was hard?"

"No reason. I would think you'd want a break once in a while though."

Jenna throws an elbow into Trent's side.

"Trent, you mean to tell me you'd get sick of seeing me if we worked together?" Jenna seems offended.

"Oh no, baby, that's not what I meant. I just meant...um..."

"Save it, Trent! I know exactly what you meant!" Jenna scolds him.

She starts to stomp off in the direction of her bedroom, and Trent follows, apologizing all the way.

"Well, that didn't take long." Matt chuckles.

"Go figure. They have such a volatile relationship. It's a wonder they get along at all," I reply.

"Well, sweetie, I think that's our cue. We should really get going."

"Oh, Drew, you don't have to go. Stay for a while," I plead.

"Thank you, Chloe, but Drew and I really should go. It's been such a fun night. Thank you for everything," Andrew says.

"You two are welcome back anytime."

We say our good-byes, and the two men walk out together but not before they give me the double-cheek kiss. Jenna and Trent have retreated to her room but soon, they too head out, probably to Trent's place. Matt and I are alone again. We start the cleanup process. Working together, Matt and I sync our actions so that before we know it, we are done. After the last dish is washed and put away, we both head straight for the couch and flop down, exhausted. I resume my place at Matt's side and snuggle in close as he wraps his arm around me and strokes my arm.

"That was fun." I close my eyes.

He pauses for a moment before he speaks. "Yes, it was."

We are both silent, relaxing against each other.

"Matt?"

"Chlo."

I smile.

"What are you thinking?"

"Hmm," he hums.

I lift my head to see his face. His eyes are closed, and his head is tilted back slightly. When I tap his chest to get his attention, he looks down at me.

"I'm not thinking anything, just enjoying the moment." He smiles, and I know he speaks the truth.

"Me too. So now what?"

"I don't know. Do you have something in mind?"

I think for a minute. "We could make out," and the words are out of my mouth before I can invoke my brain to mouth filter.

Matt sits up and turns slightly to face me, a look of shock on his handsome face.

"But I thought...You said you didn't..." He sighs and pushes a hand through is hair. "Chlo, you are the most complicated woman I have ever known."

"What? Just because I've never had sex before doesn't mean I don't want to do other things. I love kissing you, and, who knows, maybe you'll talk me into it." A broad smiles crosses my face, but it's fleeting as he stands abruptly and begins to pace, leaving me seated on the couch.

"Talk you into it? Chlo, I don't want to talk you into having sex with me. Hell, I would feel terrible, to say the least, if you did anything with me because you felt as though I talked you into it. That's not what intimacy is about."

"That's not what I meant. I just don't know how long it will take for me to stop being so afraid of sex. I don't want you to wait longer than you want to. I know that Kendall probably didn't make you wait at all and...well...I don't want you to lose interest." I hang my head and wring my hands.

He stares at me as though I've suddenly turned purple.

"Lose interest? Are you serious?" He sits back down and takes my hands, forcing me to look up at him. "I love you. You are the most interesting person I know. I don't care how long you make me wait, I'll wait. I want *you* more than I want sex with you. Do you understand what I'm trying to tell you?"

Oh my, he is really serious.

"Yes, I understand."

He sighs. "Chlo, I would love to make out with you. I would love to do anything with you. If you told me that you were in the mood to run through a field of wildflowers covered in bees, I might look at you funny, but I'd go and do it with you, because I love you."

I grin and hug him tight. "I don't feel an urge to run through a bee-infested field, but..."

He grins and shakes his head. "You are something else, you know that?"

I nod my head and press my lips against his. It's a playful gesture but quickly turns into a passionate display of our affection for each other as I fall on top of him. We continue like this for a while, but then Matt stops it and suggests we watch a movie. I make to protest but realize he might be doing this because he can no longer handle this level of intimacy without wanting to take it further. I acquiesce and find myself caught, once more, in Matt's warm, loving embrace. We lie this way until we both fall fast asleep.

Before I know it, weeks go by. Matt and I are blissfully happy, and I can't imagine my life without him. We see each other most nights, and on our days off we are always together. During our many days spent together, we make a habit of walking hand in hand through Central Park, feeding the ducks and sitting in the grass. I feel so safe and at ease with Matt by my side. It's like one long dream that I hope to never wake from.

The weather is really turning colder as the fall colors are in full bloom, and it's almost Matt's birthday. I have no idea what I am going to get him, but I want it to have real meaning.

Jenna and I have decided to go shopping and are at the mall. I am inspired, so I head into a store.

"This one, Chloe. This is perfect."

"You think? You don't think it's too much?"

"Not at all. I think he will love it."

"I wonder if it comes in red."

"I'll go ask for you."

Jenna finds a Victoria's Secret sales clerk and comes back with her. I'm so embarrassed. I've never had to think about lingerie, much less buy it.

"Hello. What can I help you with?" She's so happy it's unnerving.

"Um...er...I'm looking for something like this...but in red."

"Oh, that style is very popular. Let me show you what colors it comes in."

She opens a drawer and reveals a rainbow of underwear. Sheesh, who knew how many variations of pink there were?

"I want red, er, he wants red, I mean. It's his favorite color." And now I think I'm turning red.

"Okay. Here's something similar in the color you're looking for."

"Hmm, how about classier and less sleazy."

"Hey!" Jenna protests. "I have that one in pink!" She pouts and I shrug, but I know she's kidding.

I walk around the display to another table in the back that has sale items on it and find exactly what I'm looking for. It's lacey and low cut and pushes what little I have up and out front. The panties match the bra and have a high-cut boy-short style. Most important, it's Matt's favorite color. They place my items in a cute little pink bag, and we're off to the next store. Jenna helps me decide once again what to get Matt, and we head for home.

"Which one do you think he'll like the best, Jenna?"

"Well, I think the engraving was a nice touch on present number two, but I think present number one will mean the most to Matt."

"I hope he doesn't think he got a lemon and will want to return it."

We laugh, and I saunter to my room swaying my hips in an exaggerated way.

Tonight is the night. It's Matt's birthday, and I'm going to give him the one gift no one else can—me. I am showered and shaved, primped and curled, and very nervous. As I begin getting dressed, I almost blush when I pull on my new matching bra and panty. I have also selected the perfect outfit for tonight, a scarlet satin halter-neck dress that hangs just above the knee. The back has a sexy thick silver chain that starts at the base of my neck and trails down to fasten at the middle of my back. At the waist, there's a wide black satin sash. The five-inch pumps I've chosen show off my kick-ass calf muscles, not to mention scream sex. I take one last look in the mirror, just the right amount of everything. I peek at my watch and realize it's time to go. I take a deep breath and carefully walk out of my room.

Matt is waiting in the living room for me, and when I emerge the look on his face is priceless. His eyes are as big as saucers, and his jaw is slack. He stands up slowly, and I smile. Wow, he looks sexy in his black suit and sapphire-blue tie. I can't wait to peel it all off of him.

"What do you think?" I ask and do a little spin.

"What do I think? I think we may not make it out of this room," he replies and strides over to me. His hands find their way to my waist, where they hold me gently as he greets me with a kiss. "Oh baby, you look absolutely stunning. What could I have possibly done to deserve such a gorgeous woman?" He closes his eyes for a moment and then looks up toward the ceiling. Did he just thank God?

"Well, you look exceptionally gorgeous yourself, and you act like I'm something extraordinary. I'm just the same, Matt. The same girl you painted with mud when we were kids."

"True, but you're much more than that now—you're mine."

"And you are mine," I whisper.

He reaches into his pocket and pulls out his iPhone, taps the screen a few times, and music comes on.

"Dance with me?"

I nod, and he takes my hands, leading me into the middle of the room. With my right hand in his left and our other arms wrapped around each other, we begin to move.

We sway back and forth slowly with our cheeks touching. I hear him breathe out a contented sigh just before we swirl in our own little circle. He then lets go of my waist and pushes me outward as he spins me. I smile broadly and coil back into his arms. He places a gentle kiss on my lips and smiles. A very satisfied look crosses his face, but then it fades to serious. Lip-syncing the words to the song, he mouths, "You're more than everything I need. You're all I ever wanted." I smile a face-splitting grin and hug him as we continue our dance. At the end of the song he dips me, my hair nearly touching the floor, and then pulls me upright again.

"I love you," he whispers.

"I love you more," I whisper back.

"I seriously doubt that." He snorts.

I roll my eyes, but it's nice to know that he cares about me so deeply.

"Shall we go?" he asks as he offers me his elbow.

"Yes, lets," I say while linking our arms.

He takes me to the Park Avenue restaurant for his birthday dinner. I have told him it is way too pricey, but he insists, and I think it is because he doesn't want to be shown up by James.

The decor has changed to an autumn motif, and during dinner we reminisce about our childhood and how far we've come from those days.

"Do you remember Mrs. Smith a few houses down?" I ask.

"You mean Nosey Nelly?" he laughs. "How could I forget? She knew everything that went on in our neighborhood. In fact, she was the one who told my dad I broke out Mr. Wilson's window with my baseball. I wonder what ever happened to her."

"I don't know. Maybe she's patrolling the neighborhoods in heaven. She had to have been at least a hundred when we were kids after all."

We laugh, and it feels good to be normal with Matt. It feels like the old days, only better.

I am smiling from ear to ear. I can't help it.

"What?" he inquires.

I shake my head.

"What?" he insists.

"It's just that if someone had told me a year ago that I'd be sitting here with you, feeling the way I feel, I would've told them to go see a therapist. I'm happy, I mean, "scream your name from the top of the Empire State Building" happy."

He reaches across the table and takes my hands in his.

"Me too, Chlo." He plays with the fingers on my left hand. "Every relationship I've ever had pales in comparison to this one."

"Really?" I squeak.

"Without a doubt."

Wow.

"I wish I could say I know the feeling, but the truth is that I don't. I have nothing to compare this to."

"I'm glad you don't. I can't believe I'm the only man that you've ever kissed."

"I never said that." My mischievous grin gives me away, and his raised eyebrows beg me for more information. "Well, I did go to a party in seventh grade where they were playing spin the bottle, and Mike Klein and I—"

"Mike Klein?" he interjects. "That guy was an idiot!"

"Don't I know it. I told him I was not going to French him, and the rest of the year everyone called me No French Chloe. It was awful."

"Wait, so you didn't kiss him then?"

"No, not him. It was Scott Beck."

His mouth twists. "Do I really want to hear about this?"

I shrug. "I don't have to say anymore." And I know it's eating away at him.

"Fine, it's fine. If you don't finish the story, I'll be imaging worse than it probably is. Please continue," he concedes.

"It was at summer camp when I was twelve, Camp Yakiwi. I don't remember much about it other than it was on a wooden bridge and there was no tongue involved."

He visibly relaxes.

I laugh. "I was twelve, Romeo. How old were you for your first kiss?"

"I was thirteen," he says reluctantly, then chuckles. "And it was bad."

I'm smiling broadly.

"I can't fathom that even at thirteen you'd be bad at kissing. After all, you are the best I've ever had."

"Clearly." He snorts.

I throw a green bean at him.

We finish dinner and go back to his place. Jake is conveniently out for the night. That's good. I don't need any reason to back out of this venture.

"I almost forgot, happy birthday," I say as I present him with a little red velvet box. He looks at me, bewildered.

"You didn't have to get me anything, you know that."

"I know, but it called to me. Open it."

He cracks open the hinged lid. Inside is a pair of silver key chains in the shape of two puzzle pieces. Inscribed on the fronts are three words.

I. Am. Yours.

And on the back of each it reads:

Matt and Chloe

Matt picks one up and smiles.

"For when we are apart, to remind us both where we belong."

"It's perfect," he says and kisses me. "Thank you. You'll keep one too, right?"

I giggle. "That's why there are two, silly. I have one more thing to give you though."

"What? No, you're going to spoil me."

"It's something that only you can have."

"So it's one of a kind?"

"Priceless."

"Is it fragile?"

"Very, so please don't break it."

He thinks for a minute. "I can't imagine what it is."

"I'll show you." I grab him by his silk tie and lead him into his bedroom. He's grinning, but I don't think he has any idea. We get inside, and I shut and lock the door. His smile fades.

"No. No, Chlo. You can't be serious."

"As a heart attack." I start to unbutton his shirt.

"Chlo, stop. You can't give me this. It's too much."

"Why don't you let me decide that?" I finish with the buttons and push his shirt off of his shoulders and onto the floor. Lightly, I run my fingertips over his chest, feeling how firm his pecks are and noticing his nipples harden at my touch. He closes his eyes. I walk around behind him and keep my fingers moving all the while. His sexy back is not shy when it comes to a workout. I plant a trail of soft kisses along it as I make my way to the other side, but not before my hand brushes against his tight round ass. He moans quietly, and I continue around in front of him. I kiss his chest and then on up to his throat. He's panting as he tilts his head back for easier access, and I take full advantage.

"Chlo, stop," he commands, but his voice is raspy and I know he likes what I'm doing. "You have no idea what you're doing to me."

"I think I have a pretty good idea," I whisper in is ear. I nip the lobe, and he shutters. Slowly and gently, I wrap my arms around him. I kiss and suck his neck, all the while grinding my hips into his erection.

"Chlo, if you don't stop now...I'm not sure I can control myself."

"Okay," I agree, but continue.

"I'm...s-serious."

"I want you, Matt." I say as I look him in the eyes. "I want this, with you. I love you."

And that's all it takes. Matt coils one arm around me and the other fists firmly but gently in my hair at the back of my head. He kisses me as though we've been apart for a thousand years. He then backs me up against the bed, unzips my dress and slides it down to the floor. When he sees my red bra and panties, he emits a low, throaty growl and eases me onto my back.

"Are you sure about this?" he asks in between kisses.

"Yes, I've never been more sure about anything in my life." He exhales in a rush, and his mouth is on mine. I am about to do something I only imagined doing, and I'm doing it with the man I love. I close my eyes and surrender to my desire.

He lifts me up and gently lays me down with my head on the pillows. As he gazes down at me, he runs a hand through his hair and lets out a long-held breath.

"Chlo, that red lingerie is going to be the death of me. You look absolutely breathtaking in it," he says and traces the lace at the top of my bra.

"I know you like red so..."

His facial expression turns to desire, and he places small kisses on my neck and shoulders. He works his way down to my breasts, and I start to squirm in anticipation. While he continues on his journey, he reiterates how I can tell him to stop and he will. I say nothing, and it's his cue to progress.

Matt kisses his way south, lingering here and there. I am sure that I am a brighter version of the color of my panties as he does things to me that I never could have imagined. All I can do is throw my arm across my face and absorb the sensations. He chuckles slightly at my shock but keeps going. Soon, we are like two puzzle pieces being joined together. Even though it's a bit snug, I am amazed how we fit together perfectly. A buildup comes from within. And then there is a release that makes my toes curl, leaving me wrung out and very tired. Matt follows suit, stills, and collapses on top of me. We lie like this for a few minutes and try to catch our breath.

He rolls onto his side, smoothes a lock of stray hair off of my face, and lovingly kisses me.

"How was that?" he inquires softly.

I smile because that's all I can do to communicate right now.

"Sleep now, baby," he says, kissing my forehead, and covers me up.

seventeen

I wake up and Matt is sprawled out next to me, fast asleep. I recall the events of last night and smile. I did it, I really did it. And it wasn't this terrifying ordeal I had worked out in my mind. It was sweet and sensual and loving. I shift onto my side and watch Matt as he sleeps. He looks so peaceful, not a care in the world. I reach over and stroke his chest hair. Will it always be this way? He stirs, and his eyes flutter open. I keep still, hoping he'll go back to sleep. Nope, he yawns and rubs his eyes. Then his head swivels to look in my direction, and a sleepy smile forms on his face.

"Good morning, baby." He reaches over and wraps his arm around me while snuggling up close. His head is on my chest, and I can feel his warm breath on me. I'm playing with his hair, which is floppy and messy and...sexy as hell.

"Good morning." I yawn.

He props himself up with his elbow and kisses me softly.

"How do you feel? Are you okay? I'm sorry I had to get a little rough last night, but I had to break through your barrier. I hope it wasn't too painful."

I contemplate a few seconds before I answer.

"I'm good, great actually. I know why you did that, and it's okay, really." I smile at him, and his face mirrors mine. He's playing with my hair, and he's rolling something around in his mind, I can tell.

"What are you thinking?" I ask.

He's silent for a moment, as though he's trying to find the right way to say something.

"Matt? Is something wrong?" I'm starting to get concerned.

"No, no, not at all, I'm just...hoping you're really okay with what we did last night."

"Matt, yes. Yes, I'm more than okay with it," I confess as I stroke his face. "Remember, it was my idea, not yours. If I didn't want to then I wouldn't have."

"I sort of feel like I should've resisted a little more. I just don't want you to regret anything."

"Oh baby, I don't regret one second of anything I do with you." I pause. "I'm not sure what I was so afraid of. I should've done that years ago!" I tease.

His jaw drops.

"No, you shouldn't have!" He smiles. "Then it wouldn't have been with me!" He kisses me. "And I'm glad it was me."

"We should get up and get some breakfast," I suggest.

"Sounds good, but first let's take a shower...together."

My eyebrows shoot up. Hmm, okay. I smile a sultry smile and agree. This should be interesting. When I sit up and throw the covers back I notice some blood on the sheets, and I'm mortified. I cover back up quickly.

"What's wrong?" Matt sounds puzzled.

"Um...there's a bit of a mess," I state, turning crimson.

"Yeah, I figured there might be. It's okay, Chlo, it's just proof that you're mine alone. Proof that we love each other. Proof that you love me enough to give me something that no one else will ever have." He smiles and holds his hand out for me to take. "Come on, let's shower."

I reluctantly take his hand and stand, following him to the bathroom.

He starts the water, and the mirror begins to fog. I'm standing off to the side, self-conscience as hell. I've never been this exposed in front of anyone before, and it's unnerving. Matt is naked too as he tests the temperature with his hand and then turns to look at me. His body is truly a sight to behold. This is the first real view of him I've had, and he's beautiful.

"Hey, I'm up here," he teases and points to his face.

I turn red.

"I wasn't looking," I lie.

He steps closer. "It's okay to look at me. I'm not ashamed, and you shouldn't be either. You have a gorgeous body, and it makes me want to be inside you again," he says as he wraps his arms around my waist and kisses my neck.

I'm shocked.

"Why so surprised?" he asks, confounded.

"I don't know." I shrug.

He takes my face in his hands and stares. "You are beautiful."

I look down, unconvinced.

"Hey." I look back at him. "You are!" he says louder.

"And you're very sweet. Can we get in the shower now?" I'm trying to steer the conversation to something else.

His mouth twists, but he agrees.

The water is warm and soothing. I'm facing the stream, and Matt is behind me. His arms are around me, and I can feel his erection against my behind.

"Can I wash you?" he asks. I turn in his arms and smile sweetly.

"Only if I can reciprocate," I reply.

He nods and grabs the body wash. Pouring some into one hand, he works it into a lather. Starting with my shoulders, he rubs in circles, then he washes my arms, my back, and my breasts. When he washes them, my head goes back, and I hear a soft moan come from my mouth. His light touch sends shivers through my body, and even though the water is hot, I have goose bumps.

"Mmm, your body responds quickly. Are you interested in a second go?"

I moan, louder this time, in agreement as he persists in his mission.

"Chlo? Is that a yes?"

"Yes." And I'm a little surprised at my breathy response.

He hums his approval and turns me under the water to rinse me off.

"We don't want any soap in there." He chuckles.

I smile, and he kisses me. Our tongues are entwined and exploring each other's mouths. He stops to get a condom that just happens already to be in the shower, hmm. Deftly, he slides it on, and we are conjoined once again.

We both feel like Jell-O, still panting and clinging to each other.

"I had no idea how many ways one can do this."

"Oh baby, we've only just gotten started," he promises. I grin and kiss him but then get to thinking.

"I didn't get to wash you," I pout.

"Well, you can't do it now. I'm very sensitive."

With a mischievous grin on my face, I soap up my hands and head straight for him.

"Chlo, what are you up to?"

I make a play for his manhood, and he turns to avoid contact.

"Don't even think about it." He laughs, and I try again, this time finding my target. He gasps and turns again, grabbing my wrists.

"Oh, no you don't." Then he wraps my wrists behind my back. "You can wash me next time, okay?"

"Okay." I surrender, and we finish and exit the shower.

We are just about done with breakfast when my phone rings. It's my dad.

"Hi, Daddy."

"Hi, sweetheart. How are you, honey?"

"I'm good. You?"

"Well, I could be better. It's Gram."

"Oh no! What's going on?" I ask worriedly.

"Now, it's nothing to get too upset about. Gram had some chest pains, so they sent her to the ER. While she was there, the doctors wanted to keep her overnight. It was then that she was diagnosed with CHF—congestive heart failure. They're controlling it pretty well, but I just wanted you to know about it."

"That's awful, Dad. Is she feeling okay? Should I come home?"

"Well, Mom and I would always love to see you, but don't be in a rush. She's back at Cherry Ridge and in good spirits. If you want to plan a trip home though, I'm sure she'd be excited to see you."

"I'll look for airline tickets as soon as we hang up. Thanks for calling to tell me." I swallow. "Love you, Dad."

"I love you too, sweetheart. Travel safe."

We hang up, and almost instantly I start to cry. Matt walks over to me quickly, throws his arms around me, and kisses the top of my head.

"Shh, baby. It's going to be okay. I'm here for you." He holds on tight. "Was that about your Gram?"

I nod and repeat what my dad just told me.

"She is going to be okay. She's tough like her granddaughter."

I look up at him. "I'm anything but tough right now."

"You're crying because you're upset, not because you're weak. It helps to relieve stress. After you're done, what remains is strong and resilient. Let as much fragility out as you need to. I'll be here for you, whatever you need."

And then he kisses my tear-stained cheek.

"I love you, Matt. Thank you for always knowing what to do and say."

He snorts. "Not always."

I smile up at him. "I need to see her."

"Then we'll go, both of us. I'll make the arrangements."

"But what about our jobs?"

"We are both in a union. We're allowed to take time off. Our jobs will be there when we get back."

"No, Matt. I can't let you take time off of a brand-new job for this. She's not dying, and it's not an emergency. I'll go. I would feel terrible if you lost this job because of me."

"It won't come to that, I swear. I am coming."

"No, you're not, Matt," I interrupt with a little too much force. I tone it down a notch. "That didn't come out right. I'll go by myself this time. Maybe we can arrange another visit later in the year. Please. I'll be fine because I know she's fine for now."

He rolls his eyes and resigns.

"Fine. But call me every day with updates, okay?"

"Yes, I will. I'm not going right away though. I'll give it a week or so. That way, any testing that the doctors do will be done and the results back."

I make my flight plans for next week, and now I am off to the theater. I bump into Drew and fill him in about Gram on the way backstage.

"Oh, sweetie, that's a shame but don't panic. My uncle had that condition. It's very manageable. They'll probably put her on a water pill and tell her to watch her salt intake. I'm sure she'll be fine. Your grandma sounds like a tough old bird who might just outlive all of us."

I chuckle, which I think is exactly the reaction Drew was going for.

We continue walking toward the dressing room when suddenly my bag, which was hanging from my shoulder, gets knocked off of me and onto the floor with such force that it nearly sends me off balance.

"What the hell?" I'm confused.

"Are you kidding me?" Drew yells as he looks back at the perpetrator, who continues to walk away.

It is Kendall. *What's going on with her?* I ask myself, but then realization dawns.

"Uh-oh. I think she may have found out about Matt and me. Shit. This is the last thing I need."

"Oh hell no!" he yells behind us. "I don't care what she knows. It gives her no right to do that to you. It's not like you're a home wrecker. You won him, fair and square," he says with his hand on his hip. "Do it again, bitch, I dare you!" he says loudly.

"Drew, stop it. I know you're trying to help, but it'll only make it worse. Just let her calm down."

"Fine, whatever, but just so you know, I've got your back, Chloe."

"And I appreciate that, Drew. Thank you."

We perform another great show to a standing ovation. As I exit the stage I know that Kendall is behind me somewhere, and I'd like to avoid her if possible. When I arrive safely back in the dressing room I quickly get out of costume and back into my clothes. I'm removing my stage makeup when I hear a familiar voice.

"Yep, that's her. Don't turn your back on that one. She'll stick a knife right in it."

I ignore her.

"Not sure what he sees in her, but he'll be back, count on it."

I still ignore her.

"Maybe I should show up at his apartment wearing just a trench coat and a smile. I'm sure she's crap in the sack, or maybe she doesn't even put out."

I'm biting my tongue now. I know she wants a reaction, but I won't give her the satisfaction.

"I can tell by the way she so-called dances on stage that poor Matt has to take care of himself in bed."

I growl.

"Maybe it's for the best. Matt was a terrible lover." There's a long pause. "Hell, he couldn't even kiss worth a shit." She laughs.

"That's it!" I stand and turn to face her. "You can insult me all you want, but leave Matt out of it! This is between the two of us, not him! So what is your problem?" I'm seething.

"Wow, so the kissing comment is what finally brought you to your feet. Hmm, that must mean you guys have only kissed. You really must be cold then." She snickers.

"That's really none of your business, Kendall. What do you want from me? I didn't steal your boyfriend, if that's what you think."

"No, not you, Miss Innocent. You just happened to come along at the perfect time when Matt and I were working something out. Did you bat your eyelashes and toss your hair or did you play a damsel in distress? Which was it, Chloe? I'm dying to know your strategy."

"I didn't do any of that! We've been friends since we were kids. There's always been an attraction."

"Then why did you wait until he was mine to pounce on him?" she yells.

I cower inwardly. "Kendall, it wasn't like that. Please believe me." I start to walk into the hallway.

"Oh, no you don't." She follows me out. "We're not done yet!"

I turn around and face her.

"What Kendall? Matt and I are together. I wouldn't change that for anything. We all have to work under the same roof. We need to find a way to get along or at least deal with each other."

She snorts. "I know how I'd like to deal with you," she says as she steps closer to me. Instinctively, I back up.

"Really? You really want to teach me a lesson," I say while drawing quotes in the air. "I bet that will make Matt come running back to you," I say sarcastically.

"Maybe not, but it sure would feel good for my fist to make contact with your cute little pixie face."

"Enough!"

Both of our heads swing in the direction of the voice. It's Matt, and he's angry.

"Kendall, who I am currently dating is none of your damned business, and I'd appreciate it if you'd leave my girlfriend alone!"

Matt's face is turning a rather menacing shade of red as he steps in between us.

"We were just having a discussion, Matt. I wasn't trying to bother her. I was...congratulating her on landing such a great catch." She smiles sweetly at him. I feel sick.

"I'm not some sort of fish to be caught. Now I think you should go home, Kendall."

"That's where I was headed." She looks at me. "Congrats again, Chloe."

I roll my eyes as she walks away. Then Matt turns to me.

"Are you all right?" he asks with concern in his voice.

"I'm fine. She doesn't bother me. I guess this means our secret is out though."

Matt puts his arms around me and pulls me close.

"Yes, I think it is. I hope you're okay with that. It'll be nice to not have to hide my affection for you."

"Yeah, I know what you mean."

He pats himself down in search of something. "Oh great, I left my phone by the light board. I'll be right back and then we can go. Stay here, okay?"

I agree and sigh and enjoy the view as he walks away.

It takes several minutes for Matt to reappear, and he seems a little irritated when he reaches me.

"What's wrong?" I'm puzzled.

"Nothing." His tone is clipped. He puts his arm around me, and we head out in the direction of Matt's place.

eighteen

I wake up earlier than Matt does, and the sunshine is streaming through the windows of his room. I watch as little particles of dust float through the beam of light as if they have no place to go and all the time in the world to get there. Matt is lying on his stomach with one arm draped over me in a protective manner. I don't move, as I do not want to disturb his slumber. I love admiring him. His face is chiseled like a male model's would be, and his shoulders and biceps are muscular, although not overly so. His light brown hair is tousled and looks just as good now as it does when he doesn't have sex hair. I sigh with contentment. Does it get any better than this? I don't see how it could. I'm getting rather warm, so I try to free one foot from the blanket, but my movement causes Matt to wake. He lifts his head, sleepily looks at me, and grins.

"Good morning, beautiful," he says as he squeezes me.

"Good morning." I smile.

"Did you sleep well?"

"I always sleep well next to you."

"I'm glad you decided to stay the night. I really like waking up to you."

"I'm glad I did too, although it wasn't really a conscious effort. It was more like I passed out afterward."

He hums and rubs his nose back and forth against mine, and then he plants a gentle kiss on my lips. We both have morning breath, but neither of us seem to mind. My heartbeat increases just at that simple gesture of love.

"We should shower. You can go first, and then we'll decide what to do for breakfast...er...lunch, um, whatever you want to call it. Now off you go. If you're not done by the time it's my turn then I might just have to come in with you."

My eyebrows shoot up.

He chuckles. "Just get moving."

"Okay, okay, I'm going. Sheesh, bossy, aren't you?" I giggle.

I stand up to leave, and he swats my derrière.

"Hey!" I yelp in jest. And he laughs.

In the shower I stand under the hot water and absorb all that has transpired. As I wash I note that I am still a little sore, but it reminds me of the truly intimate connection that we now have. After I'm done, I wrap myself in a towel and peek into Matt's bedroom.

"I'm all finished. Can I borrow some clothes again?"

He stares at me for a moment like he has X-ray vision, and I feel self-conscious.

"Um...yeah...sure. I'll g-get some out for you." He stumbles through his words, and I smile inwardly. As I get dressed, Matt leaves to take his shower. I wander into the living room and see his phone on the coffee table. Just then it chimes, announcing an incoming text. It startles me, but I pick it up and can't resist taking a look at who it is. I frown at the number on the screen. It's Kendall.

It was good talking 2u. I'm looking forward to lunch this week. C U then!

What? He talked to her? And they're having lunch this week? I feel the need to sit down, so I do. What on earth were they talking about? Were they discussing me? Maybe he called her to tell her he's with me now and that she should back off. If that were true, then why are they getting together for lunch? My head swims with unanswered questions. Maybe I should just ask him about it. No. I'm going to gather more information while he has no clue that I know. It feels dishonest, but it's the only way I'll know for sure. I hear the shower shut off so I turn off Matt's phone and put it back where it was. A few minutes later he appears in the hall dressed only in a towel. Wow, the sight of him does odd things to me.

"I'm done. Do you want to go to lunch before work?" he calls out.

"No, I can't. I promised Jenna that I'd have some overdue girl time with her today."

"Okay." He nods and disappears into his bedroom.

I am tempted to look closer into all of his messages but I refrain, thinking that's just too invasive.

On the way home, I'm contemplative about what I just saw. I'm confused because Matt and I connected so well last night. Well, I thought we did anyway. Then this morning I see the text from her and that tells a different story. The bad part is that my brain always gravitates toward the negative, so all I can think about is Matt and Kendall together. I'm hoping Jenna has some advice that will be useful.

When I walk in the door, Jenna is sitting on the couch watching TV. She glances over at me and nods as she stuffs a chocolate-covered pretzel in her mouth. Oh no, that usually means man trouble.

"Jenna, is something going on with you and Trent?"

She looks at me with a look of despair and shovels more chocolate in. I walk over to sit next to her and throw my arms around her as she begins to cry.

"Oh, honey, what happened?"

She sniffles and cries harder.

In between crying, sniffling, and eating, she explains that she and Trent broke up because his ex-girlfriend came into town and they more than likely hooked up.

"That's awful, Jenna. Is there anything I can do?"

She sits up and wipes her tear-stained cheeks with her shirt.

"No. There's nothing anyone can do. He's just a giant ass!"

"Tell me what happened," I say softly.

"Well, we were hanging out at his place when there was a knock at the door. He answered it, and there she was. She was really pretty and very forward. He no sooner opened the door when she burst in, grabbed his face, and kissed him. And it wasn't just a peck either."

"Oh my God, you're kidding? What did Trent do?"

"I wish I were. He pushed her away, of course, and looked back at me to see if I was watching. When he saw my face I know he was ashamed. How could he do this to me, Chloe?"

She's crying again.

"I don't know, honey. Could there be another explanation for his behavior? I mean he didn't initiate the kiss, so maybe he didn't really want it. And he did push her away."

"I don't know, but I didn't stick around to find out. I grabbed my purse and went running out. He's been trying to call me ever since, but I refuse to talk to him and ended up shutting my ringer off."

"Okay, that's fine for now, but eventually you'll have to talk it out."

"I don't think I want to hear anything he has to say."

We sit in silence for a few minutes.

"I need to hear some good news. Tell me what's going on with you and Matt."

Oh boy.

"Oh you know, same stuff, different day." I laugh uneasily.

She looks at me and gasps.

"Chloe, you did it, didn't you?"

How does she know?

"What? How—"

"I'd know the look a mile away! You did! So how was it?"

"Um..."

"Details! I want them all!"

"Jenna! I'm not going into details but it was...good, really good. It happened on his birthday." And I can feel my face turn red.

She squeals and claps her hands like a seal, and I laugh. I tell her in vague terms how it went. I don't want to share too much because it's such a personal thing that happened between Matt and me. I tell her enough to satisfy her but not enough to make me feel as though I've betrayed him.

"But..." she prods.

"But what?"

"There's something else going on, Chloe. I can feel it. Something you're not telling me."

How the hell?

"Well, I'm just afraid that he still wants Kendall."

"What? Why would you think that?"

Reluctantly I tell her about the text I saw. I know that right now her view on it could be biased because of her situation with Trent. I'm surprised when she tells me not to panic and that there might be a logical explanation.

"What makes you think that, Jenna?"

"Look, we've known Matt forever. He's not like that. If he's planning to meet with her then it's probably to make sure she understands that you two are together and there's no hope for her."

She does have a point.

"Maybe you're right. I don't know what to think anymore. Too much thinking makes my brain hurt." I chuckle.

Just before I leave for the theater, I get a text from Matt.

We need 2 talk.

My pessimistic nature kicks in, and I begin to worry.

Okay, about what?

There are no further texts from him, and I feel sick. I need to talk to him right away.

When I get to the show, I don't see Matt at all. He usually finds a way to wish me luck on the performance for that night but not tonight. Kendall, however, is everywhere, much to my dismay. She is making it very clear that she doesn't like me, but I don't care.

We go on to perform the first act. During intermission I get a strange vibe. I am reapplying my stage makeup when Kendall walks in. Great, what does she want?

"Chloe." She says in a condescending tone. "I just wanted to say that no matter how things turn out, there are no hard feelings."

I turn toward her in utter confusion. "What?"

"I mean, I know you think you know Matt very well, but if he chooses me then I don't want there to be any animosity between us."

The nerve of her! Okay, I'll play. "And if he chooses me?"

She pauses, laughs, and then stops with a resolute face. "Oh, you're serious. Well, the fact that we've been talking and that he's considering coming back to me speaks volumes, don't you think?"

I'm fuming but the second act starts in five minutes so I need to calm down. "Whatever Kendall. I'm not worried," I lie.

She snorts. "You should be."

And with that we go back out on stage, all the while my stomach is in knots.

The show is done for the day, and I'm back in the dressing room removing all evidence of being a performer. I still haven't seen Matt, but then again, I haven't made it out into the hallway yet. As I exit, Drew stops me just outside the door.

"Hey, sweetie, I heard about your confrontation with the Tasmanian she-devil. Are you okay?" Drew asks with a tilt of his head.

"Yeah, I'm fine. She just really gets to me, you know? The nerve she has to insinuate that Matt is going to leave me for her! Ugh!"

"Don't let her upset you, Chloe. She is running out of options, and she knows it. Desperation takes on many forms. She's trying to put doubt in your head. Don't let her."

"But, Drew, what if she's right? What if Matt really does want her back."

He gives me a look of skepticism.

"No, really, listen. He always sends me a good luck message before show time, and today he didn't. In fact, I haven't even seen him here. And then, there's the text I found in his phone; it was from Kendall. Apparently they've been talking and they're having lunch sometime soon."

His mouth pops open.

"And finally, there's what we did."

"Oh? What did you guys do?"

"It."

Now he's speechless.

"Oh, sweetie, she's pulling out every trick isn't she?"

I nod.

"Well, we need to come up with some major damage control now."

"No. I'm not going to do anything. If he truly wants me, then he'll take me as is. I'm not stooping to her level to win Matt. I'm not playing games. This is too important."

He agrees. "All right then, let's go home," Drew decides.

We start walking down the long hallway, but when we turn the corner my heart stops. There, about fifteen feet away from us, is Kendall and Matt in a lip lock that anyone would envy. Drew gasps and covers his mouth, at the same time grabbing my arm either to brace himself or hold me back. I think I'm going to throw up. I too cover my mouth in shock. Matt breaks off the kiss and looks straight at me. The look on his face is...anguish. In disbelief, I take a couple steps back.

"Chlo!" Matt calls.

But I want nothing to do with him. I take a few more steps back so that Drew is now in between us.

"Chlo, don't go!" Matt calls again and takes a few steps in my direction.

I turn and run full speed toward the exit, and all I hear are the voices of Matt and Drew in the distance.

"Leave her alone, you asshole!"

"Get out of my way, Drew. I need to talk to her!"

I hear a scuffle, and Matt's haunted voice echoes down the hall. "Chlo!"

nineteen

I hit the bar on the outside door and push through it to the street. I know Matt will chase me, and hailing a cab might take too long, so I start walking in the direction of my apartment. Tears are free falling down my face as people on the sidewalks stare. I don't care; I'm just too angry. I am walking purposefully with a long stride so I can get as far as possible and disappear into the night. I know it's dangerous, but in the emotional state that I'm in right now, no one would dare mess with me. I am reminded of the last time I escaped from Matt in this very place. That turned out to be a wonderful thing, not so this time. Hearing the sound of the same door I just went through open and close, I'm hoping I'm far enough away that he can't see me.

"Chlo!" I hear Matt call me. "Chlo!"

I'm not sure if he sees me or if he's just screaming my name out of frustration. I learn the answer soon enough. As I hear someone's footsteps running behind me, I quicken my pace even though I know he will catch up.

"Chlo, stop walking, now!" he shouts and grabs me by the wrist. I twist around and yank my arm from his grasp.

"Fuck you, Matt!" I spit. And for a few seconds he looks as though I've slapped him. "I don't want to hear anything you have to say! I'm done!"

I resume walking. He recovers and walks beside me.

"Chlo, what you saw...it wasn't—"

I stop walking and face him.

"It wasn't what, Matt? It wasn't you kissing Kendall? Because that's exactly what it looked like to me!" I stare blankly at him and resume walking.

"Chlo, I...I'm so sorry. I don't—"

"Save it! I'm not listening anymore."

"But I love you. Please, let me explain."

"You love me?" I snort. "That was so obvious when you had your tongue in Kendall's mouth!"

"Yes, Chlo." He grabs my arm again, and we stop walking, but I won't look at him. "I love you." He touches my face to wipe away a tear. I ache for his touch, but I just can't take it right now.

"Sometimes loves not enough. Don't call me, don't text me, and no e-mails. I'm done," I reply and free my arm again. I see a taxi parked a few feet away and get in it. Giving the driver my address, I use my peripheral vision to look at Matt. He's frozen on the sidewalk in disbelief, and at that moment, I feel a twinge of pain for him.

The ride home is long, well, it feels long. I am tortured by what I saw and what I said and what I did. I just broke up with the only man I've ever loved. What did I do? I sob all the way back to my apartment, all the while wiping my face with my sleeve.

Jenna isn't home, or maybe she's already in bed, either way I'm grateful for the alone time. I just want to slip into a hot bath and soak my troubles away. I start the water and pour in some bubbles. I am reminded of the bath Matt arranged for me and get teary-eyed again. No. Stop this. He betrayed me. I need to feel anger to get through this. I slide into the water, close my eyes, and try to relax.

It's early in the morning, and I am working at Mangolinas. Olivia called to ask me to cover her shift today and I agreed. I figure the busier I am, the better. My body isn't used to this early hour, so I pump myself full of caffeine and do my thing. I am pretty much floating through my day in a daze. The only thing that lifts my spirits is focusing on my impending trip home tomorrow. It'll be good to get away for a while. I've already put in for my leave of absence so they'll get a sub for the shows I'll miss.

I am about to approach my next table when a familiar face walks in.

"James!" I say with a smile and a hug. "What are you doing here?"

"Hi, Chloe. I was hoping to run into you," he replies warmly.

"Well, you're lucky you found me. I have only been filling in here since I got into *Chicago*."

He chuckles and looks embarrassed.

"Yeah...I know. I've kind of been stopping in every so often to...um... see you. And I've been to the show a couple times."

Oh. I had no idea.

"Have you? Did you like it?"

"Absolutely! You are a fantastic dancer."

I blush. "Well, thank you. So are you staying to eat?"

"No, I'm not. The only reason I'm here is because I wanted to see you...and talk to you."

"Oh? What about?"

"Nothing in particular. Just wondering how things are going."

"Great! Good. Everything is fine." Boy, that didn't sound convincing. "I have my dream job with one of my best friends. My other best friend is a disaster, but she'll be fine, and I get to go see my Gram tomorrow."

"Wow, that sounds great."

"Yeah," I say with a sigh.

"So what about that guy you're dating? You didn't say anything about him. Are you still together?"

Oh no, try not to look upset.

"We're...not together anymore."

"Oh, I'm sorry," he says with a sympathetic face. "Are you okay?"

"I will be. It just happened so...it's still kind of fresh."

"I see. Well, if you need a distraction..."

I smile.

"Are you asking me out again?"

"I wouldn't dare, unless you'd say yes, in which case I guess I would be asking you out." A very wide grin crosses his face, and he looks utterly pleased with himself.

"A friendly date?" I ask.

"No, not this time. If you're not dating anyone, then I'd like my chance to show you a good time. But I know you're probably still reeling from your breakup, so we'll keep it casual. What do you think?"

Hmm, what do I think? It's really soon, I don't know. But maybe this is exactly what I need. I take a deep breath.

"Okay."

"Really?"

"Yes, really. When do you want to go out?"

"How about tomorrow night?"

"Oh, I can't. I'm going back home to Ohio to visit with my Gram. I'll be there for about a week."

"I didn't realize she lives out of town. Well, how about after you get back then? We can go to dinner, or I can cook for you at my place."

"You cook?"

He grabs his chest. "You wound me. Of course I can cook."

I grin broadly. "Sorry, I had no idea. Dinner at your place sounds good. I'll call you when I'm back in town. We'll set it up then."

"It's a date," he says as he hugs me. "I'm going to go. Please have a safe trip."

"I will. Thank you."

The flight itself isn't that long, but I'm exhausted from the trip. All I have with me is carry-on luggage, so until I get to the point where the public is permitted, I have to carry this heavier-by-the-minute bag by myself. I'm excited to see my parents, but I'm troubled with the fact that Matt has made no attempts to contact me. I know I told him not to, but in the back of my mind I'm surprised and disappointed that he hasn't. Maybe I should've let him explain. Maybe there's a logical reason that he kissed Kendall. Ugh! That image is permanently burned into my brain. And then there's James. He's so... uncomplicated. It feels good when we're together because there are no expectations. I am so confused. I hope talking it all out with Gram will help.

As I walk down the long corridor that leads to the mob of loved ones, I see my dad waiting in the crowd. He's six feet two inches tall and hard to miss. He smiles when we make eye contact, so I hurry through the crowd toward him and throw my arms around his neck.

"Daddy!" I squeak out.

"Hi, honey. It's so good to have you home. How are you?" he says and lets go.

"I'm good, Dad. I've missed you," I say with tears in my eyes.

"Aw, honey, we've missed you too. How was the flight?"

"It was fine. A little bumpy, but it was good. Did Mom come with you?"

"No, she stayed back to make dinner. You know how she is."

I smile fondly. "Yes, I do. I'm so happy to be home."

On the fifteen-minute ride to my parents' house, I look out the window at all of Ohio's familiarity. I see railroad tracks and shopping centers and patches of forest that line the highway. Even the smell screams I'm home.

"Gram is doing much better now," Dad interjects. "They have her on some new meds that seem to be working. She's supposed to cut down on the salt, and she hates that, but at least her feisty nature tells me she's back to her old self again."

"When can we go and see her?"

"We'll go tomorrow after a good night's sleep."

As we pull into the driveway, I hear mom shout my arrival. She meets us at the front door.

"Chloe! I'm so glad you're home!" she yells as she hugs me. "Come in, come in. Make yourself comfortable. Dinner is almost ready."

"Thanks, Mom. It smells wonderful. What is it?"

"Chicken with roasted potatoes and green beans. One of your favorites, I believe."

I smile at her. "Mom, I like anything you cook, you know that."

"I'll take your bags up to your room sweetheart," Dad says as he slings the heavy duffel over his shoulder. "Jeez, honey, what do you have in here?"

"Nothing much. Just girly stuff," I reply.

"I'll take your word for it." And he disappears up the stairs.

"Becca, that meal was delicious. I'm so stuffed I'm not sure I can make it to my chair in the living room."

"Thank you, and I'm sure you'll find a way to get there." She waves him off with her hand, and he takes his cue.

"So, honey, what's going on with you? How's the show going?" Mom asks.

"It's going great, Mom. It's hard to believe I get paid to have so much fun."

She smiles warmly. "And the rest if your life?"

Oh no. Here comes the interrogation.

"It's fine, Mom, really."

"Are you and Matt still an item?"

Ugh.

"Not at the moment. We're taking a break. We both needed some space."

I look up through my eyelashes to see if she's buying this. Whew, she is.

"Well that's good. You know there are more fish in the sea besides that boy," she states.

"I know Mom, and you'll be happy to know that I found another fish."

"Oh? Who?" Her curiosity is piqued.

"His name is James. He's trying to break into broadcasting or something. I'm not really dating him. We went out once, and he is very nice. We're just friends right now."

"Well that's nice, honey. I'm happy to see you didn't decide to settle down with your first boyfriend. "

"I know, Mom."

Mom has always liked Matt but never saw him as a potential boyfriend for me. I think she's hoping I'll marry a doctor or lawyer and then she won't have to worry about me making my own living. She and I differ in opinions on this point.

After helping Mom with the cleanup, I excuse myself and retire to my old bedroom. It looks the same as when I left it. Pink walls, beige carpet, pictures of tigers plastered all over, home. As I lie in my childhood bed, I almost feel like a teen again. I drift off, remembering what it was like to love Matt from afar.

twenty

The phone rings. When I answer I immediately recognize the voice.

"Matt!" I say with a huge grin. "I've missed you. I knew you'd call."

"Hey, Chlo. How have you been?"

"I'd be better with you in my life again," I reply. "We need to talk things through. I was wrong not to let you explain. Can I see you?"

"Uh, Chlo? I have something to talk to you about. I need to tell you—"

"I know. It's okay. I forgive you because I love you."

"Chlo, stop. I...I'm back with Kendall. I love her. That kiss made me realize it. I'm sorry."

The phone goes dead.

Silence.

Tears fall like rain down my cheeks to my chin and onto my lap. What? This can't be real! He can't love her. I think I hear the sound of my heart breaking.

The phone rings again. I try to answer, it but it just won't stop ringing.

"Are you going to turn that noise off?" says a voice.

"No. Please, don't hang up," I moan and then I realize I'm back in Ohio in my bed, my dad's gentle voice coaxing me from slumber.

"Wake up, honey. We're going to visit Gram soon."

I am up, dressed, and downstairs eating all within ten minutes. My dream is lingering in the back of my mind. Dad is driving me up to

Cherry Ridge Senior Living Facility today to see my Gram. I've missed her so much.

When we arrive, it's obvious that this is a newer building. The outside is a light-colored brick. There's an overhang with a semicircular driveway for pickups and drop offs that's held up by very tall pillars. As we walk through the automatic sliding glass doors, I can see several elderly people milling around. Straight in front of us is the front desk, and to our left is an activity room where bingo is already in progress. To our right are couches by a large fireplace and tables with chairs for sitting and visiting. Beyond the front desk is the dining room. The employees are pushing vacuum cleaners and resetting the tables for lunch. At one grouping of chairs sits a woman who is speaking what I think is German with another woman in an electric wheelchair. I can't tell what they're saying, but they seem to be enjoying themselves. There's another woman with a silver walker heading over in our direction.

"Hello there!" she greets us warmly. "Are you here visiting today?"

I smile at her and say, "Yes, we're here to see my grandmother."

"Oh, that's great! My name is Faye. What's yours?"

We tell her and make small talk. She points us in the direction of the two hallways of individual apartments.

"Your grandmother is in B hall. Have a nice time!" she says as she continues on her way. Dad and I come up to Gram's room, and I knock gently. Slowly I open the door. She's lying in her hospital-style bed, but she's awake and watching a movie.

"Gram?"

She turns her head, and a slow smile forms on her sweet face.

"Chloe, is that really you?"

"It's me, Gram." I walk over to her. Her arms are outstretched, and she gives me a tight hug that almost smothers me and seems to go on for days.

"How've you been, baby?" her muffled voice asks as she speaks into my shoulder.

"I'm good, Gram, real good."

"How's Matt? Is he behaving?" She chuckles.

Oh no. Change the subject, now.

"Oh, Gram, we can talk about him later. How are you feeling?"

She releases me and looks over at her son.

"I feel fine baby. Did your father scare you into coming here?" she asks, clearly irritated.

"Mom, I just told her what your doctor told me. I didn't scare her into coming. She loves you and thought it would be nice to see you," Dad states.

She eyes him speculatively.

"Really, Gram, I just missed you so much and needed the time away. That's why I came, honestly."

"Oh, sweetie, I don't care why you came, I'm just glad you're here."

"How about if I step out and let you two catch up? I'll find us some coffee," Dad says as he exits.

"So, Gram, how do you like it here? You have a nice view of the pond," I say as I look out the large window.

"Chloe, what's going on with you and Matt?" she says.

"Gram, I didn't come here to talk about Matt. I came here to see you." I smile unconvincingly.

"There is something not right going on, and I want to know what it is."

I sigh. She can always tell when things are amiss.

"Aw, Gram, we had a fight. I saw him kissing an ex-girlfriend of his and...well...I flew off the handle and didn't let him explain. I told him I was done and that he should never contact me again," I say, now breathless.

She motions for me to come closer to her while she swings her legs off of the bed. I sit next to her, and she puts her arm around me.

"Baby, he's crazy about you. I know he is. You need to talk to him. When you get back, I want you to go to him. You need to make the first move. That way he'll know you care enough to start the conversation."

"I don't know," I say.

"Trust me. I know you two will work things out eventually."

"I love you, Gram." And I hug her tight.

"Now come on, baby. Let's go find your dad."

We walk out of her apartment and down the hall. Dozens of elderly people wander about. Some smile as we go by, some wave, and some greet us kindly. There's a very tall, very handsome man walking with a walker; his sons follow behind him with his wheelchair just in case he needs a break. All three seem very nice. The older man sits down in his wheelchair as they say hello.

"Hi, Don. I'd like you to meet my granddaughter, Chloe. Chloe, this is Don and his boys, Brian and Mark."

"Hello. It's nice to meet you," I say, extending my hand.

"Hello there, young lady. How are you today?" Don replies and takes my proffered hand, kissing the back of it.

"Oh my, such a gentleman. I'm fine, thank you."

"Your grandmother is quite a woman, you know," he says as he winks.

"Now, Don, don't start puttin' on the old charm. It doesn't work with me, and it won't work with her either," Gram scolds him with a grin.

"But it's true. She's also feisty," he teases.

She laughs, and I can tell they have a sort of routine. It's fun and flirty, and it's sweet to watch.

"It was very nice to meet you. Perhaps we'll see you again soon?" he inquires.

I smile and nod, and we continue on our walk.

Gram shows me around, and before I know it, it's time to go.

"I'll come by again tomorrow, Gram. Maybe we'll go shopping or something."

"I'd love that. See you then. I love you, baby!" she calls out as she waves.

"Okay, I love you too, Gram." And then we're gone.

The next few days fly by. I visit Gram every day. Sometimes I take her to lunch, sometimes we eat there. Today we go shopping. Apparently, even seventy-nine-year-old women need to refresh their wardrobes every now and then. As I enter the facility, I greet several residents I have gotten to know.

"Hello there, Reinhardt!" I call out. "Anything new going on?"

He smiles at me and replies, "Nope, not today. Taking her out again?"

"Yes, shopping. A girl can't have too many clothes." I chuckle.

I continue to make my way to Gram's room when I come across Lillian.

I open my bag and stealthily slip her a bag of mint-flavored M&Ms. I'm not sure if she's allowed to have candy, but she seems so happy to know someone cares enough to break the internal laws on her behalf.

"Thank you, dear," she whispers.

"I thought you'd like to try my latest addiction, Lillian."

"Yes, I would. My son isn't due to bring me goodies for another week. This should hold me until then."

I smile and nod and continue on my way. When I get to Gram's room, we exchange greetings and leave quickly, eager to start our adventure.

We make a day of our shopping excursion by starting at the major department stores in the mall and end with a late lunch at Applebee's. We are having a great time talking about some of the residents at Cherry Ridge, and I giggle when I realize that Gram does a great impression of my dad when he's trying to scold her. It feels so good to sit and talk with her that I almost forget why I came back to Ohio. It makes me sad to think that someday I will lose her. Enough of those thoughts, I will make the best of the time I have left with her. As we exit the restaurant I hear someone call my name so I turn around. It's Matt's dad, Joe.

"Chloe, wait up," he pants as he jogs over to us. "Hi, Thelma, long time, no see."

"Hi, Joe. How's Maggie?"

"She's good, thank you."

He turns to me in a seeming hurry.

"Chloe, I don't mean to skip the small talk but have you talked to Matt recently? I know you two have been sort of an item, but I talked to him a few days ago and he seemed...off. Is there something wrong? Do you know what's going on?"

Oh no. The last person I want included in my and Matt's personal life, or lack thereof, is Joe.

"Mr. Masen, forgive me, but I haven't talked to Matt in almost a week. We—"

"They were going to come back home together, but Matt's job required that he stay in New York. He's probably just missing Chloe something awful," Gram interrupts.

I look at her dumbstruck.

He lets out a long-held breath. "Oh good, I'm glad that's all it is. He really sounded terrible. I was very worried that something was horribly wrong with him."

I smile because I don't know what else to say right now.

"I'm late for an appointment, so I've got to run. It was nice to see you again Thelma." She nods. He takes my hand. "Chloe, take care of my boy, eh?"

"Yes, sir, I'll do that."

He smiles and kisses my cheek.

"I always knew you two would end up together," he whispers in my ear.

Gram smiles at me, and I chide her.

"Why did you stop me from telling Mr. Masen the truth? I think he deserves to know that we aren't together anymore."

"Why? You know as soon as you get back to New York you're going to sit down and talk to Matt. You'll get back together and live happily ever after."

"What? You don't know that!"

"Yes, I do." She winks.

Bewildered, we get back in the car and head for home.

I'm daydreaming as I drive—not a clever combination—but Gram's words befuddle me. How can she know? She can't. It must be wishful thinking.

"You know you have to go home on the next flight to New York," Gram interrupts my thoughts.

I look at her in confusion.

"No, I don't. He's not mine to worry about."

"He's always been yours; he always will be. Go to him. Save him from himself. I'll be fine. I'll see you at your wedding."

My mouth pops open. "Gram!"

"Oh, like you've never tried on his last name!"

I smile.

"Go on, say it...out loud."

My grin broadens. "Chloe Masen."

We both giggle.

"Again."

I say it again and again, and our giggles turn into gut busting laughter. When we are finally all laughed out, Gram turns to me and says, "Baby, please go to him. It's important to me. I know you two love each other."

"But, Gram, sometimes love is not enough."

She places her hand on my leg and replies, "Love is always enough."

I get her back home and say my good-byes, promising to go straight to Matt's when the plane lands. Mom and Dad are disappointed that I'm cutting my trip short, but they plan to take vacation in my neck of the woods sometime soon.

In the air all I can think about is what I'll say to Matt when I see him. The time passes very quickly, and before I know it, I'm on the ground at La Guardia. I turn my iPhone back on and instantly see I have a missed call from....Jake? Hmm. I give him a quick call back. He answers on the second ring.

"Chloe?"

"Hi, Jake."

"I'm so glad you called. It's Matt, he's out of control. He's been drunk for a solid week, and he's missed so much work. I've been covering for him, but please help. I don't know what to do."

"What? Why?" I exclaim.

"I'm not sure. He keeps saying your name, but he doesn't make any sense. Please, Chloe, you're the only one who can help!"

"I just landed at La Guardia. I'm on my way."

twenty one

When I reach Matt and Jake's apartment, I pay the cab driver and step out. I look up at the building and take a deep breath. I'm nervous about seeing Matt and what condition I might find him in.

Jake buzzes me in, and I go up. I'm standing in front of their door, frozen. I know I have to do this, but I'm shaking. What if he is so angry with me that he refuses to see me? What if we fight again? What if...Oh hell, here we go.

I knock softly. I no sooner put my hand back down to my side when Jake opens the door in a rush.

"Chloe, come in." He takes my arm. "I'll take you to him."

"Um, okay," I say in a fog.

Jake leads me through the living room, and I recall my first time in this apartment. I look at the couch and smile sadly. We trek through the hallway that leads to Matt's bedroom. I look to the left and remember the bath that Matt had drawn for me. His bedroom door is closed when we get there. I can hear music coming from the other side. My heart pounds wildly in my chest, but I must go in and save him from himself, as Gram put it.

"I didn't tell him you were coming. I'll be out in the living room if you need anything," Jake says, and as he walks away, leaving me to my work, I see a hint of concern on his otherwise handsome face.

I tentatively knock but don't wait for an invitation. I just walk right in.

Matt's room is a mess. Dirty clothes lie all over the floor like a carpet, and in between them are dozens and dozens of crumpled, empty beer cans. Empty bottles of hard liquor line up on the dresser and night-stands, and it reeks like a sewage plant. The curtains are drawn shut, and I see Matt sitting on the edge of his bed. His back is to me. The radio that is playing is directly to my left, so I reach over and turn it off.

"Jake, leave me the fuck alone. Can't you see I'm busy?" he says without turning around. He takes a large swig from a bottle containing amber liquid.

"Busy doing what exactly, drowning yourself?" I ask. He stills but doesn't turn around.

"Chlo, you're back."

"Yeah, early actually. I was approached by your dad, who asked me to get to the bottom of your recently strange behavior," I say dryly. I'm pissed.

"Sorry about that. I didn't ask him to get in touch with you. So what are you doing here?"

"I'm here, apparently, to sober you up and help clean up this pigsty," I say rather acidly.

"Yeah, well, don't waste your time. I'm not interested in doing any of that."

I fly around to the other side of the bed and stand in front of him.

"Guess what. You don't have a choice." I yank the half-empty bottle of Jack out of his hand and slam it down on the dresser. I reach down and grab his foot and begin to peel his socks off. Ugh, they smell like ten men's locker rooms put together.

"What are you doing?"

"I'm taking your socks off right now, and then you're getting in the shower!"

"Chlo, stop it."

He's fighting me, so I lift his foot up, tipping him backward onto the bed. From this position, I am able to get both socks off and then I grab his sweat pants from the bottom and pull hard.

"Hey! What are you doing?" he shouts and tries to hold onto his waistband.

"Don't get shy on me now, Matt. You're getting in that shower if I have to undress you myself!"

"Okay, okay, I'll go shower."

I step back. He staggers to his feet and sways several times on his way to the bathroom. Once he's inside, I go to the kitchen for garbage bags and Clorox wipes. Then I start a full pot of coffee. I return to Matt's room and begin the massive cleanup. I don't have to pour out much booze, as Matt has already consumed most of it. His clothes go in the hamper, and the beer cans and bottles go in the trash. I am vacuuming his floor when he reappears in the doorway in a towel. I swallow. God, he's hot.

"Wow, you're fast. This place was a disaster a little while ago," he says.

"Yes, it was. Get dressed. I'll come back and finish when you're done."

I shoulder past him, but he grasps my arm to stop me.

"Thank you," he says softly.

My mood shifts slightly. "You're welcome," I say and continue on to the kitchen.

It takes him only a few minutes to get dressed, and I hear the door open. I walk down the hall with a mug filled with black coffee.

"Here," I offer and push the cup at him. "Drink it, and when you're done, pour another. I made a whole pot, and from the look of you, you'll need every bit of it," I say, irritated.

I walk past him and back to his room to finish my work. I've stripped his bed and am in the process of remaking it when he slinks in.

"Chlo?"

"What?" I answer absentmindedly.

He takes the opposite side of the sheet to aid me in the task.

"I'm sorry."

"For what?"

"Getting shit-faced, letting you see me like that, allowing you to clean up. But mostly, I'm sorry you had to cut your trip short. I know you wanted to stay longer but because of me..."

"Don't worry about it," I dismiss him.

"I am worried about it, Chlo. You shouldn't have to deal with this. Why should you? I mean, I don't deserve you. You're so...good, and I'm... not. What I did...I..." He sighs. "It wasn't what you think."

"What was it then? Because I know what it looked like." I'm angry again.

"I can't tell you."

What?

"You can't, or you won't?"

"Won't."

"Why not? Matt, you've always been able to talk to me about anything. Why can't you talk to me now?"

"It's complicated."

"I'm sure I can keep up. What's going on with you?" I go to his side of the bed, and I bid him to sit with me. He complies. Holding one of his hands with both of mine, I look into his tired eyes. "Talk to me."

He exhales, bows his head, and briefly rests it against my shoulder.

"I hate this. We were so happy. And then Kendall..." He stops.

I narrow my eyes. "Kendall...what?"

"Nothing. It's not important."

"The hell it's not!" I spit. "If that little bitch has anything to do with this I'll—"

"You'll what, Chlo? What would you do?" he interrupts.

"I don't know, but I'm sick to death of her interference. It's not fair." A single tear rolls down my cheek. Matt lifts his hand to my face and gently wipes it away.

"Don't cry, Chlo. We'll get through all this. We have to. I can't live without you."

Another tear falls, and then another, and another until I am sobbing. Matt wraps his arms around me and lets me cry. He coos softly into my hair as he smoothes it away from my face.

After a while, my weeping stops, but he keeps his arms around me.

"Better?" he asks.

I nod, but we haven't resolved anything. "Are we getting back together?" I ask, hopeful.

He sighs. "Not yet."

"Why?" I exclaim as I lift my head up quickly to look into his sorrow-filled eyes.

"I told you, it's complicated."

I pull away from him.

"Chlo, please just remember I love you. That's all you need to know."

"Are you with her?"

There's a pause.

"Yes."

I squeeze my eyes shut as I feel a stab of pain in my chest. "This is a waste of time. I need to go. If you can't—I mean, won't—tell me what's going on, then I have nothing more to say."

"Chlo...I...I'll see you at work."

Really. That's it?

"Fine." And with that, I pick up my bag and walk out.

On the ride home I contemplate all that went on today. He said it's complicated a few times. The words "not yet" rattle around in my brain. What does that mean? Why not yet? I don't understand. He also says he loves me. If he didn't want to be with me, he wouldn't have said that, surely. Ugh, men! I decide I just have to stop thinking about it for a while.

Days pass by like minutes. When my time off from the show is finally over, I am faced with the knowledge that I will be seeing the Matt and Kendall show all week, maybe longer. I cringe at the thought. At the theater, Kendall is making a point to show me that she and Matt are a couple again. If she's not talking about him, she's making attempts to see him and then telling everyone who will listen how much he loves her. A thought crosses my mind. If you feel the need to tell everyone how much your boyfriend loves you, are you trying to convince your audience or yourself? My deduction brings a little victory smile to my face.

I see Matt every now and then backstage. He offers me a smile, except for when he's with her. I've got to be missing something. Suddenly, Drew comes up to me in a rush.

"Chloe, did you hear about Maxine?"

I shake my head.

"She got fired for having drugs."

"What?" I say a little too loudly. "You're kidding! When?"

"A little while ago. Gina saw her picking up her stuff and crying. When she asked her what was wrong, she wouldn't say, but she did say good-bye to everyone. Josh told me that he overheard her say something about being framed."

"Oh my God, that's terrible! Poor Maxine. I had no idea she even did drugs."

"I don't think she does. Maybe Josh was right. Maybe she was framed."

"Who would do that?"

"That seems to be the six-million-dollar question," Drew says.

Another week passes, and life at the theater is really getting to me. My stomach is in constant knots knowing that Kendall will be flirting and pawing my now ex-boyfriend/best friend. I will always love him, but all of the turmoil has made me push away from him emotionally. I need a hobby, something to get my mind off Matt. I don't know how long he and Kendall will remain a couple, but I'm not willing to put my life on hold for him anymore. I need to let him go. I pick up my phone and call James. He is pleased to hear from me and welcomes me back home. I feel a little guilty for not telling him I've been back for a while. We make arrangements to have dinner at his place. I'm nervous that he will make assumptions but confident that I can handle things if I need to.

It's Monday night, my only day off. James picks me up in a silver Eclipse.

"Good evening, Chloe. You look wonderful, as always."

I blush.

"Thank you, James. You look dashing as well." I smile.

"Thank you. I wasn't sure what kind of food you like, so I went for traditional."

"Oh?"

"Spaghetti."

"Mmm, I love spaghetti."

"Good." He pauses. "And I thought we'd make it ourselves. Is that okay?" His face is hopeful.

"That sounds like fun. Then I can assess your cooking skills," I tease.

"I'm not sure how confident I am in my abilities, however, I can boil a mean pot of water."

We laugh, and my nerves begin to settle.

"How was your trip back to Ohio?"

"It was good and much needed. I really miss my family sometimes. I know I have Jenna, but it's not the same, you know?"

"I know what you mean. I take an annual trip out to California to visit my mom. It's not exactly the same because I didn't grow up there."

"Did you grow up in New York City?"

"Yes. My mother moved away when I was in high school. She wanted us to come with her, but I just couldn't leave my dad."

"Yeah, I get that. It was hard for me when I transferred to NYU. I knew I'd miss my parents, but it was Gram I was anxious about. She's getting up there in years, and I was...am afraid that I'm not going to be around when she needs me." I sigh and look out the window.

"Chloe, are you okay? Are you sure you're up for this today? We can reschedule if you—"

"No, it's okay," I interrupt. "I'm fine. Let's go to your place, cook till our hearts' content, and have a wonderful evening," I say with enthusiasm.

He chuckles. "Okay then, let's go."

He steps on the gas, and the car shoots forward. Before I know it we're pulling into a parking garage. He parks and gets out. I am checking my makeup in the passenger visor mirror while he walks around to my door and opens it.

Oh my. Nice touch, Mr. Chivalry.

Holding out his hand, he says, "No need to worry, you're gorgeous."

I smile and take hold of his hand while emerging from the car.

We walk over and get into a waiting elevator. He pushes the button, and we are whisked up eleven floors. The silence is awkward, but soon enough the doors open to reveal a long hallway. He takes my hand and looks down at me.

"This is our stop," he says and leads me to the right. We walk until we come to room eleven twenty-eight.

"Here we are, my home sweet home."

James unlocks the door and pushes it open.

twenty two

I step inside James's apartment as he turns on the lights. It's a very modern, but very modest place. It's small but the open floor plan makes it feel big inside. The living room has a large picture window next to the sliding glass doors that lead to a small balcony. I can see another apartment building across the way.

To my left, a small breakfast bar spills out from the kitchen with its all-white lacquer cabinets. A bouquet of fresh white roses is on the counter. Their aroma scents the entire area.

"You have quite a place here, James."

"Yes, it is quite a place." He chuckles. "I've had it for a few years. It could use an update."

"I think it's great. No improvements needed." I turn back and smile. He mirrors my expression.

He walks over into the kitchen, and I hear him open a bottle of wine. Within minutes he's back and offers me a glass.

"Thank you," I say as I take it from him.

"Would you like to sit for a while or shall we begin?" he says, motioning toward the kitchen.

"Let's get cooking."

We start by assembling our ingredients and utensils. I'm opening cabinet after cabinet looking for what I need. I know I could just ask him where things are, but it's kind of fun snooping. We aren't saying much, but it's not uncomfortable, it's...nice. It's also good to know that neither one of us feels the need to fill the silence with mindless chatter.

The pasta is in the pot, the sauce is too, the cheese bread is in the oven, and our salad is nearly done. I lean my back against the counter with my arms crossed and see him grinning.

"What?"

He smiles bigger.

"What?" I ask again.

"Nothing."

My mouth twists, and my eyes narrow. "What's your middle name?"

He looks puzzled now. "Anthony."

"James Anthony Hale, why do you have that ridiculous grin on your face?" I say, teasing him.

"Hey, no fair using my middle name. My mom uses that when I'm in trouble. Am I in trouble, Miss Shepherd?"

I snicker. "You will be if you don't fess up, now spill it, Hale," I tease again.

"You really want to know why I'm smiling?"

I nod as he saunters closer. "You really want to know?"

I nod slowly this time, and he comes to stand right in front of me. He puts his hands on the countertop on either side of me and looks into my eyes. I swallow involuntarily. He's so close that I can see the all the detail in his beautiful, ice-blue eyes.

"I am smiling because I'm currently entertaining the most beautiful woman I've ever met, and I'm about to kiss her if she so chooses."

He pauses millimeters from my lips as though he's waiting for permission. I'm breathless, but I subtly nod and shut my eyes. Slowly he closes the gap between us, and his soft lips brush gently against mine. My heart is beating so fast that I'm sure he can feel the vibration, and there's a warming sensation all over my body. He leans in more now, and the fingers of his left hand weave slowly through my hair. When our mouths connect it's like someone has sucked all the air out of the room. His slow, seductive kiss is making me want more. Then his right hand wraps gently but firmly around my waist, pulling our hips together. This maneuver pushes me through some sort of wall, and I thrust both hands into his hair and deepen the kiss. God, this man can kiss! My brain has ceased all cognitive functions, and I hear only the sound of my heart thumping in my ears. Then, like a bucket of cold water, I imagine it's Matt that I'm kissing. After what feels like an eternity, I pull back, panting.

"Chloe, I'm...sorry. I didn't mean for that to get out of hand."

He releases me in a daze. What the hell just happened?

"Chloe? Are you all right?"

He grabs both of my shoulders and jostles them slightly to get my attention.

"What?" I'm stunned. It's almost as though he put some sort of spell on me.

"You okay? You look...disoriented."

"Um, yeah. I mean, no, I'm good," I reply as I turn from him and finish making the salad. It takes only about three seconds for James to turn me back around, take me by the hand, and motion for me to sit with him on the couch.

"Chloe, we need to talk. If I've hurt you in any way, I'm sorry. That was never my intent. In fact, I hope you don't think I invited you here to seduce you because although I would like nothing more than to take you back to my room and make love to you all night long, I know that we don't know each other well enough to do that yet. That kiss was not planned. It just felt like the right time to do it. I'm so sorry if I upset you."

I look at him and blink a few times. I think my brain is shutting down. I need time to think; I need to buy myself some time to think.

"You didn't...upset me. I'm just a little...in shock, I think. Let me process what just happened. Let's finish making dinner and eat."

"Okay," he says softly but eyes me suspiciously.

We get done cooking and sit down to consume our masterpiece. The conversation is minimal and mostly safe topics like the weather and work. He helps me clear the table and wash up our work area. After a while we sit back down on the couch with a glass of wine. I'm feeling apprehensive, but I don't understand why. It was a great kiss. We definitely have chemistry, but something's not quite right.

"Tell me what you're thinking, Chloe. Did I read signals that weren't there? Was that a kiss good-bye?"

My head swings up swiftly to look at him. Do I want to say good-bye to James? No. No, I don't. I like him, really like him. I'm still hung up on

Matt. That's what this is. Oh, James, how can I say this to him without sounding like a jerk?

"No!" I say rather hastily. "It wasn't. I...I'm just really confused right now. Look, the kiss was really good." He smiles slightly. "No, it was great. I don't regret it in the least. It's just, this...thing we have going on right now is moving really fast, and I'm not ready to...take the next step. I just got out of an intense relationship and got my heart stomped on. You'll have to excuse me for being a little gun shy."

A look of relief washes over his face.

"You're nervous? That's what this is—nerves? I can deal with this." He exhales. "Chloe, I like you a lot. I'm sure you can tell, and I don't want to push you in any direction you're not willing to go. I won't kiss you again."

What? I start to open my mouth, but he holds his finger up to silence me.

"Let me finish. I won't kiss you again until you ask me to because then I'll know you really want it."

I pout.

"What's with the pouty lip?" He reaches out and strokes my bottom lip, which I am purposely sticking out to exaggerate sadness.

"But I really did enjoy our kiss."

He smoothes away a rogue lock of my hair.

"I know, but if you were truly ready for it, this conversation would be going a lot differently right now."

He's got a point.

"Okay, fine. I get it. You're right."

"I'm right? Something tells me I'd better record you saying that for future playback."

I smile. "Yes, maybe you should."

We both laugh, and our mood instantly shifts.

By the end of our date we are laughing so hard that my stomach muscles hurt. I haven't had this much fun in a long time. By the time he takes me back home, I have a new perspective about my relationship with James.

I find Jenna waiting up for me when I get into our apartment.

"Hey, Chloe, late night for you, eh?"

"Yeah. I guess it is pretty late." I smile.

"What's with the huge grin?" she asks.

"I just got back from James's place."

Her eyebrows shoot up. "Oh? How'd it go?"

"Good. It was fun. We made dinner together."

"Are you going to see him again?"

"Yes, I am. He's really nice."

"And he's hot." She smirks.

I giggle. "Yes, that too."

The next night when I arrive at the theater I feel more confident for some reason. And the usual Kendall drama just rolls right off my back. I'm no longer bothered by her repeated attempts to irritate me by dangling her relationship with Matt in my face. I feel liberated in a way.

"Hi, Kendall," I say as I walk by her. The stunned look on her face is priceless. I laugh inwardly.

"Well someone woke up on the right side of the bed today," she says spitefully. But I don't care. Let her say what she wants; she won't get a rise out of me.

After the show I gather my things and leave the dressing room to go home. I'm looking down at my phone when I have to stop abruptly because I almost run into someone who is stopped right in front of me.

"Oh, sorry." I apologize and then look up. When I do, I'm starring into the handsome face of James. He's grinning from ear to ear and holding a bouquet of white roses.

"Hi!" I squeak, sounding like a twelve-year-old girl at a pep rally.

"Hi, yourself," he replies and kisses me on the cheek. "These are for you." He presents me with the bouquet, and I happily take it. I'm not sure how he got back here, but I'm glad he did. I put my nose inside one of the roses and inhale. Mmm, it smells wonderful.

"Thank you, James. That was very sweet of you. Did you come to see the show again?" I stifle a grin.

"No, I just came by to give you these." He points to the flowers. I smile, I can't help it. He's so...thoughtful. Just then, Kendall comes strolling out into the hall. She stops dead in her tracks when she gets an eyeful of Mr. Wonderful. It's funny to see her mesmerized with her mouth hanging open. She's been starring long enough that I feel like it's rude not to introduce her to James.

"Kendall, this is James. James, this is Kendall."

"It's very nice to meet you, Kendall."

He extends his hand for her to shake but she still hasn't found her voice.

"Um, yes, it's n-nice to meet you too," she stutters while accepting his proffered hand and shakes it. "I didn't quite catch who you are."

I roll my eyes.

"James. I'm Chloe's boyfriend."

Boyfriend? Hmm, boyfriend. Okay, we'll go with that.

"Oh! Her boyfriend, I had no idea. She never said she had a boyfriend." She's trying to make me look as though I've been hiding him.

"Well, it's fairly new, so I can understand why no one knows yet."

Ha!

She has a small look of defeat on her face that is quite satisfying.

"Ready?" I ask.

"Yes. It was nice meeting you." He raises his hand to say good-bye.

As we walk away, I link my arm through his and we stride toward the exit. And I know it is eating away at her that I am with such a hot guy. We round the corner laughing about how stunned she looked and run, almost literally, into Matt.

He looks at the two of us and then down at our linked arms, and a frown mares his face.

"Oh, sorry, please excuse us. We didn't mean to carry on and get in your way," James says and smiles down at me.

I peek up at Matt and the look on his face is a combination of hurt and horror. It makes me sad, and I just want to leave, now.

I turn my gaze to James and say, "We should go."

"Okay." Then he looks back at Matt. "Sorry again." James puts his arm around me, and we continue walking.

I want to look back, but I'm afraid I'll provoke Matt. I decide to keep moving and hope that Matt isn't stupid enough to—

"Hey!" Matt shouts.

Oh no.

We both turn and see Matt coming toward us. I close my eyes and pray silently that he doesn't start any trouble. He comes to stand in front of us and looks at me.

"Aren't you going to introduce me to your *friend,* Chlo?"

He accentuates the word friend. I can tell he's pissed but is trying not to look like it.

"Um...of course. Matt, this is James. James, this is—"

"Chlo's ex-boyfriend. It's nice to meet you." He reaches out and shakes James's hand. James looks shocked at first but recovers quickly.

"It's nice to meet you...Matt, is it? Huh. It's funny. She's never mentioned you."

Matt looks as if he's going to boil over, and I'm getting anxious that this confrontation could get ugly. I need to diffuse it.

"Okay, now that introductions are done I think we should go," I say to James.

"Where are you two lovebirds off to? Gonna take her to Wendy's? Burger King perhaps? Taco Bell?"

"Matt, stop it now!" I scold him. "This really is none of your business!" I take James by the hand. "Let's get out of here."

"Wait," James says calmly. "He doesn't intimidate me. I don't feel the need to justify my actions to him. Because he screwed up, I have the opportunity to be with you. I should thank him. His loss is my gain."

Oh, this isn't good.

Matt is kneading his fists, and I know that his hot temper is going to explode.

I step in between the two men.

"Matt, go home. You obviously need time to cool off. James, thank you for the flowers. I'll talk to you tomorrow."

I begin to walk away but James insists on walking me outside. Matt doesn't follow, and I'm glad. It upsets me that I've hurt Matt, but the truth is, if he felt an ounce of what I felt seeing him and Kendall together, it was worth it. Maybe Matt got a little bit of perspective tonight. James and I exit, and he hales a cab for me.

"Are you sure you won't let me drive you home? My car is not parked far away."

I smile; he's always so thoughtful.

"No, thank you. I appreciate the offer, really, but I'll be fine in the taxi. Call me tomorrow, okay?"

He nods and bends to kiss my cheek.

"Sleep well, Chloe."

"You too, James."

I enter the waiting cab and blow him a kiss. As we pull away from the curb, I see him standing there watching me get further and further down the street until we finally turn and he's out of sight.

While en route, my phone rings.

"Hello?"

"You're dating him?" Matt snaps.

"Hello, Matt. How are you?" I ask in a patronizing voice.

"Don't start. I asked you a question."

"Yes, there was a question in there somewhere. Too bad it was barked at me." I'm irritated.

"Chlo, just answer me." Now he sounds exasperated.

I sigh. "Yes."

He says nothing. All I can hear is his breathing.

I break the silence. "Why do you ask?"

"Is it serious?"

What?

"It's very new," I reply.

"Why do you have to dodge every question?" He's calmer but still agitated.

"Maybe because you're asking questions you really don't want the answers to."

Silence again.

"I'm hanging up now, Matt."

"Chlo, wait," he says quickly. "I'm...sorry. I didn't mean to come off as such a prick. I'm trying...I really am, but it's...hard to see you with someone else when I'm still..."

"Still...what?" I ask slowly.

"It doesn't even matter anymore, Chlo. It's for your own good...I mean it's...for the best. I gotta go. I'll see you around."

"Matt, wait! What do you mean for my own good? Matt? Matt?"

He hangs up. What the hell is this about? My own good? What does that mean? I am more confused now than I ever was. I sigh and sink into the seat of the taxi.

twenty three

The next few weeks are just about the same. James and I take turns hosting each other for our dates. Once in a while we'll have lunch or coffee out. I am having a great time getting to know him. We laugh a lot, and we're really getting closer. A few days after the confrontation with Matt, I asked James to kiss me. I don't imagine that he's Matt anymore, although, he usually crosses my mind at some point. James has made a habit of meeting me backstage once a week after the show to hand deliver a bouquet of flowers. It's such a sweet gesture. The cast is jealous, and Kendall rarely sticks around to witness it anymore. Matt and I hardly ever speak. I don't think he can handle the thought of me dating James, and he'd rather just stay away from us than start any more trouble. I really do miss him. I sometimes see him in the halls, and I smile and wave at him. He smiles back, but it's a sad sort of expression that makes me feel terrible. I wish I knew what he is thinking. He and Kendall are still dating, but no one can really tell by looking at them. They ignore each other most of the time. The only telltale sign of their relationship status is that they walk out the door together.

My phone alerts me to a text. It's from Drew.

I'm coming over right now with some information. C U in 10!

Hmm, that's odd. I'm going to see Drew tonight at the show, why does he want to see me now?

Ok. I'll B here. C U soon.

At almost ten minutes exactly after his text, Drew arrives at my apartment. I open the door and he rushes in.

"Guess what I heard?"

"Hello to you too." I smirk.

"Oh, sorry, sweetie. Mwah, mwah." He kisses me on both cheeks and takes off his jacket. I gesture for him to sit on the couch, and he does.

"Drink?" I offer.

"Yes, please, water," he responds.

"You know how Maxine got canned a few weeks ago for having drugs on her?"

"Yeah, what about it?" I shout from the kitchen.

"Well, Maria, who is good friends with Maxine, told me that Maxine has never done drugs and that she said she was set up."

I walk back into the room holding two bottles of water and hand one to Drew.

"Thanks, sweetie."

"Yes, I think you told me that initially."

"Well, Maria also told me that about three months ago, Maxine got into a terrible fight with someone from the cast. She said that Maxine was in line to get a principle role, but at the last minute she got put into the ensemble. No one could understand why, and to this day Maxine and the perp don't speak."

"You're kidding?" I interject.

"And do you know who the perp was?"

"Who?"

"Our very own Kendall Shay."

"Get out!" I exclaim and shove his shoulder. "Do you think Kendall had something to do with Maxine not getting a principle?"

"I'm not sure. She'd have to have some pretty good connections to accomplish that, but you never know."

"I wonder what they fought about."

He shrugs his shoulders. "I don't know, but if she has that kind of influence, I'm glad you two are not at odds anymore."

"Yeah." And I wonder what else she's capable of. "Drew, you don't think she's—"

"Doing something similar to Matt?" he finishes my inquiry.

We stare at each other in disbelief. Has Kendall threatened Matt in some way? "Could she get him fired?"

"I don't see how that would benefit her. I mean, if she said, 'Date me or I'll get you fired,' she could potentially lose him, both personally and at work. And he doesn't seem like the type to be intimidated by something like that," he states. "She would have to threaten him another way to get him to respond."

"Yeah, you're right. This is my dream job, not his." And then realization dawns on both of us simultaneously.

"Chloe, I bet she has threatened to get *you* fired!"

"Now that makes sense. The things Matt let slip during the course of our conversations...I get it now."

"What did he say?"

"Well, when I asked him about kissing Kendall, he said that it isn't what I think and that it's complicated. He said that a couple of times. And I asked if we were going to get back together, and he said not yet."

"It fits now that we know the reason. Anything else?" he asks.

"Yes. He said we were so happy and then Kendall...and he just stopped, midsentence, and said he wouldn't say anymore. Oh, and when I started to cry he said we would get through this, he couldn't live without me, and I should remember that he loves me. This has got to be it!"

"I think so too, sweetie. It's the only thing that makes sense. Kendall threatens Matt to get you kicked off the show unless he gets back together with her. She knows how much he loves you and how much you love this gig. If this is true, do you realize what Matt has sacrificed for you, Chloe?"

"Yes, too much. But what do I do about it?"

We both sit back and think.

"I have to confront Matt about this. I have to get him to admit it." I turn to face Drew. "Thank you so much, Drew. I can never repay you for being such a gossip!" I smile broadly.

"Thanks a lot!" he chides.

"You know what I mean." And I hug him.

"Will you talk to Matt tonight at the show?"

"No. I don't want to risk Kendall overhearing us. Hmm, I have a coffee date with James tonight. Maybe I can go and see Matt tomorrow during the day."

"Where does James fit into all of this?"

I frown. "I don't know. I don't want to hurt him. But Matt's right, this is complicated."

Later at the theater, Drew and I have a whole new view of our traitorous cast mate, Kendall. Everything about her irritates me now. The way she flounces around, the way she plays with her hair, even the way she sits as if she's royalty or something bugs me. I see Matt at a distance and wave to him. He gives me a halfhearted wave back and then goes back to what he was doing. My heart aches for him and what he has done for me. I wish I could tell him I know everything, but really, what good would that do? Kendall could hear us and make good on her threats. No, I'll wait until tomorrow to talk to Matt in private.

After the curtain call, we all file out as usual and head back to the dressing rooms. To my surprise, James is waiting for me just outside the room.

"Good evening, beautiful. Another job well done, I presume," he says, and he plants a passionate kiss on my lips and dips me backward slightly. Afterward he hands me one red rose.

"Hi! Thank you. You're early today," I reply and take the proffered flower. I note that it's the first time he's given me just one single flower. I raise it and ask, "What's the occasion?"

"Do I need an occasion to show my girl how much I care?"

I swallow, feeling guilty that I haven't really been thinking about James much at all lately.

"Of course not." I smile. "I'll be back in a few minutes, and then we can go."

"Okay, no rush."

James and I arrive at the coffee shop that he picked out. It's not far from my apartment, and it happens to be the same one that Matt and I went to eons ago—or so it seems. He picks out a couch to sit on instead of a table with chairs, and I suspect it's so he can sit closer to me instead of across.

"I'll go get our drinks," he says. He already knows what drink I want. I sigh. Something is different tonight. I don't feel as strong a connection with James as I have before. It might be the memory of my time with Matt in this place. I glance over at the table where Matt and I sat. There's a couple sitting there. They are holding hands and smiling at each other. I imagine it's Matt and me. To an outsider, did we look like a couple? We weren't back then, but I wanted to be, as I wish we were now. James comes back and interrupts my daydream. He hands me the cup, and I thank him.

"Chloe, is something wrong tonight? You seem as though you're not completely here."

"What?" I snap out of my daze. "No, I'm fine. I'm just tired, that's all. So what made you pick this place?"

"You don't like it?"

"It's fine, I just wondered."

"Well, it's one of only a handful of cafés that's open so late, and it's close to your place."

I nod.

"Chloe, I wanted to talk to you about something." He takes the cup out of my hand and places both our coffees on a side table. He then holds both of my hands in his, and looks into my eyes.

"Okay."

"We've been dating for a while now, and I really like you. I know we're not exclusive but...would you be my girlfriend, officially? I mean, I have no desire to see anyone else, and I'd like to ask you to do the same. Chloe, I've fallen in love with you."

I'm stunned into silence. What do I say to that? This has come at the worst time. If he had said this to me a couple of days ago, I would've jumped up and down and said yes but now...

Just as I am about to reply, I hear something smash to the floor. I turn around to see a very drunk Matt with shards of a decorative vase at his feet.

"Matt! What are you doing here?"

I look back at James, and he is on his feet.

"Jeez, Chlo, everywhere I go, there you are, swapping spit with Mr. Mogul. Get a room already," he slurs.

James jumps in between us in a protective stance. "Leave now," James commands.

Matt puffs out a short burst of air in mockery. "Are you gonna make me? Last I checked this was a public place."

"Matt, he's right. Go sleep it off. I'll call and check on you tomorrow."

James's body position is that of a gladiator. His chest is sticking out slightly, his arms are at his sides but back a little and out away from his body, and one foot is in front of the other. This is very angry James, and I recognize that this is his fight pose. James is more than willing and able to take on Matt, but I'm not sure who I'd put my money on. James's muscles are slightly bigger, and he is a little taller but Matt knows how to street fight and his muscles are nothing to scoff at either. I'm not sure how Matt would do though, considering his current condition. I have to intervene. Just before I step between the two volatile men, Matt swings at James and makes hard contact with his jaw. James's head is shoved to the side in reaction. He is forced to take a step back but recovers quickly with a right hook to Matt's left eye. It opens up immediately, and blood drips from it. Matt then lunges forward, and the two are locked in battle.

"Stop this! Both of you!" I scream, as other customers clear out of the way. The two men stop fighting and look at me. "I'm tired of being the object of your rage for each other! Matt, step outside and wait for me," I say and push him toward the door. I turn to James. "I'm so sorry about all of this. Are you okay?" I examine his jaw, and he nods. "I know this is not how you wanted this evening to turn out, but I should take him out of here. I need to get him home before he hurts himself or someone else."

James reveals a hurt expression, but my instincts tell me Matt needs my help more right now, even if he's being a complete ass.

"You're going with him?" he says in exasperation. "He started it. He always starts it, and you're leaving with him? Chloe, you're not the person I thought you were."

"James, please don't."

"Don't what? Tell it as I see it?"

"James, please, we'll talk about this tomorrow. I'll call you, okay?"

He shakes his head. "No, please don't. I don't know what's happened over the last day or two, but something has changed. I'm leaving now. Good luck sobering this asshole up."

He walks away from me and smacks shoulders with Matt on the way out. Matt starts to walk after him, but I grab his arm and halt his progress.

"James!" I call after him, but he just keeps going. I'll deal with him another time. For now, I've got my hands full. I offer an apology to the barista and hand her a hundred dollars in hopes that it will cover the cost of the broken vase and convince her not to call the police.

Outside, I hail a cab and pour Matt into it. I climb in after him and give the driver Matt's address. It takes no time at all, and we're there. I shell out more money in cab fare and yank Matt from the car. When we get inside, I shove my hands into Matt's pockets in search of his key. He's got his one arm around my shoulders to steady himself, and he chuckles a little at the movement of my fingers.

"Get over it Matt. I'm just looking for your key, not a good time."

I find it, and we stumble through the door. I have just enough strength to lead him down the hall to his room and deposit him on his bed. He falls onto his back and is nearly ready to pass out.

twenty four

They say people are truthful when they're drunk, and I decide to test that theory now before Matt passes out completely. I start my interrogation.

"Matt, look at me."

He opens his glazed eyes and reaches up to touch my face. "You're here. You're really here."

I impatiently push his hand away. I need answers before he's down for the count.

"Matt, I need to know, did Kendall threaten you?"

He mumbles. Ugh!

"Matt!" I raise my voice to get his attention again, and he tries to focus on me. "Tell me, is Kendall forcing you to be with her?"

"Kendall...an evil bitch. I want...you're the one, Chlo." He's almost incoherent.

I smile slightly. "I know. Tell me what Kendall said."

"She...if I won't be her boyfriend, she'll...get you kicked out of the show. Fired, Chlo! I can't let her do that to you! She's awful," he slurs. "And now I'm...stuck with her until I can figure out a plan. And I'm also stuck seeing you with your mogul. I hate watching you be happy with someone else. You should be mine. I love you, but shh...don't tell." He fades out, and he's dead to the world.

I knew it! That bitch! If I knew her address I might march over there right now and let her have it! Ugh! Okay, calm down, Chloe. One thing at a time. I need to get Matt undressed and back in bed. I start with his socks and pants. They come off easily because they're dress pants and they slide. Then I go for his shirt. It's a white button down, thankfully, so I don't have to try to get it over his head. I get behind him and push him into a sitting position so I can pull it off of his arms. Then I lower him back to the bed. He's wearing only his boxer briefs, and I can't help but admire his physique. I run my fingers over his tight chest and start to feel aroused, so I stop. Wow, he really is beautiful. I kiss his right peck, and he stirs. I see the cut above his left eye. I should clean the wound a little so he doesn't get blood on his sheets.

Reappearing from the bathroom with a first-aid kit in hand, I first gently wipe the area of all dried blood. Next I put some antibiotic cream on it and top it off with a bandage. There, he never felt a thing. I pull the covers over him and kiss his forehead.

"Good night, Matt. Sleep well, baby," I whisper.

He mumbles and shifts onto his side. "You're...the best, Chlo. I love you."

I smile because I know in his dreams we can be together. Now we just have to work on reality.

I don't want to go home because it's so late, so I resolve to sleep on Matt's couch. I set the alarm on my phone so I can be gone before he knows I stayed here. As soon as my head hits the pillow, I'm fast asleep.

I wake slowly, my eyes refusing to open fully to the bright sunlight streaming through the windows. I feel a warm blanket being pulled onto me and I sigh. For a few minutes I am ten years old and at my parents' house. My mom covers me up and kisses my head. As I wake a little more I realize I'm not at home. I'm not in my bed either. Where am I? Oh yeah, I stayed at Matt's. My eyes open abruptly in realization. My alarm! It didn't go off! I bolt upright, adrenaline pumping hard and fast through my veins.

"Hey, take it easy," Matt says softly. "It's still early. Go back to sleep."

I look at him, bewildered.

"I woke up with a sudden urge." He gives me a wry smile. "And on my way back to bed I saw your dance bag so I came in here looking for you and saw you asleep on my couch. You looked cold, so I found you a blanket and covered you up. I didn't mean to wake you."

"What time is it?" I ask.

"It's eight in the morning."

I rub my eyes and sit up the rest of the way.

"I have to go."

"Why?" He sounds a little panicked.

"Because I didn't mean for you to see me here. I was going to be gone before you got up. I have to go."

"No, stay, please. I'll make us some breakfast."

I look at him skeptically.

"Please, Chlo? It's the least I can do. I ruined your evening again, and I'm sorry."

"Seems to be a habit with you lately," I tease.

He blows out a sharp breath. "There are a lot of things I'm doing lately to screw things up."

"I know all about it."

He stills. "You know about what?"

"Matt, I know all about Kendall's ridiculous plan to get me fired. Drew and I figured it out."

He stands up. "I don't know what you mean."

He starts to move away from me, but I grab his leg to stop him. "It's okay," I say as I climb to my feet. "She doesn't have any power anymore."

"Like hell she doesn't! Chlo, are you willing to risk your job on that theory, because I'm not!" He grabs me by my shoulders and sits me back down as he follows.

"I'm so sorry that I couldn't tell you about this. I know how hard it was for you to see me kissing her. I know because every time I see you with James, a little piece of me dies. But to make it appear real, I couldn't tell you about it. I'm trying to come up with a plan, but it's not easy."

"Two heads are better than one." I smile. "We're in this together now, okay? No more secrets between us."

"I saw him kiss you last night...in the hall outside the dressing room."

Oh.

"I'm sorry you had to see that."

"It's okay, Chlo. It's not your fault. I pushed you away when I should've told you what was happening. I thought I could protect you, but I only made things worse, for both of us."

I touch his face. "Hey." He looks at me. "It's over. Anything that happens now is small stuff. I know now, and that's what's important. Is that the reason you got drunk last night, because of that kiss?"

"Yes. I'm not proud of myself. In fact, I'm ashamed of my actions. Please apologize to James for me."

I let out a sarcastic laugh. "I doubt he'll speak to me again." He looks puzzled. "Ah, of course you wouldn't remember. After I broke up your fight I told him I'd talk to him another time and then I escorted your drunk ass home. I don't think he was pleased with my decision."

"So is that why I woke up in just my underwear?"

I nod slowly on purpose while raising and lowering my eyebrows for a sultry look.

"We didn't—"

"No!" I laugh. "Not that I wasn't tempted, but you could barely stand up let alone anything else being able to stand up."

He grins like a loon, and then his smile fades.

"Thank you yet again for taking care of me. I wish it were the other way around," he says with regret. "And for being my own personal doctor." He points to the cut on his eye.

"Anytime, sir. I'll send you my bill," I tease.

"Can I pay it off in trade?" He raises his hurt eyebrow seductively then winces. I laugh loudly, and he smiles.

He takes my face in his hands. "I love you, Chloe Shepherd. Always have and always will, forever." He kisses me softly and slowly it turns into one of the most heartfelt expressions of love I've ever known. I lay my hands on his chest and melt into his touch. He pulls back suddenly. The desperation in his eyes startles me at first. Then he smoothes a stray hair out if my face, looks me in the eyes, and says, "Marry me."

twenty five

"W-what?" I stutter.

"Marry me, Chlo. We both love each other, and we've known each other our whole lives. It's the only thing that makes sense. Marry me, please." His hopeful eyes sear into me like hot blades.

"Matt, I—"

"Wait, don't answer right now. I know I've not made it easy on you lately and I don't want any of that to cloud your judgment. Just think about it, okay?"

I don't know what to say or do. Hell, thinking is even a problem at this moment. Marry him? Is he insane? We're not even dating and he pops the question? But why now? It seems to me that he might be doing this out of fear, the fear of losing me. He has said he can't stand watching me get close to James. Maybe he's afraid if he doesn't act quickly, I may ride off into the sunset with him. I can't marry this man, not right now.

"Matt." I take hold of his hands. "I love you, you know that, and yes, we've known each other a lifetime."

"But..." His face falls.

"But I'm not ready for you to propose to me. We have a huge obstacle to get past before we can even show up together in public. If Kendall catches wind of this, then all of your effort to stay away from me has been for nothing. Besides, this really isn't the manner in which I envisioned my future husband asking me that question." I give him a wry smile. He looks hurt, and I feel terrible. "Oh, Matt, please don't be upset. Don't think of it as me turning you down. Think of it as a rain check for some time way in the future."

He sighs. I know that's not the answer he wants, but for now, that's all I can give him.

"So does this mean we are not getting back together?" Matt quietly asks.

"Not yet," I reply, raising one eyebrow and standing upright.

"Funny," he replies sarcastically. "You know, you're lucky I like you. You're an awful lot of trouble," he says and joins me standing.

"Yes, I am very lucky you like me." And I throw my arms around his neck. "Promise me something."

"Anything, Chlo."

"Promise me you won't sleep with Kendall. I don't think I could do this if I knew you were still—"

"You won't have to worry about that, Chlo. I wouldn't be able to anyway because I'm in love with you." He smiles and touches the tip of my nose. "I'd like to ask you to do the same," he adds.

"That's assuming I've slept with James in the first place," I retort.

He cringes. "I know it's none of my business and I have no right to ask but..."

"But..." I goad him purposely.

I can tell he's very uncomfortable, wanting to know, but not wanting to know.

"Chlo, give me a break here. Did you or didn't you?"

I try to prolong his agony.

"Well I thought you and I were done, and I was with him for over a month, so what do you think?" My face is repentant, but I smile inwardly.

He covers his face and groans into his hands as he sits back down on the couch. I can no longer keep a straight face.

"Matthew Aaron Masen! Do you seriously think I would jump into bed with the first guy who brings me flowers?" I stare down at him in mock disappointment with my hands on my hips.

His head pops up, and his eyes shoot straight to mine in guilt, but then narrow when he figures out I am messing with him.

"Oh. My. God. You really had me going. I can't believe you did that!"

My smile is triumphant but fleeting as I realize he's about to chase after me. I turn and take three steps to no avail. Matt has his arms like a vice around me as he begins his delicious tickle torture. I laugh and gasp for air. Eventually he stops and kisses me. It's not the ordinary variety, though. Somehow it feels like more, a promise of some sort. I'm glad we could lighten the somber mood I put him in by rejecting his proposal. Maybe someday I'll be Chloe Masen, but not now.

"So how do we get out of this predicament?" I ask.

He sighs.

"I don't know. I've been trying to think of ways to change Kendall's mind. I've tried talking to her rationally. I told her I don't love her so why on earth would she want to be with me and all she says is that I'll grow to love her."

I make an expression of disgust.

"That's sad. I wouldn't want to be with someone I had to talk into loving me."

"Yeah, no kidding. I just wish I knew what leverage she has, if she really has any."

"I have a little bit of information." I reply, and his eyebrows shoot up.

"Oh? What do you know?"

I tell him all I know about Maxine and Kendall.

"There's got to be more to the story than we know right now. Maybe I'll ask Drew to poke around and see who knows anything about this. He has an uncanny ability to get people to gossip." I chuckle.

"Okay and I'll see what I can find out as well." He holds my face in his hands and our eyes meet. "We are going to figure this out, and when we do, we're going to be together and nothing is going to come between us ever again."

Oh my.

"I hope you're right, but until then we'll have to pretend that nothing has changed between us."

He rests his forehead on mine and sighs in frustration.

"I know. That's the part of the plan that will be the hardest," he admits.

I pull back and smile.

"Hey, it's going to be okay, you'll see. Good always wins out." I've said it, but I'm not so sure I believe it. "I'm gonna go home and call Drew. I'll tell him to start putting his ear to the ground so we can resume what we started five years ago."

He agrees but tells me to be careful. One more kiss and I head home.

"Drew, see what you can find out, please. I want to end Kendall's reign around that theater," I state angrily.

"I'm on it, Chloe. I just knew there was a logical explanation of why he would dump you for that home-wrecking bitch. Stop worrying. You can count on me."

"You're the best, Drew."

"Just remember that, Shepherd." He snorts.

"Always," I respond lovingly.

We hang up and my brain gets to work, but I just can't seem to think of how she is doing this. Matt said that Kendall never told him exactly how she could get me fired, just that she could. What if she's bluffing? What if the power she holds is just an empty threat and my job has been safe the whole time. Matt's right, I'm not willing to risk it. Until I get more information, I'll act as if nothing has changed. Then again, a lot has changed. How can I explain the absence of James? Surely Kendall will eventually notice he's not coming around and start to question me about it. I guess I'll just say we broke up. I'm sure as hell not going to make up with him just to keep up appearances. That would be wrong on so many levels. Ugh, I'm going to have to play it by ear, I guess, and for now, try not to dwell too much on it at least until Drew gets the scoop. I get ready to go, and I leave for the theater.

The next week or so is very difficult. I see Matt at the show and my heart tells me to run into his arms and kiss him passionately, but my head tells me I will ruin everything if I give in to my desires. I know my head is right. The look of longing on Matt's face mirrors mine, and I'm anxious for the day when we can hold hands in public again. Kendall's smug face irritates me more than ever now. She hangs all over Matt, which makes me feel nauseous. In the back of my mind, I am clinging to the hope that Matt will keep his promise. I'm fairly certain she has more experience with sex than I do, and it makes me wonder how he really felt about her before I came back into his life. Did he love her or at least care about her? Was she good in bed? Was she better than me? Is there something she did for him that I don't do and he misses it? I'm not sure why these negative thoughts pop into my head; it's self-doubt, I'm sure. I need to lose this train of thought before it drives me crazy. Matt loves me, of this I'm sure, and I need to focus solely on that right now. There is no room for doubt.

Today is the eighth day that's passed since Matt confessed Kendall's extortion plot. I have only seen him in passing at the theater, but we've spoken most nights via phone and text. I have just arrived at the Palace when I see Kendall flouncing about as she makes her way to the dressing room.

"Hello, Chloe, have you smelled something rancid? That look on your face is not the most flattering."

What I'd like to tell her is that the scent of arrogance and jealousy is far worse than anything I can think of, but I refrain and blame it on having allergies.

"Eww, good thing Matt no longer has to put up with that ugliness," she says as she wrinkles her nose.

It takes everything I have not to lunge at her, fists balled tightly.

"Give it a rest, Kendall. You've already got Matt, what more can you do to me?"

She laughs.

"Yes, I do have him. And we are getting closer every day. In fact, I wouldn't be surprised if he asked me to move in with him."

I snort and roll my eyes as I head to my dressing area. If she only knew how Matt really feels about her.

During intermission, Drew finds me.

"Meet me by my dressing room immediately after the show. I have information," he whispers discreetly.

I nod in compliance and shoot Matt a quick text.

The little birdie learned a new tune.

Matt replies almost immediately.

Looking forward 2 hearing it.

The second act feels longer than usual but I know it's just anticipation and hopefulness. The curtain call is finally done and I rush to interrogate Drew. On my way there, I am careful not to let Kendall see where I'm headed. I reach my very resourceful friend.

"Drew," I pant. "What have you found out?"

Just as he is about to say something, Matt walks up on us.

"Hi, Drew. What information do you have?"

"Shh, you two! Do you want to screw this all up?"

We look at each other, puzzled.

"Sorry. I'm just a little impatient," I state. I turn to Matt. "You should go, we shouldn't be seen together."

"I know, but I want to hear this too," Matt says.

"I understand, but this could blow up in our faces if Kendall comes around the corner."

"Quiet, both of you! Look, this is not a safe place to talk. Meet me at my place in an hour. Oh, and bring some wine." And with that, he leaves us.

I offer Matt a small smile, and we touch hands before departing, each in separate directions.

Almost an hour later, I stand in front of Drew's door, rapping on it with my knuckles. It opens.

"Come in, come in." Drew grabs me by the arm.

"Hi, Drew. Has Matt arrived yet?"

"Not yet. Do you want a drink?"

That's Drew, always polite, but I'm not here for anything but news, good news I hope.

"No, thank you. Can you just tell me what you've heard?" I'm growing more curious as the minutes pass.

"We'll wait until Matt gets here so I don't have to repeat everything."

Just as he finishes his sentence there's a knock on the door. Drew opens it and ushers Matt in.

"Hey Drew," he greets him.

Matt looks further into the apartment and spies me. Without hesitation he rushes past Drew, over to me, and unapologetically wraps his arms around me and buries his face in my neck. His skin has a slight chill to it because of the cool weather but he smells divine, like some sort of musky cologne and his own intoxicating scent.

"Hey, Chlo," he whispers.

"Hey." I close my eyes and smile.

He picks up his head and lifts my chin with his fingers. Staring into my eyes briefly, he places his lips on mine, and slowly, gently, he kisses me. My head spins as our tongues do a subtle dance and his hand glides through my hair.

"Ahem," Drew speaks up. "Are you two quite finished?"

We stop kissing and smile at each other and then at Drew.

"Sorry. We don't get many chances to see each other without prying eyes being on us."

"Well, I'm all for the Romeo and Juliet stuff, but we've got business to attend to, or do you two want to stay in hiding forever?" he chides us.

"No, definitely not," Matt states vehemently.

"Good, then let's get started."

We make our way over to the beautifully decorated dining table and each take a seat.

"Okay, so I was talking to Lexie who was pretty good friends with Maxine. She is convinced that Maxine would never do drugs and that it was a set up. She also said that Maxine was extremely happy just before she got fired and Lexie thinks it was because of her love life."

"So why is that significant?" Matt speaks up.

"Well, it's not important that she was happy, it is important who she was happy with."

"I'm not following you," I say, puzzled.

"Maxine never told Lexie the name of the guy she'd been dating. It was all sort of hush-hush."

The confused looks on our faces beg Drew to continue.

"A week or two after she was fired, Maxine was spotted picking someone up post-show. It was Tom Weeks, one of our producers."

Hmm, where does he fit in?

"Wait, you mean *before* she got fired?" I want to clarify.

"No, *after.*"

"I don't understand. She was fired, why would she come back?" Matt interjects.

"I didn't get it either until I thought about it. Don't you see? Maxine and Tom must have been having an affair. Tom just divorced his wife."

"Okay, but extramarital affairs are not illegal, and I still don't get the connection."

"Okay fine, I wanted you two to work this out for yourselves, but I'll lay it all out there for you."

Drew takes a deep breath.

"I think Maxine and Tom were sleeping together during Tom's marriage. Someone found out and blackmailed Tom, stating they'd tell if Maxine got a lead role, hence her being put into the ensemble.

Tom decided he was going to end his marriage, and after it finalized he tried again to put Maxine in a lead role. His blackmailer no longer had leverage, so they did the one thing they had left to do..."

"Get Maxine fired," I say in my light bulb moment.

"Yes, and that move was out of pure spite. The perp had nothing to gain by getting rid of Maxine, just satisfaction."

"That means that more than likely it was someone else Tom was fooling around with, before Maxine," Matt realizes.

"Yep. Any guesses as to who it could be?"

"Kendall," Matt and I say in unison.

"That makes sense." I stand up and pace back and forth. "Drew, you told me before that Kendall and Maxine hated each other and in fact got in an argument a few months before we were hired."

"Matt, did she ever talk about her past boyfriends?" Drew inquires.

"Not really. No, wait, I do vaguely remember her mentioning that the last relationship she was in ended badly. She also told me he worked in the field. It's gotta be Tom she was referring to. When she talked about him, you could see the irritation on her face."

"Okay, I get her involvement in getting Maxine fired, but do you really believe she'd go to such lengths to get back at Matt for dumping her?" I'm hoping the answer is no.

"Chlo." Matt takes my hands. "Hell hath no fury like a woman scorned. She's been rejected twice in a matter of a few months. She's very capable of blackmailing Tom and me so she can hold on to who she thinks is hers. Tom took away her power; you took away...me. I know it didn't happen exactly that way, but in her mind it did."

"He's right, Chloe. She's dangerous, and I have no doubt that she would do something to get you fired in a heartbeat if she finds out we know."

"Then what do we do?" Exasperated, I cover my face with my hands. This is overwhelming. I feel so trapped. Matt engulfs me with his arms in a warm supportive embrace, and I turn and bury my face in his chest.

"I don't know right now, but we'll think of something," he coos.

"Maybe I should just give in and quit the show."

"No!" the men say together.

"Chloe, she gonna keep doing this until someone stops her. You quitting the show would be like extra birthday presents for her."

"Drew's right. We need to put our heads together and come up with a plan."

"Do you think Tom would talk to us?" I inquire.

"I doubt it, sweetie. I'm sure he wants to stay as far away from Kendall as he can. Besides, if you or Matt is caught even breathing the same air as Tom, she may get suspicious and jump the gun. I think we need to record her confession somehow."

"I'll do it. I'll get her drunk one night and...figure out a way to make it happen," Matt says angrily.

"Ugh! No way! You will do no such thing! I'm not going to let you lead her on just to get her to talk about it. I can only just stand you two walking out of the theater together, I think I'd lose it if I knew you were flirting with her while she was drunk and doing God knows what else."

"Chlo, I'm not talking about sleeping with her, if that's what you mean."

I wrinkle my nose.

"Drew and I will try first. We can get a rise out of her pretty easily, so it shouldn't be hard," I insist.

"That sounds like fun!" Drew claps his hands. "I have a voice-acti-vated digital voice recorder we can use. That bitch won't know what hit her!"

Drew laughs, but when I look at Matt, he's not so sure.

"It's gonna work. It has to," I say softly to Matt.

He sighs. "I hope you're right."

twenty six

The next night, stationed outside of the dressing room, Drew and I begin our purposeful, contrived conversation, hoping Kendall's interest is piqued enough to eavesdrop.

"Oh, Drew, I can't take it anymore. The sight of Matt with Kendall is really getting to me. Why do they have to flaunt their love in front of me?" I lower my head and roll my eyes where no one can see me. Ugh, even just saying those words makes my stomach roil.

"Chloe, it's gonna be all right. You deserve better than him. We've all been there Sweetie, although most of us don't have to watch it up close and personal."

It's working. I see Kendall standing in the doorway, off to one side with her ear toward us. I wink at Drew.

"Nobody understands how miserable this feels. I wish I could go back in time and change things."

Kendall comes into view, perhaps to join the conversation.

"What's wrong, Chloe? Are you all sad and weepy because Matt's in love with me?" Kendall says with faux sympathy.

"Stay out of it, bitch," Drew spits. "Isn't it bad enough that you took her boyfriend, do you also have to rub it in her face?"

"Excuse me, but if you recall, he was mine first. In fact, he doesn't even mention you anymore. Oh wait—he did say something about you, Chloe. He said how happy he is to be back with me instead of his prude little ex-girlfriend."

I gasp as if this news hurts me and cover my face with one hand. Drew scolds her on my behalf.

"Kendall, you have no idea how it feels to be dumped, and then have your ex-boyfriend parade around in front of you flaunting his new relationship," I add.

"Don't I? What about when Matt broke up with me to be with you? Trust me when I say those were not my favorite days. I'm just glad he came to his senses and dumped you for me. Now he knows that he's back where he belongs. He and I are extremely happy and in love."

Ugh! I think I may throw up.

"That's not the same thing," Drew interjects. "You got him back. Chloe will never get Matt back."

"Damn straight, she won't."

I let a fake sob escape.

"See, Kendall, you can't understand how I feel right now."

"Oh, boo-hoo, Chloe, it's not like it's the first time this has happened. You are not the only one who has ever been dumped. It happened to me before I got together with Matt, so you do not have a monopoly on the feelings you're having. Grow up already. This is how life works sometimes."

"Seriously, I don't believe anything you say," Drew goads.

"I don't care if you believe me or not. I am not going to talk to you about my entire love-life history. Look, I've learned from my mistakes in the past. That's probably how I was able to get Matt back. You just have to know how to treat a man. Then maybe one will stick with you, Chloe."

I've had just about enough, and Drew knows it.

"Whatever, Kendall, go ahead and live in your fantasy world. Let's go, Chloe. We don't need to hear anymore."

Drew takes a hold of my arm and escorts me down the hallway and around the corner where no one can hear us.

"Damn it! We didn't get anything! Why did you pull me away?" I'm really frustrated.

"You were about to go postal on her ass, I could tell. I couldn't let you blow this whole thing. She wanted to get to you, and she was successful."

"Of course she got to me. The sewage spilling out of her mouth was ridiculous and untrue."

"Exactly, Chloe, it was untrue. That's why you just need to ignore her. You know how Matt really feels, so don't worry about what she says."

He's right, of course.

"I know. I just wish this was all over."

Drew hugs me.

"It will be, sooner rather than later, hopefully."

As Drew is consoling me, Matt walks around the corner. He looks at me, and I shake my head to let him know we got nothing. He gives me a look of sorrow and regret. I know he wishes he could be holding me right now. I know because I wish the same thing.

"C'mon, Chloe, let's get out of here," Drew murmurs, and we head for Drew's house.

We get there, and Matt has yet to arrive.

"I'll text him," I say, and I grab my phone.

Where r u? We were supposed to meet up at Drew's.
R U coming?

His reply is short and to the point.

On the way.

I know that a text like that is anything but sweet and romantic but any response from him makes my heart beat faster and my palms sweat. The notion that he gets closer and closer with every second that ticks by thrills me.

"He's coming," I inform Drew, and he leaves his door ajar.

While we sit waiting, Drew and I discuss other possibilities for beating Kendall at her own game.

"We need to get inside her head, you know, see what would make her talk."

"Yuck!" Drew wrinkles his nose. "I don't want to get anywhere near her head. That has got to be one screwed-up place."

I laugh.

"Yes, I suppose you're right, but what else can we do? I want this to be over."

"Trust me when I say I can't wait for her to get what's coming to her, but we still need to be careful," Drew retorts.

"Yes, we do. This time I'm going to be the one to get her confession," Matt says as he walks through the unlocked door.

Matt is here. I smile broadly and leap to my feet, greeting him with an over exuberant hug. His returning embrace is equally ardent.

"Hey, baby," he whispers.

"Hey, back," I reply.

"So what were you two talking about?" Matt inquires.

"We were discussing our next move," I reply.

"You mean *my* next move. I am the only one who can get Kendall to talk."

"Matt, no. Please, let me try again. I'm sure it'll work this time," I whine.

"No, it's gotta be me, Chlo."

"But—" I feel Drew's hand on my shoulder, stopping me midsentence.

"Chloe, let him try," Drew says softly. "He'll probably be more successful than we were. I know you can't stand the thought of what he might have to do to get her confession, but he's not going to let it get that far. Look at him." Drew gestures toward Matt. "He's in love. It's you he wants to be with, not her. You need to trust him."

I glance over at Matt; he looks tired. The stress of all of Kendall's shenanigans is taking a toll on him. In my heart I know Matt would never break his promise to me. I know he won't sleep with her. I need to give him the freedom to do this...for us.

"Okay. Do what you have to. I'll find a way to deal with it," I mutter and look down at my hands.

I feel his fingers under my chin as they lift my head. Reluctantly, I look into his eyes. He has a small smile on his beautiful lips.

"Hey, Drew's right. I'm not going to do anything with Kendall that I wouldn't do with you standing in the room. I love you. When are you going to realize that?"

A shy grin appears on my face, and I hug Matt, holding on for dear life.

"I know and I love you too, just please do what you have to and get out quickly."

"You know I will."

"Okay now that we're done with the lovey-dovey portion of this meeting, can we discuss the plan?" Drew insists.

Drew always knows exactly how and when to lighten a mood.

"Yes, please, let's figure this out," I say, and we get to work.

Collectively, we decide to wait until the weekend to put our plan into action. Matt will borrow some recording equipment from the sound crew. After getting her loosened up with alcohol, Matt will take Kendall back to his place. They'll start talking about the cast and the scandal surrounding Maxine. He's not sure exactly what he'll say until he starts, but he's confident he can get her to tell him everything. After that, we should be able to live our lives without the fear that Hurricane Kendall could strike at any time. I suggest they go out for dinner—that way she will behave herself. Matt agrees, but Drew still believes going somewhere private will make her more willing to talk. I am very uneasy about all of this. Matt keeps his hand on my leg as we discuss this. It makes me feel more connected to him and calms me.

"All right then, I think we're set," Matt says. He looks at me and smiles. "Hey, don't be such a worrywart. It'll all work out."

I offer him a small smile. "I hope you're right."

"Of course I am. In fact, when it's all over with, I'm gonna say I told you so." He crosses his arms across his chest and looks pretty damn proud of himself.

"Really now," I add. "Do you want to make a little bet?"

"Hmm. And what exactly are we betting on?"

"Well, I don't think I will feel safe until Kendall is completely out of our lives, so I guess we should bet on that."

I imitate Matt and cross my arms too.

A smile slowly develops on his handsome face. "Okay, say that I can get Kendall completely out of our lives and you're saying I can't do it, is that right?"

I nod.

"And the wager?"

I think for a moment. "The usual."

His grin gets wider. "You're on."

We shake hands, and he stares into my eyes with determination.

It is Saturday night. Our plan will take place tonight after the show. Matt has borrowed a digital recorder for the occasion and now it's all a matter of waiting. I have been attempting to reason this whole thing out in my head. I know deep down that Matt is doing this for me, for us, but I am worried about how far he will have to go to get her to admit what she has done. Drew has been great; he is going to stay with me tonight until Matt is done. I suspect that he will try and keep me busy to get my mind off of things. Matt said he'd come straight over to my house afterward so we can all hear what, if anything, he recorded.

The performance concludes, and Drew meets me outside my dressing room.

"Hey, sweetie, are you ready to make like a baby and head out?"

I chuckle, but it's halfhearted.

"Yes, I guess so. I was hoping to see Matt before we leave, but I don't know where he is."

"I think he's still with the guys in lighting." He puts his hand on my shoulder. "It's going to be fine. Matt will get the job done, and you two can live happily ever after, you'll see."

I sigh. "I hope you're right. No, I know you're right. I am vowing to think positively for the rest of the night." I turn and square my shoulders toward Drew. "If I start woe-is-me-ing, you have my permission to slap me or shake me or something."

He smiles. "You've got yourself a deal, Shepherd. That'll be payback for so many things."

I laugh loudly, and it feels good.

Drew and I begin walking down the hall toward the exit when he suddenly stops and looks at me.

"What?"

"Nothing, just stay right here. I'll be right back."

How strange. What is he up to? Just as I see Drew round the corner and disappear, the custodian's door behind me opens and a hand reaches out and grasps my wrist, pulling me inside the closet. It happens so fast that I only let a squeak out. A hand is placed over my mouth, and I attempt to pry it off.

"Shh, Chlo, it's me," whispers a familiar voice.

I stop struggling and turn to look directly into the eyes of Matt. Without a second thought, I throw my arms around his neck and squeeze.

I heave a long-held sigh.

"Matt," I whisper back. "I'm so happy to see you. I didn't think I'd get to before, well, you know."

"I know. I texted Drew and asked him to lead you here. I had to be with you before I left."

He places his hands on either side of my face and presses his lips to mine. When I part my lips, our tongues do their dance. I'm certain he is feeling as anxious about tonight as I am. He breaks the kiss off but continues to hold my face, caressing it gently.

"I love you, Chlo. I'm gonna do what I need to and come straight home to you. Then we're going to spend the rest of the night in bed enjoying our victory, okay?"

"Okay, I know. I love you too, Matt. Please don't forget that."

"Back at you Chlo."

He kisses me again, and there's a small, rhythmic knock at the door.

"That's my cue. I'll see you later."

I nod, and he's gone.

After a minute or so, the door opens.

"It's time to come out of the closet, Chloe," Drew says ironically.

I give him a wry smile and exit the tiny room.

"Thanks for that, Drew. You always know exactly what I need."

"You owe me! Now come on, let's go back to your house and hit the sauce."

When Drew and I get to my apartment, he immediately starts distracting me. The first thing he does is open a bottle of wine that he brought with him. It's a Cabernet Franc Ice Wine that is more on the sweet side. It's delicious and goes down quite easily. As we drink a couple of glasses each, Drew tells me that he has also brought a bottle of sparkling wine as well.

"For celebration purposes."

"Champagne? I hope we get to taste it." I snort.

"Don't make me slap you, Chloe," he replies with a smirk.

I smile and take another sip.

"Did you know they can only call it Champagne if it comes from Champagne, France?"

"Are you trying to impress me? I had no idea."

"No, it's true. Andrew knows his wines. Apparently his last boy-friend was a vintner. Jonathan, I think his name was. He was a whore."

I nearly spit out my wine while trying not to laugh. He notices and shoots me a look.

"Well, he was!"

"Okay, okay, I'm not saying he wasn't. I just never thought of gay men as being slutty."

"Being a slut isn't exclusive to being straight. There are plenty of homosexuals who can't keep it in their pants either. He was a cheater," he states with irritation.

"I'm sorry, Drew. I know that someone's sexual orientation and their ability to be monogamous don't go hand in hand. I didn't mean it to come out like that. It's just that you two seem so happy together, and the thought really never crossed my mind. I can't even imagine Andrew with someone else."

"Apology accepted. Now let's put in a movie. I'm in the mood for a sappy love story."

"Ugh, I'm not sure I'm up for that."

"Yes you are. You need to see that even though couples go through rough spots, there's always a happy ending for those who were meant to be."

I make to protest but he shushes me.

"Letters to Juliet it is!" Drew pops in the DVD, and we snuggle under a blanket on the couch.

As I sleep, I feel a hand gently push tendrils of hair off my face. Soft, warm lips brush against my forehead, placing a single kiss on it. Sleepily I stir and open one eye.

"Shh, baby, go back to sleep," Matt whispers.

I mumble something I don't even understand and start to drift back to sleep, but not before I hear Matt's amused chuckle.

twenty seven

I wake to feel cold feet nestling up against mine.

"Drew, get your cold-ass feet off of me," I whine.

"Sorry, but yours are nice and warm, and since you stole the covers most of the night, I figure you owe me...again."

We both fell asleep on the couch last night, one at each end with our feet in the middle.

"Drew, I mean it. If you don't retract your feet, I'll lance you open with a toenail I've been meaning to manicure."

"Okay, okay! Sheesh, Matt's a lucky man to have to wake up to you and your sunny disposition," he says sardonically.

Now I'm wide awake.

"Matt! Is he here?" I sit upright and glance around the room until my eyes settle on a heap of blankets on the recliner. The only telltale sign that there's a human being underneath is the slow rise and fall in the middle.

"Drew," I gently kick him. "Get up, Drew."

He protests but sits up.

"Ugh, morning comes way too early in the day," he mumbles.

"Drew look." I point in the direction of the chair. "He made it here. I wonder if he got anything last night."

Drew raises an eyebrow at me.

"I didn't mean it like that. I'm dying to know how it went with Kendall," I whisper.

"I wonder what time he got in," Drew yawns.

"I don't know. I fell asleep somewhere into the second movie. Should I wake him?"

"No, let the poor man sleep. I'm sure he's had an eventful evening. He'll wake when he's ready. What time is it anyway?"

I check my phone for the time and see an unread text message from Matt sent at five o'clock in the morning.

I'm on my way. I can't wait to curl up next to you and tell you all about it.

"Holy shit." I stare at my phone.

"What?"

"I got a text from Matt at five saying he's on his way here."

His eyebrows shoot up.

"Wow, that took longer than I thought."

"Yeah. I wonder what took so long."

I hear Matt stir, so I put my finger to my lips to tell Drew to be quieter.

"I'm going to get up and make a pot of coffee. Are you hungry? I could make breakfast." I am starving.

Drew nods and gets up to help me.

It's almost ten in the morning now and even though I hate to do it, I have to wake Matt up. I kneel down next to him. He looks so peaceful and almost childlike. With gentleness, I stroke my fingers down his cheek. He wrinkles his nose, and I stifle a giggle. When I touch him again his eyes flutter open.

"Hi," I say.

"Hi," he says with a sleepy smile. "What time is it?"

"Nearly ten."

He yawns and stretches.

"I didn't want to wake you but—"

"I know. It's okay. I needed to get up."

"Are you hungry? Drew and I made pancakes and saved some bacon for you. There's a second pot of coffee that's just about done too."

He looks at me and reaches for my face.

"So beautiful and so domestic."

I roll my eyes.

"Enough with the sweet talk. Get up and eat," I say with a smirk.

His hand cups the back of my head and gently pulls me in, and he kisses me softly. Then he pulls back and looks into my eyes.

And in that moment, all is right in the world.

After a few minutes of reconnecting, Matt stands and heads for the bathroom. I return to the kitchen to pour him some coffee. When he joins us, he holds a small digital recorder in his hand. My heart beats out of my chest. Did he beat Kendall at her own game or was he unsuccessful as we were?

"Breathe, Chlo."

I hadn't realized I was holding my breath. I take in a gulp of air.

"I hope you got that bitch to admit to something," Drew chimes in.

I stand paralyzed, staring down at the small device.

"I think you'll be happy to know that I did, in fact, get her to talk."

My eyes shoot straight to Matt's face, and he's grinning. I throw my arms around Matt's neck, and Drew claps his hands in celebration.

"Yes!" Drew shouts, and I squeeze Matt tightly.

"How did you do it? Tell me all about it," I insist.

"Let's sit down and we'll talk."

We sit at the dining table. Matt begins to eat his breakfast while Drew and I wait anxiously for the full report. A few minutes pass by, and Matt says nothing, he just continues to devour his pancakes.

"Well? Are you going to say something or are we going to have to start playing charades?" Drew says and glances at me. I shrug my shoulders, and Matt looks up from his plate.

"Oh, are you waiting for me?" Matt gives us a faux innocent look but can't keep a straight face for long. I throw a dish towel at him.

"Funny, very funny, Matt. Now start talking."

"Okay, okay. Where should I start?"

"How about the beginning, Romeo. I have a show to get ready for, and I want to know which Kendall will show up there." Drew's patience is clearly stretched thin, probably from lack of sleep.

"All right. We started out going out for a drink or two. I took her to some dive bar not far from the theater. I knew my best bet to get her talking was to keep the alcohol flowing. We stayed there for about an hour and a half when she suggested we go back to my place."

Ugh.

Matt looks at me and reaches for my hand.

"I'm fine. Go on."

He nods. "When we walked through the door to my apartment, I gave Jake the get-lost look and he left. To make a long story short, I got her drunk and started talking about Maxine. It didn't take her long to open up and tell me all the sordid details. You guys were right. She was blackmailing Tom."

"I knew it!" Drew bangs his fist on the table, startling me. "Oh, sorry, sweetie."

"It's okay." I turn my attention back to Matt. "So she told you everything? Just like that?"

He nods. "Pretty much."

"And does she know you recorded her?"

"No, she has no idea. I figured we had one more show today before we're off on Monday. I also wanted her to be sober when I confronted her."

"Oh."

"Oh? Chlo, you're unusually quiet. What's on your mind?"

Hmm, it sounds too easy. He's leaving something out. It's a detail he doesn't want me to know, and I'm frightened of what it might be.

"Are you sure you're telling us everything?"

"Do you want to listen to it?"

"Hell yes, we do! I want to hear that her reign of terror is over," Drew interjects.

I laugh. "Yes, please, let's listen to it."

"Okay I'll play it, but, Chlo, keep in mind, you may not like everything you hear. I said only what I had to, to get her to talk."

"I understand."

He takes the device out of his pocket.

"What you're about to hear is when we got back to my place. She's already got a good buzz going."

He takes hold of my hand and presses play.

Matt: "So that was really strange about Maxine. I had no idea she did drugs."

Kendall: "Well you never can tell how people really are, Matt. You think you know a person and then they prove you wrong."

Matt: "That's for sure. Whatever, I didn't really like her anyway. I heard she is dating one of the producers. He just got divorced, and I wonder if she's to blame."

[Momentary silence]

Matt: "Kendall? Do you know something about it?"

Kendall: "Can you keep a secret?"

Matt: "Of course I can. What's this about?"

[Another moment of silence]

Matt: "Kendall. You can tell me anything, you know that."

Kendall: "I know. Okay, I'll tell you, but only because you don't like her. You might actually get a kick out of it."

[She snorts]

Kendall: "She was having an affair with that producer—his name is Tom—and I found out about it. I was so mad because, well, don't think I'm a slut but he's my ex. I know it was wrong to date a married man but he didn't tell me he was married at first and when I found out, I was already in love with him."

Matt: "Kendall, I don't think you're a slut. You can't help who you love. It wasn't in your control."

Kendall: "That's what I think too! Anyway, I was upset to hear he had moved on to her, and I tried to talk to him. At the time I wanted him back. He rejected me, and I was enraged."

Matt: "I am so sorry you had to go through that, honey, but go on."

Kendall: "Aww, thank you, baby. I am so glad you understand."

[Muffled rustling]

Kendall: "Okay, so then I heard that he was about to move Maxine into a lead role."

Matt: "No way!"

Kendall: "I know! Ridiculous, isn't it? Well, I just couldn't let that happen so I threatened to expose his affair to his wife if he did that. And it worked. He left her in the ensemble. Then when auditions came up, I told him I wanted in the show, and that son of a bitch put me in the ensemble with her! I wanted a lead but he said there were no lead roles available. He told me that he could move me up later if a spot came open. Anyway, I got the job and the rest is history."

Matt: "Wow. But that doesn't explain how Maxine got hooked on drugs."

[She giggles]

Kendall: "Well, now that's the funny part. She doesn't actually do drugs."

Matt: "What? Then how did she get caught with them? Wait, did you plant drugs on Maxine?"

Kendall: "Shh, not so loud. Yes, I did."

Matt: "Oh my God, you're kidding!"

Kendall: "Nope, I'm not kidding."

Matt: "But why? I don't understand."

Kendall: "Well, let's just say that I don't handle rejection very well. Tom told me he was divorced from his wife and that I no longer had anything to hold over his head. I was furious. He said he was going to put Maxine in a lead role and this time I couldn't stop him. He was wrong. I couldn't let them win so I bought some cocaine off of some guy I knew and put it in Maxine's dance bag. Then I called up another executive and tipped him off. The look on Maxine's face was priceless when they dumped her bag and out popped a bag of white powder."

Matt: "That's crazy. I can't believe you got away with it. I guess I better never cross you."

[He chuckles]

Kendall: "No never cross me, I told you that before. I will not be rejected again. Besides, you seem to have accepted our little arrangement just fine."

[Muffled sounds]

Matt: "Yes, I know exactly what I've got standing before me, and I know how I feel about you."

Kendall: "Aww, Matt, I knew you'd come around. I knew you'd forget about Chloe once I forced you to look at me instead of following her around like a lost puppy. I'm much better for you anyway. Look at what lengths I've gone to for you already. You were stuck in a rut with her, unable to get out. I freed you, and look at how happy we are now."

[Muffled sounds]

Matt: "Kendall, tonight you've made me so happy. I'm glad you told me all about Maxine. And you know, my feelings for you haven't changed a bit."

Kendall: "I love you too, Matt."

[Muffled sounds]

There's a click and it's done, her confession caught for anyone to hear.

"Diabolical bitch, isn't she? I can't believe she confessed it all so easily. It's like she was telling you about the weather. She's crazy," Drew says.
"I know."
Matt looks into my eyes.
"Chlo? Are you okay?"
I hesitate before answering.

"Yes, I'm okay. It's just weird for me to hear a conversation between the two of you. I'm glad you were able to get her to tell you everything though."

He lets out the breath he'd so obviously been holding.

"I don't love her, Chlo. Hell, I don't even like her."

"I know. It's okay. It's over now, and that's the prize worth the struggle."

"So what do we do next? I mean, when are you going to let her know she's busted and we are together?"

"I'm planning on confronting her after the show today. I'm taking the recorder with me and I'll pull her aside and play a portion of it to her. Do you want to be there with me?"

"No," I say forcefully. "I don't."

"Make at least one copy of it, Matt. That chick is psycho. I wouldn't put it past her to grab it and run," Drew adds.

"I've already thought of that. I've sent a copy to my e-mail address and to Chlo's."

He turns to examine my face. Putting both hands on either side of it, he says, "It's over. Now we can be together. And maybe now you'll consider that question I asked you." Matt smiles, and I smirk. We kiss. "I have to go."

"I know."

"I'm outta here too, Chloe. I'm glad everything worked out in your favor."

"Thanks, Drew. I am too."

I turn back to Matt.

"Will I see you tonight?"

"Bet on it," he says with a playful smile and a wink.

I grin and shake my head, scolding him slightly, but he's so charming that I just can't help it—a little giggle escapes.

Another quick peck on the lips and he heads for the door.

"Bye, Chloe. I'll see you later," Drew calls out.

"Okay, bye, Drew. Bye, Matt."

Matt turns and gives me that all-American-boy smile that makes my heart melt, and I blow him a kiss as he shuts the door behind him.

I am so happy that Matt got Kendall to admit what she'd done. Now it's just a matter of threatening to take the recording to the powers that be if she makes any attempt to get me or anyone else fired. I hug myself and look forward to a relationship with Matt that will never again be interrupted by her.

Later that day, after the show, I witness Matt talking to Kendall in the hallway. They then walk around the corner to a more private place. I sneak over so I can spy on them, though I can't hear what they're saying. I watch as Kendall's body language goes from loving, to upset, and then to angry. Matt takes the tape out of his pants pocket and plays it for her. She covers her face and wipes tears that stream down it. She's arguing with him now, and he's shaking his head. He too looks angry now. I can tell they are fighting, and Matt keeps pointing to the recorder. Finally, she runs toward me. I duck back and pretend I wasn't watching their heated exchange. She doesn't even notice me as she sprints past, her makeup running down her cheeks, and she continues down the hall until I can no longer see her. After a beat, Matt comes strolling toward me. Without saying a word, he grabs me around the waist and lifts me off the ground. I squeal, as I'm not expecting it. Still holding onto me, he looks up into my smiling face.

"Now it's over. Kiss me."

I do, and it's like we've not seen each other in forever. The kiss is so passionate and so primal. I am certain there is no one else left on the planet. He sets me back on my feet, and we hold hands, walking toward the exit. Drew is standing just down the hall in the doorway of his dressing room. He claps and, if I'm not mistaken, wipes a tear from his eye. As we leave the theater, I feel that I'm the luckiest girl in the world. We hop into a waiting cab and head toward my apartment.

twenty eight

The sun is streaming through my bedroom window. Its warm beam of light heats the blankets that are draped over Matt and me as we lie here, skin on skin. When we arrived back here yesterday, we couldn't keep our hands off of each other. We made love over and over again. But for a reason I don't understand, I'm not tired, I feel energized actually. I relax with my hands folded behind my head, my elbows out to the side. Matt is still asleep. His head is on my chest, and his arm is wrapped around my waist. He snores quietly, and surprisingly, it's a soothing sound. I reach down and twist a small lock of his hair and wonder how we got here. Not so long ago I felt hopeless. Now I feel like anything is possible. When I think about Matt's proposal it makes me smile. Was he serious? And if he was, am I ready to say yes? I just don't know. Everything about us has moved so fast. I would like to enjoy this time in our lives and make it last as long as possible. On the other hand, being married to Matt would be an adventure I would also love. It's all so much to think about, but with Kendall out of the way, it's a lot less stressful.

After making love yet again, we go about our day off as if we are newlyweds. We start with breakfast. Matt insists on making me French toast and even cuts the bread into the shape of hearts. I laugh and tell him he's crazy. "Only for you," he replies, and I melt. While we eat, a thought crosses my mind.

"Matt?"

"Yes, baby?"

"You don't think Kendall is plotting her revenge, do you?"

He thinks a minute. "I don't know. I'm not sure what she can do. We still have the confession. She doesn't have any cards left to play."

"Unless she's got an ace up her sleeve." I'm a little worried.

"Hey, let's not talk about her. It's our day. No one else matters."

I smile in agreement.

"Matt, you know that question you asked me before?"

"Yes, what about it?"

"Does it still stand?"

He smiles. "Yes, it does. Why, do you finally have the right answer?"

"Not exactly."

He frowns.

"Oh, don't give me that sad face. I have a compromise if you're willing to consider it."

"Oh? What have you been brewing in that gorgeous head of yours?"

I give him a wry smile with one eyebrow raised.

"Well, the truth is I'm not sure I'm ready for marriage, but I do enjoy waking up to your handsome face. How about if we move in together? I'll have to clear it with Jenna, but she's never here anymore now that she has made up with Trent, and it just seems like the next natural step." I cringe inwardly and close my eyes in anticipation of his response. There is a long pause. I open one eye and then the other. He's grinning from ear to ear.

"Were you afraid to ask me that question?"

"No...maybe...yes," I sigh.

"Well, I think it's a great idea."

"You do?"

"I do." He winks at me, and I suddenly get the double meaning of those two words.

"Ha-ha, very funny."

He comes around to my side of the table, leans in, and kisses me.

"When would you like me to start moving?"

"As soon as you want to. But don't think for one minute that this means I'm going to do your laundry and clean up after you. You'll have to buy the cow for that to happen."

He laughs loudly and kisses me again.

"I'm the one who is ready to buy the cow. You're the one who is still on the fence. And by the way, you're in no way a cow, a horse maybe."

I smack him in mock disapproval.

"You're the horse's ass!"

He laughs, I laugh, and we are back in our happy, fun-loving place.

One phone call to Jenna, and it's a done deal. Matt and I go shopping for extra towels and things he'll need that he can't take from Jake's. Lunch at Lombardi's is even better than the first time. No texts to interrupt us and even though the waitress still stares at Matt a little too long, I don't care because he's mine. After a stroll through Central Park we end up back at our place. Jenna has prepared a celebration meal where we tell her all about our misadventures with Kendall. She is shocked but relieved to know everything has worked out.

For the next few weeks it is the same. Matt and I love falling asleep together after a lengthy lovemaking session and subsequently waking up wrapped around each other. Our daily routine is even choreographed in such a way that you would think that we'd lived together for years. Jenna remarks more than once that we behave like an old married couple.

Work is awkward at first. People are confused to see Matt and me walking hand in hand, but it only takes a short time for the whispers to stop. Kendall avoids us like the plague. She barely even looks at me and never says a word. I like it that way but hope that someday she can get over it and move on.

Then one crisp November day, we are getting ready to go to work.

"Chlo, have you seen my gray striped tie?"

"No, but why are you wearing a tie today?"

"No reason," he calls from our bedroom. "Can you look around for it?"

"Yes, as soon as I'm done with my hair." I finish and go in search of the tie.

"Here it is," I say as I walk into the room and hand it to him.

"Thanks, baby," he says and gives me a peck on the lips. "We've got to go. Are we still going to our favorite little coffee shop after the show?"

He's tying it all wrong, so I turn him around to help him.

"Yes, that's the plan," I say as I finish the perfect Windsor knot.

"Okay, well, I need to pick something up before then, so can we just meet there?"

I make a funny face.

"I guess so."

"Okay, great. Thanks, baby. Are you just about ready to go?"

"Yep, let's roll!"

We jump into a cab and head to the theater.

To my delight, Kendall has called in sick today, and I think my turns are better, my leaps are higher, and I'm in an all-around good mood. Drew is equally as chipper as he reveals to me that he and Andrew are now engaged.

"Oh, Drew, that's terrific news! How did he propose?"

"Well, it wasn't the most original proposal, but it worked for me. He put a ring in the bottom of a glass of champagne and got down on one knee. It was so romantic."

I hug him tight. "I'm so happy for you, Drew. You deserve all the happiness in the world."

"Thanks, sweetie. Are things still good with Mr. Wonderful?"

"They're the best. I never thought I'd ever be this happy."

"I hear ya, honey. Do you want to grab a bite to eat later?"

"I'll have to take a rain check. Matt and I are meeting for coffee after we're done here."

"We'll do it some other night. Talk to you later."

"Okay, congratulations again, Drew!"

He waves his thank-you as he walks away. As I turn to walk back into the dressing room I collide head on into Jill, another dancer from the ensemble. The coffee she'd been holding is now all over the front of my shirt.

"Oh no! Chloe, I am so sorry. Are you okay?"

I am drenched but luckily the coffee was only warm so I didn't get burned.

"I'm okay, Jill, it's fine."

"I feel terrible. Here, let me get you some paper towels."

She goes into the bathroom and comes back out with a large wad of brown towels.

"Thanks." I take them and dab off the already soaked-in liquid. "Looks like I'll have to go home and change before I hit the coffee shop."

"Oh jeez, I'm sorry again Chloe."

I just smile and nod.

I take out my phone and shoot Matt a quick text.

I'm going home to change. Then I'll meet you for coffee.

He replies.

Okay sounds good. Be careful.
C U there in about an hour? ILY

Oh, Matt, I love you too.

Yes, an hour sounds fine. ILY2

I stow my phone and walk out to a waiting cab. When I get home I see Jenna. She laughs when she sees my shirt, assuming that my clumsiness was responsible. After changing into a tight T-shirt and blue jeans, I walk back out into the kitchen.

"Hey, Jenna, I'm walking over to meet Matt for coffee. Don't wait up," I smirk.

"You're not taking a cab?"

"It's only a ten-minute walk. I hate to spend the extra money for cab fare if I don't have to."

"Okay, well, be careful and call me when you get there."

"Yes, Mother," I say as I smile and walk out the door.

The evening air is cold, so I pull my coat closed and begin my trek. It's dark and a little scary, but I'm aware of my surroundings so I keep my head up and pick up the pace. The streets for the most part are empty. There's the occasional pedestrian but I just keep walking along. I am anxious to see Matt. I'm surprised that even though we see each other day and night that I still look forward to being with him. I hope this feeling never ends.

I'm halfway there when I hear a noise behind me. I turn to look, but there's nothing. It's probably just a stray cat. I continue on my journey, now acutely aware of every noise. Ugh, I'm just being paranoid. I quicken my pace again but relax a little when the café is in sight. I'm less than fifty feet away from the love of my life. I pass an alley and hear a loud crack. Suddenly I'm on the ground. My head feels like it's going to explode. I curl up into a tight ball, squeezing my eyes shut and holding my head. Feeling a warm ooze trickle across my fingers, even in my confusion, I know it's blood. Besides hearing my rapid heartbeat pounding in my ears, I hear hushed voices and feel like I'm being dragged and then frisked. I stay curled up, hoping whoever it is just takes my bag and leaves. There are footsteps now that sound like they're getting further away, but I could be wrong. When I open my eyes, I can still see the light from the café, but it's getting blurry. Any minute now, I am going to pass out. I reach inside my coat pocket for my phone, but it's gone. I have to get to the café. If I stay where I am, no one will find me. I could die here, and Matt would never know what happened. I begin to crawl back into plain sight slowly, inch by inch, every movement a monumental effort.

There's a lot of pain in my right shoulder, and I note that it is almost useless. It must be broken from the fall.

It feels like I've been crawling like this for hours, though I know it hasn't been that long. I'm hoping that Matt notices I'm late and comes looking for me, but in reality, I know he has no idea that I stupidly made the decision to walk. I stop moving because I no longer have the strength to go any further. I feel dizzy and nauseated, and when I look toward the café, I realize that my vision is getting worse. Oh what am I going to do? Just then the door opens, and two people walk out—or are there four? Whichever it is, I need to get their attention. Struggling into a sitting position and waving my good arm, I try to call out, but when I do, my head pounds thunderously, so I stop. They don't see me and walk away in the opposite direction. I sag against a light pole that I managed to reach. I'm in trouble, real trouble, and I know that in a matter of minutes, I am going to be rendered unconscious. My befuddled brain recollects the events of the past few months. I concede that they have been the best and worst of my life and that I wouldn't trade them for anything. Is this how all of my hard work and determination will pay off? Am I going to die here? No, Matt and I have come too far to have it end like this. Holding onto the pole for support, I climb shakily to my feet. I am pleasantly surprised to discover that my legs are fully functioning, so I gingerly begin to stumble toward the coffee shop. As I get closer, the light that comes from it is blinding, and I squint but keep moving. I'm at the corner of the building now and hold on to it for dear life while taking a short break. Suddenly, the door opens again.

"What do you mean, she walked? Why would you let her do that, Jenna? I'm going outside to see if I can find her. Call me if you—" Matt stops in midsentence as he turns, and his eyes land directly on me. "Oh my God!"

Dropping his cell phone, he rushes over to me, and I immediately collapse. He catches me just in time and lowers me to the ground.

"Chlo, what the hell happened to you?" his agonizing voice asks.

I say nothing. It just feels good to know Matt's here. All I can do is rest my head on his chest as his arms envelop me. My eyes are closed as I absorb the feeling of safety.

He tilts my head back, and his thumb is caressing my cheek.

"Chlo, baby, look at me. I need you to open your eyes," he softly commands.

Reluctantly, I do as I'm told. When I look up at him, the worry, then relief, on his face makes tears well up and roll down my cheeks.

"Talk to me baby, please. Just say...something."

His wavering words come out sounding as if he is about to cry, and it's shocking. Do I really look that bad?

"Home," is all I can muster.

"Hospital," he replies, but I just want to be back at our place, with him. I shake my head slightly.

He snorts.

"Baby, you don't have a choice in this."

I feel him lift me, and I try to stay awake and enjoy his embrace, but it's no use. Soon darkness surrounds me, and I hear myself whisper, "I love you."

I wake up slowly, feeling like my head is in a vice. Opening my eyes, I can tell I'm inside a room, but it's just too blurry to make anything out. It smells sterile, like a dentist's office—no wait, a doctor's office. Am I in a hospital? I look down at my right hand, there's tubing taped to it, and I recognize it as an IV line. That same arm is restrained in a sling, and when I try to move it, I wince. As I look around the fuzzy images become a little clearer. Yes, it's definitely a hospital. It's then that I notice my left hand is pinned down or trapped under something, it's Matt. Thank God he's here. His forehead is resting on the hand that he's holding, while he sits on the chair beside the bed. I think he's asleep. I try to free my hand when he suddenly looks up. Holy hell, he looks awful. His hair looks as if it hasn't been combed in a week, and the dark circles under his eyes tell me he hasn't slept either.

He breathes in a sharp breath of air and raises his hand to touch my cheek.

"Good morning, beautiful," he greets me. His voice is shaky and his smile is wistful.

"Morning?"

"Yes, baby, it's morning. How do you feel?" He is talking in a soft, soothing voice.

"Um, ouch."

He snorts.

"I can imagine. Do you know where you are?"

"Hospital?"

"Yes. Do you remember what happened to you?"

I think for a few minutes.

"I'm not sure."

"It's okay, baby, don't push yourself. I'm going to call a nurse."

He reaches over and pushes a button but then returns to the place he was.

"You look terrible," I inform him.

He laughs. "I bet I do. But you, you look beautiful, as you always do."

"Lies." I'm trying to be funny.

He chuckles.

"No, I mean it."

"I'm sure," I say sarcastically. "What happened?"

"You were mugged, Chlo."

"Oh."

"Yeah, I went to our café and waited for you. I got worried after a while and tried to call your phone. It went straight to voicemail. Then I called Jenna. She said you had left almost an hour before...on foot." He looks down at me, and I know he wants to scold me. "It was then that I knew something was wrong. I went running outside, intending to retrace your steps. That's when I found you."

His face looks pained, and I squeeze his hand.

"I'm okay. You got to me."

"Chlo, why would you walk around New York at night by yourself? Don't you know how dangerous that is? You have a concussion, and your shoulder was dislocated. It could've been much worse."

I can tell he's angry, but he's trying not to raise his voice.

Just then a nurse comes in.

"Good morning, Chloe. How are you feeling?"

"Like crap."

"Well, you'll have that with your injuries. I'm going to check your vitals."

She gets to work, and in no time she's done.

"I'll check in with you later," she promises, and then she's gone.

Matt's back at my side, his head resting on my hand.

"I'm sorry, Matt. I didn't mean for this to happen."

He sighs. "I know, I'm sorry too. This is my fault. We should've left the theater together. God, Chlo, when I turned and saw you standing there like that, I was so afraid. Then when you collapsed in my arms I thought I was too late. Your eyes were closed and you weren't talking and I thought..." He rakes a hand through his hair. "I don't know what I would've done if..." Matt takes my hand and places it on his face. He closes his eyes and turns, kisses the palm, and lets out a long held sigh. "I'm so sorry it took me so long to go looking for you."

"Matt you can't blame yourself. How were you to know some psychopath would do this to me?"

He shrugs his shoulders and pulls himself together.

"By the way, did you see who hit you? The police questioned me, but whoever it was left before I found you. They said it looked like you were hit on the head with some kind of blunt object," he says as a pained look crosses his handsome face.

"I have no idea." Then a thought hits me. "Do you think it could be Kendall?"

He half-smiles. "I thought of that too, but it turns out she was sick and in bed with the flu. Her roommate told the police she stayed home to take care of her. I guess it was just some random thug."

"Oh. So I have a concussion, and I screwed up my shoulder. Anything else?"

"Three stitches in your head, you'll be off work for a week or so. I've already called in and told them all about it. They told me to wish you well and they'll see you soon."

"Thank you."

"For calling you off work?"

"Yes, but thank you for saving me too."

"Hey, it was my turn, right? Besides, I'm not sure I saved you as much as found you—not nearly as useful."

"You're my hero."

"All in a day's work, ma'am."

I giggle, but it makes my head pound so I wince.

"Go easy baby." He's still worried, I can tell. It's very sweet, and at that moment I realize that I can't imagine my life without him in it.

I take a deep breath. "I love you, Matt. Marry me."

His eyebrows shoot up.

"What?"

"You heard me. Marry me."

He chuckles.

"That guy hit you harder than I thought."

"I'm serious."

He kisses the back of my hand.

"I know you are, and it's sweet but...no. It's like you said. We're not ready yet. Let's just take our time. Besides," he raises one eyebrow, "that's not very romantic."

I roll my eyes, and he laughs.

"Funny, real funny."

I take a full week off of work. Matt takes a week off too just to take care of me. He dotes on me and makes sure my every need is fulfilled. Drew stops by to give me a lecture on New York at night. And Jenna says that if I ever decide to do that again she'll drag me back inside by my hair. I am feeling good, and I'm itching to go back to work. My stitches come out on Friday, which means the show must go on.

Matt and I ride to the theater together. He's wearing his gray striped tie again. I laugh inwardly and think that maybe that particular tie is bad luck. Kendall has recovered and actually tells me she's glad I'm feeling better. I'm surprised and think maybe she is finally getting over Matt.

We end the show, and the bows have all been taken but strangely, the giant red curtains don't close. The cast keeps waving, waiting to be concealed but they remain open.

"What the heck is going on?" I say to Drew.

He is as perplexed as I am. "I don't know—a glitch?"

Just then, the single beam of a spotlight shines down, and a man walks out into the circle of light. I strain to see what's happening, and to my shock, it's Matt.

"What is he doing?"

"Oh, sweetie, I'm not sure, but whatever it is, it's big."

"Chloe Shepherd, will you please join me downstage?" Matt has a microphone. My legs are wobbly as it hits me: I think he's going to propose again. I feel faint as I am pushed through the crowd toward him. I reach his smiling face, and he holds out his hand for me to grasp.

"Ladies and gentlemen, this very beautiful young woman is the love of my life. We've been friends ever since we were kids, and I just recently found her again, in more ways than you can imagine. Like most couples, we've had our share of troubles, but I would go through them all again if it meant that we would end up together. Chlo, I love you more today than I did yesterday, and I'll love you even more tomorrow. I've told you before that I can't live without you, and I sincerely meant that. My heart belongs to you, and nothing in this world could ever change that."

He gets down on one knee and pulls out a ring.

"Chloe Grace Shepherd, will you please do me the honor of marrying me?"

I hear several gasps, and then the room that is filled with nearly two thousand people is absolutely silent. They are all waiting on my reply.

A slow smile creeps onto my face as I reply, "Yes."

The room erupts into cheers and whistles. Matt places the ring on my finger and stands to embrace me. He lifts me off the ground and twirls me around before setting me back down and kissing me passionately. The cast gathers around us; everyone congratulating us. Drew spins me around and hugs me tight.

"Now we can plan our weddings together!"

I laugh and hug him again.

"Yes, we can."

The curtains close, and the crowd starts to disburse. I turn to my fiancé.

"I love you, Matthew Masen."

"I love you more, Chloe Masen."

"Impossible," I reply.

"Don't start with me, Mrs. Masen. You still have to make good on our bet."

And I'm grinning like a loon as we end the show but begin our lives together.

Epilogue

"Do I really have to do this?"

"A deal is a deal. We bet, and you lost, now here's the mic," Matt replies.

"But I never had to use a microphone before."

"Call it a modern upgrade. Now sing."

Ugh, how embarrassing. I grab the microphone out of his hand and give him an exasperated look. I guess it's now or never. I look out at the audience. Everyone I care about is in this small room. I know that they support me no matter what, but it's still nerve-wracking to have to get up in front of them and open myself up in a way that makes me feel inadequate. I'm a dancer, for heaven's sake, not a singer. The music starts and seems to echo off of the walls of this karaoke bar. Matt has threatened to call me a chicken for the rest of my life unless I go through with the consequences of losing our bet. In all the years that we've known each other, he has only ever lost a bet with me once. It was so satisfying to hear his prepubescent voice crack over and over again while singing for all of our friends. I'm not thrilled about doing this, but it's what we've done our whole lives. It makes me feel safe in a way because it feels ordinary and silly. It reminds me of the kids we used to be, before life got complicated and stressful. Well, I guess it's show time. I begin to sing.

"Daisy, Daisy, give me your answer true. I'm half-crazy over the love of you. It won't be a stylish marriage. I can't afford a carriage, but you'll look sweet, upon the seat of a bicycle built for two."

The song goes on and on, it seems, three verses in all. After it ends my friends and family cheer loudly, and Matt comes back onto the small stage and takes the mic.

"How about another round of applause for my girl. She was a good sport."

The crowd claps and whistles again, and I'm sure I'm a lovely shade of red. Matt puts one arm around me and kisses the top of my head. I lean up and whisper in his ear, "I'll get you up here eventually, Matt."

He smiles down at me. "Wanna bet?"

I smack him, and he pretends that it hurt. Then he kisses me again.

We mingle with the small group of people who came to witness my awkward performance. Among them are my parents and Gram. Matt had flown them into New York knowing he was going to propose. I didn't know they were there until after the show. When I got out of the dressing room, Gram pulled me off to the side to say, "I told you so." It's funny how she always knew that Matt and I would end up together. My mom cried, and my dad gave Matt a congratulatory slap on the back. They, too, have always loved Matt.

Drew tells me that a few days after that performance, Kendall left the show for good. No one knows why, but I suspect it was because of us.

Matt and I have decided to stay with Jenna for a while yet. We talk about getting our own place, but good apartments are hard to find and it just makes more sense to keep splitting the rent. And as for our wedding, we haven't set a date yet. We figure that it took us this long to realize our feelings for one another—a little longer won't hurt. We want to get it right the first time so we're going to take our time and enjoy ourselves on our journey to our forever.

She stands in front of the window, an outsider, looking in. Her tear-stained cheeks are black from the mascara that is streaming down. She inhales the cold air forcefully through her nose and wipes it with the back of her hand. They all look so happy, she thinks to herself, and why shouldn't they be? After all, they have everything they've ever wanted and she has nothing, nothing but a canyon-sized hole in her heart. She wishes she were the one inside the karaoke bar, acting like a fool, swooning over every touch and every smile that Matt has to offer. Instead, she is forced out into the cold, cruel night. But she'll get him back, she just has to bide her time and wait for the package to be delivered. Matt would never deny his child or the mother of it.

Kate Squires was born and raised in Ohio, where she still resides with her husband and children. She has always loved writing but never, ever thought her life would someday lead to sitting in front of her laptop for hours on end creating stories other people would read. As a child she hated reading until a certain series turned that all around for her. Now she can't get her hands on enough books. Kate has dabbled in all sorts of odd jobs, ranging from dog groomer to dance instructor and even a chicken farmer, but her true passion is creating characters out of thin air and making them do her bidding. *That Promise*, the sequel to *That Kiss,* is also available. Visit her website for more information about her books and upcoming events: www.KateSquiresAuthor.com

Made in the USA
Charleston, SC
03 June 2014